TOUCHED BY SIN

SINS OF THE FALLEN

BOOK ONE

HARLEIGH BECK

This is a work of fiction. Names, characters, organizations, places, events and incidents are either products of the author's imagination or are used fictitiously.

Cover design: 3Crows Author Services

Editing/Proofreading: Spooks Proofs & Passion Author Services

Graphics: Quirky Circe

*Not suitable for readers under 18

For the readers out there who support me on my writing journey. You're all amazing! I love you, and I hope you enjoy this sprinkle of darkness.

TRIGGER WARNINGS

This is a *dark* PNR romance, and it contains scenes that can be incredibly disturbing to some readers.
I trust that you know your triggers.

The warnings include but are not limited to dub/non-con, sexual violence, sexual power games, humiliation, degradation, kidnapping, blood play, breath play, cheating, stupid decisions, and graphic murder.

Please read responsibly.

AUTHOR'S NOTE

Thanks for being here on this journey with me. If this is your first time, welcome. There are a few things I would like to point out before I shove you down the rabbit hole. Firstly, you won't find your Prince or Princess Charming within these pages. These characters are not meant to be likable. They're selfish, volatile, and have a knack for making stupid decisions. I mean, you're about to take a trip down to Hell, where morals technically don't exist, right? The sexual content in this book is dub and non-con throughout. There's also a lot of it. If you're not into that, you won't like this book. You also won't like this book if you're not into male characters who finish on your face and call you a slut. Just saying.

Now with that being said, enter at your own risk.

Love,

Harleigh

PROLOGUE

AURELIA

The tall, golden gates shimmer in the afternoon sun. Beyond lies the unknown, a world of misery and pain. Or so I've been told. Ever since I was a young girl, I've been curious about what lies on the other side.

Eden is perfection; it's Heaven, and the elders tell me I'm one of the lucky few born in paradise. They're right. Everything here is beautiful. The tall trees sway in the wind, and the sweet fragrance from the colorful flowers drifts on the warm summer breeze.

Eden has never known pain and misery. Us angels live a sheltered life here, which makes me curious to find out what's on the other side. Back when I was younger, I used to climb the trees near the gates to peek at the landscape beyond the tall walls. The Garden of Eden is surrounded by a dense, dark forest with tall, spindly trees and a penetrating silence you can sense beyond these walls. Even now, I can hear it calling me, urging me to scale them.

"Aurelia, what are you doing?" Freya, my best friend, asks,

causing me to startle and snap my white wings shut behind me.

She laughs. "Sorry, I didn't mean to scare you."

My heart is still in my throat as I drag my gaze away from the tall gates. "I thought I heard something."

Freya follows my line of sight, and her throat jumps before she circles her fingers around my arm, steering me back to the path that leads to the village. "You know we shouldn't be out here."

"I know."

"You can't tell anyone I let you talk me into coming along. The elders won't be happy."

"No one will find out," I reassure her. She hates it when I sneak out to the gates, but she's too kind to stop me.

"We shouldn't lie," she says, her white wings fluttering with unease behind her. "The elders have banished angels for lying."

"We're not lying to anyone."

"You're trouble," she tells me, but then she smiles, and we giggle nervously.

"Why do you always come out here?" she asks as I tuck my blonde hair behind my ear. Freya doesn't understand why I feel so drawn to the gates. I don't, either. It's a deep-rooted curiosity. Ever since I was a little girl, the elders have told us stories about a place called Hell, where the fires never stop burning and cast out angels like us, with dark wings and sharp fangs, torture human souls. Their lands lie beyond the dark, sinister woods. It's a place of misery, sin, and depravity. I'm curious, and it makes no sense why Freya is not.

"I want to see for myself what's beyond the gates."

Freya stumbles to a halt, and her wide eyes land on me. "Are you crazy? Why? You have everything you need here. Why would you wish for such a thing? It's dangerous, not to mention foolish. You're an angel, Aurelia. You live in heaven, the highest ascension. Why would you want to jeopardize it?"

We're close to the village now, and a group of angels, sparkling with light, walk past us. I wait until they're out of earshot before replying, "Aren't you curious about what's beyond these walls?"

"No!" she exclaims like my question is absurd. "The thought has never crossed my mind. I'm happy here. How can I not be when I live in a place of eternal happiness and unconditional love."

I step closer and lower my voice. "You speak of such things, but how can you know happiness and love when you've never experienced pain?"

The look on Freya's face is comical. She walks away, calling out over her shoulder, "I worry about you sometimes. You know that?"

My bare feet pad on the soft grass as we step off the trodden path and cut between two houses. "There's no need to be concerned. I'm not going to do anything stupid. Sometimes I just like to come out here and listen to the silence in the woods. Can you not hear it?"

"How can you *hear* the silence?" she asks, her soft, bare skin glowing in the sun. "Silence has no sound."

We reach the village square and hurry over to the spot on the nearby field where classes are in full swing. The teacher rolls her eyes when we plop down on the grass. It's not the first time we've been late because of my burning curiosity. I lean in, whispering in Freya's ear, "Silence screams sometimes."

Freya is only half listening. Her eyes are on Oliver, a couple of rows in front. "I want to marry him," she says dreamily.

Oliver, with his blonde hair and blue eyes, looks like any other angel here.

"His wings are so big," she swoons.

I giggle when she rests her head on my shoulder. His white wings are impressive, and he knows it. No other angel boy comes close to his wingspan.

"Last week, we looked at Corinthians. Can anyone tell me what unconditional love is?" the teacher asks, looking expectantly around the group of students. Freya has her hand up in the air, eager as always to shine.

The teacher smiles at her. "Go on, Freya."

"Love is patient and kind. It always protects, always trusts, always hopes, always perseveres."

"Very good."

"You're a teacher's pet," I tease, leaning in.

"I don't deny it."

"Aurelia," the teacher says, and I snap to attention. "How does fear relate to love?"

"There is no fear in love. The one who fears is not made perfect in love."

"Very good."

I preen, too. How can I not when my teacher looks at me like an exemplary student? I'm not. I'm too restless and curious-minded to be a teacher's pet like Freya. I'm always pushing the boundaries of what's acceptable here in Eden with my endless questions and wandering feet. It will get me into a lot of trouble one day.

CHAPTER 1

AURELIA

"Show us your wings," Freya says to Oliver after class, batting her wispy eyelashes. My attention is elsewhere as I stare longingly at the path that leads to the gates.

"Wow," she gasps behind me, "they're amazing!"

I walk away, my feet padding on the soft grass. Freya won't notice I have left. Not when Oliver flexes his impressive wings. He'll have the pick of the crop one day when it's time to choose a wife. I wouldn't say no, but he doesn't excite me either. Unfortunately, there's not much choice here in Eden unless you're into blonde-haired boys with blue eyes that shimmer like the fish pond in my backyard.

I've never seen a dark-haired boy. They only exist in the fairytales we're told around the campfire about dangerous boys with hellfire in their eyes and sin at the touch of their fingertips—the fallen angels, banished from the Garden of Eden.

It doesn't take me long to reach the tall and majestic gates lined with white roses. They shimmer gold up ahead, the flowery fragrance tantalizing my senses as I near. Birds sing in the trees, and the breeze lifts my hair off my shoulders. I'm closer than ever. Close enough to be in serious trouble if anyone sees me.

I look behind me, but there's no one around except a deer munching on the grass by the tree line. It flicks its ears as I reach my fingers out to trace the green leaf of a white rose. The petals shimmer like everything here in Heaven.

I draw in a breath and my hand retreats but soon moves back in to slide over the gate's smooth surface. To my surprise, it creaks open enough to allow me to slip through. I hesitate for a brief moment. Will I find my way back if I leave? What if I get lost? What if Freya comes looking for me?

Before I can think it through, I sneak out. The air is different out here, denser somehow. It's colder too, and shivers run down my back as I step further away from the gate. The dark, gaping forest, with trees that appear like demons with claws and fangs, draws me closer until I stand at the edge with my heart in my throat, barely daring to breathe. My arm brushes up against the scratchy branch of a tree as I debate turning back.

I don't.

"Come closer," the darkness whispers, reaching for me like tendrils in the night, long, crooked fingers tangling in my hair and pulling at my pale skin. I gasp and step back. My heart thunders in my chest, and I'm more alive than I've ever been. I should turn around and walk back to safety, but I step forward instead.

With one last glance behind me, I disappear into the shadows, my wings kept tucked close to my body. My cascading hair snags on the branches, and it's not long before damp leaves and twigs stick to the tangled strands. It's silent in here except for my racing heartbeat and the throb of it in my ears. It's chilly, too. My breath is visible in the air and my skin swells with goosebumps. There's no bird song, no deer munching on leaves, and no hares twitching their ears. It's just me and the tall, spindly trees that reach for my limbs and tangle in my hair while whispering untold secrets.

I keep walking deeper into the forest, pulled forward by my own unsatiated curiosity. The woods whisper my name, welcoming me home. As though I were a visitor in Eden, and this is where I belong.

There's a sudden sound to my left—a twig snapping—and I whirl around, stumbling back when three boys emerge from the shadows. Boys unlike anything I've seen before. Boys with hellfire in their dark eyes and sin at their fingertips.

"Well, well, what do we have here?" the tall boy to the right asks, cocking his head to the side and smiling cruelly.

The boy in the middle chuckles darkly. "Are you lost, little angel?"

My feet carry me backward until my spine connects with a tree. I try to move around it, but the boys are faster.

"Where are you going, pretty little thing?"

Dark hair, darker eyes, black wings. They're fallen angels, the monsters from the fairytales of my youth.

"What's an innocent little thing like you doing out here?" one of them asks as I back away. They circle me like predators circle prey. "You never know what monsters lurk in the shadows."

I dart to the left, but one of the boys steps in front of me, causing me to stumble back against a hard chest. Big hands grip my pale arms. "You're far away from home, little angel."

I walked much farther than I intended to, and now I don't know where I am or which way leads back to Eden.

"What shall we do with her?" the boy in front of me asks, and the one off to the side says, "I think we should keep her."

"A souvenir," the boy behind me agrees, his nose buried in my matted hair. He breathes me in.

"Let me go!" I hiss, my small tits jiggling as I fight his grip on me.

"Look at that." The boy in front of me palms my breasts. "It's true what they say. All true angels are naked." His dark eyes collide with mine. "Inside those gates, do you really not realize you're naked?"

His rough fingers have me fighting twice as hard. No boy has ever touched me before. Not like this. "Get your hands off me," I snarl, surprising myself. I've never felt this unpleasant, aggravating emotion before. I'm not happy or content. I want to hurt him. I want to claw his face and draw blood.

Chuckling knowingly, he grabs my chin and inspects my face. "She's pretty."

"Are you surprised? She's a true angel. They're all supposed to be beautiful." The boy standing to the side sounds bored.

"How am I supposed to know? I've never seen one before."

The boy with the bored expression pushes off the tree he's leaning against and drawls, "Let's go already before they notice that she's gone."

"I can't believe we're stealing an angel," the boy behind me says excitedly as he drags me away.

Digging my feet in, I lash out and strike him repeatedly. If they take me, I'll never find my way back home. I'll never see Freya again. "Let me go!"

I'm lifted up and carried fireman style. The boy is insanely strong, not breaking a sweat. I try to fight him but find myself face-to-face with the black wings on his back. I've never seen anything like it before. They're so dark, and I can already tell that they're big.

"Speechless?" one of the boys asks, eyeing me curiously.

It's dark in the forest, as if night fell while I was walking further away from safety. That can't be right. It was only past lunchtime when I snuck out.

"You'll regret this!" I hiss.

"I count on it." He winks.

"It's true," the boy whose shoulder I'm on agrees. "Nothing good can come from stealing an angel."

"Besides the pleasure of defiling her?" the bored-looking boy at the front asks. I can't see him, but his deep voice sends shivers down my spine. The boy in front of me grins, flashing white teeth in the darkness. "Welcome to Hell, little angel."

CHAPTER 2

AURELIA

I'm placed down on my back, and the cold stone floor bites into my bare skin. We're in a large sitting room with a fabric couch and two armchairs. Damask wallpaper peels away from the corners near the door. The chandelier on the tall ceiling is cast iron, with white cobwebs hanging from the candle sticks.

The boy with the bored expression lowers himself down onto his knees in front of me and says, "You're in Hell now, sweet angel. Your God can't save you. His power doesn't extend outside the borders of Eden." The boy eyes my white, dirt-smeared wings with a satisfied smile. He caught his prize and wants to revel in his victory. His big hand lands on my naked skin and calloused fingers skim over my collarbone and down my chest, over the soft curves of my breasts. "Do you know why you're here, little angel?"

I stay silent.

"Do you know about my kind?" He pinches my nipple and smiles when I whimper. "We're fallen angels cast out from the garden you call home." Trailing his touch lower, past my belly button, his fingers hover at the apex of my thighs before dipping between my legs. "Have you ever been touched, little angel?" he asks, sliding his fingers over my pussy.

I haven't been touched—I'm not a sinner—but the shameless, feminine moan in the room is mine. It comes again when he pinches the swollen nub between my legs.

"Feels good, doesn't it?"

My eyes flutter, and the insides of my thighs dampen.

"Such a good little angel," he praises, his eyes burning red. "Spread your pretty legs for me. Forsake your God."

His two friends, seated with their legs spread like kings of their domain, laugh on the couch. I've never seen fallen angels before, but everything about them is dark.

Dark hair. Dark wings. Dark eyes that flicker with flames. Even their shadows are dark. Angel boys are different. Light blue eyes, blonde hair, and sparkling white wings that reflect the sun.

"You're cruel," one of the boys comments, placing a cigarette between his lips. With a flick of his fingers, he conjures a ball of fire. The embers spark as he inhales deeply and extinguishes the flame.

"Maybe," the boy in front of me replies, sliding his finger knuckle deep inside me, a wicked smile on his lips, "but she enjoys it."

He smells of embers and firewood. I like it. It's the scent the fairytales told me about as a child. The danger lurking in the woods that our elders warned us to stay away from.

"Don't you, sweetheart?"

A second finger. I can't breathe. My heart gallops in my chest, and my pussy contracts around him. I would be cast out if the elders found out about this. I've been touched by sin, and I'm no longer pure.

"Please, let me go," I whimper.

"No can do," he replies, sliding his glistening fingers back out. As I watch, he licks them clean, groaning darkly. "So fucking good."

The air thickens with swirling cigarette smoke.

"You stole her. What now?" the boy who carried me here asks, his feet propped up against the black glass coffee table.

"I don't know," the boy admits, cupping my chin with his wet fingers. He inspects my face as if he's never seen an angel before. He probably hasn't. We don't visit the underworld. "I was bored."

More laughter. "You're always fucking bored."

"I want to dirty up her face. She sparkles, for fuck's sake. What's that shit about?"

One of the boys shrugs as he lights up his own cigarette. It amazes me how they can conjure up hellfire with their hands.

"Must be the holiness shining through." He laughs at his own joke.

The boy in front of me considers this. "Maybe it'll dull if we fuck her?"

"Maybe," the boy on the couch agrees.

"Would you like that?" he asks me, jostling my face when I try to peer at his friends. "Want us to corrupt you beyond repair?"

I stare at the small horns peeking through his mussed-up hair. Does he have fangs too, like the stories say?

Leaning in, he whispers against my lips, "When we're done with you, your wings will be dark with sin."

"You won't get away with this!"

His sinister chuckle makes me tingle in unfamiliar ways. It's masculine and raspy—a pink tongue and a hiss from the coiled snake that lures me deeper into the woods.

Come closer.

"Baby, baby, baby," he breathes, his hot breath tickling my

ear. "You're not in Eden anymore. You're with the fallen angels."

I try to crawl away, but he circles his warm fingers around my ankle and drags me closer. Back home, I wasn't aware of my nakedness. Now I want to cover myself. The boys are dressed in dark material, their arms covered in intricate tattoos, symbols as ancient as time. I've heard about 'clothes' in our stories—pants, T-shirts, belts—but I never truly understood nakedness.

Now I do.

"Where are you going, sweetheart? We're not done playing."

"Please," I beg, "let me go."

He studies me for a moment before crawling on top of me and staring down at my face. His hair falls in his dark eyes when his lips curve into a smile. The white gleam of his teeth sends sparks down to my core. His hands are on either side of my head, his arms straining. I've never noticed a boy like this before.

"Never had a man lie on top of you," he observes, echoing my thoughts.

"You sound pleased," I retort.

The urge to claw him strikes me out of nowhere as his wings spread out behind him, dark and magnificent. When I gasp, something hard twitches against my thigh.

He seizes my chin, rolling his hips against me. "You're so fucking innocent."

His friends laugh while lighting up more cigarettes.

"Daemon, just fuck her already and get it over with."

Daemon.

"No," he breathes out, his eyes flicking between mine. "I've never had an angel before. Let's see if we can break her first."

his eyebrows raised.

"I'm not."

"Sure."

"Shut up!"

Ronan watches me closely, then, "Have you ever seen an erect cock?"

Alaric chokes on his drink and starts laughing. My cheeks burn, but I refuse to look weak in front of these fallen angels. I hold his gaze, pretending to be braver than I am.

"Answer me!"

Daemon leans forward and grabs a beer as I shake my head.

"No."

They exchange an amused look.

"Never seen a hard dick, huh? How do they make babies in Eden?"

"I don't know," I reply, feeling foolish when they laugh. "We're born of the Light." I lower my head so they can't see my burning cheeks.

Daemon clears his throat. "Did I say you can look down?"

I glare at him, and he flashes a hint of fang as he smiles.

"Come here," Ronan tells me, putting his drink down on the coffee table. I go to stand, but he shakes his head. "Crawl to me, little angel."

I look between them uncertainly.

"What are you waiting for?"

My hands connect with the cheap rug, and it scratches my palms as I slowly crawl over to Ronan. His shoes come into sight, and when I'm settled on my knees between his spread legs, he lifts my chin with his hand. His fingers land on his belt, and I fight the urge to look down. The sound of his belt buckle being undone has my heart racing in my chest. After sliding down his zipper, he shifts. "Look down."

My throat is dry, and I try to swallow past the strange

lump. I'm growing wet between my legs.

"Look. Down."

My eyes fall on his thick, veiny length against the black fabric of his T-shirt. And as I watch, he fists his cock and strokes his hand over the length.

"Keep watching, little angel."

A white liquid collects on the tip. He swipes it, letting go of his cock to dip his thumb into my mouth. "Suck."

It's salty and delicious. I try not to look too eager.

He's back to stroking his cock. "I'll let you watch today, little angel."

I glance up at him, but he slaps my cheek, ordering me to keep watching. I'm aroused. I've never felt anything like this overwhelming desire to let these men use me.

His hand moves faster, jerking the length with expertise. "Do you know what happens when a man comes?"

I shake my head.

Behind me, Daemon chuckles. It's a low, masculine, and gravelly sound that speaks to something nefarious inside me. "You should give her a demonstration."

"Trust me, I fucking intend to," Ronan replies breathily, his hand sliding into the back of my hair. He sits forward and brings his cock closer to my mouth. "Stick your tongue out like a good girl, little angel. It's time to stuff your hot little mouth full of my cum."

Curiosity gets the better of me and I comply, looking up at him.

"Fuck," he groans, stroking his length one more time.. then twice.. three times. "Spread your wings. I want to see them."

His grip on my hair turns painful. It only hurts more when he stiffens and jerks his hips forward. A hot liquid shoots over my face. I startle, but his hand in my hair prevents me from moving. "That's it," he breathes, milking his length.

"Look at me, little angel. Such a good little whore, so greedy for my cum."

Two more spurts of his white, salty liquid. One on my tongue and one over my nose and cheek.

"Hell, that was something else!" He zips himself away and falls back against the couch. I don't know what to do or how to act. His release is sticky on my skin and it's humiliating, but that's what he wants. I like the way he looks at me right now, satisfied and smug. He is pleased to have marked me in front of these other males. Even if they're his friends. It's a primal claiming.

Alaric blows cigarette smoke up at the roof. "Do you like being our whore?"

I'm taken aback by his question. "Whore?"

Alaric gestures at me. The release on my face. "You're an angel covered in semen. *Cum.* So I'll ask you again, do you like being our whore?"

Do I?

I look between them. First Daemon and then Ronan, who watches me from beneath lowered lashes.

Alaric throws his empty beer bottle at the wall and shouts, "DO YOU?"

I yelp when the glass explodes, and he asks again with a devilish smile, "Do you?"

"Yes."

"Is that so?"

"Yes." My voice trembles.

"Why?"

"I don't know."

"At least she's honest," Daemon drawls, peeling off the label on his beer bottle.

"Come here." Alaric sinks back down further on the couch. "Show me."

I slowly crawl over to him, settling between his legs and

awaiting further instructions.

"Open your mouth."

I do.

He sinks his fingers inside, pumping lazily. When I gag, he smiles. "An angel who likes humiliation. We hit the jackpot, guys."

"She's fucking perfect," Daemon agrees behind me.

"We're not good guys," Alaric informs me, as if I didn't already know. "We ruin pretty things like you." His fingers slip down my throat, and I choke as his other hand fists my hair. "We'll pluck your wings, sweet angel."

I moan even as salty tears seep out.

"We'll hurt you and make you cry."

My clit throbs painfully.

"Do you want that? Do you want us to make you cry?"

I nod eagerly.

He slides his long fingers out and grabs my chin. "Open your mouth."

I do, clinging to the darkness in his eyes that will lead me ashore.

"Do you want us to hurt you?" he whispers, leaning in.

I nod again.

"Such a good girl." His voice is a dark promise, and I know I'll never see the light again.

He spits in my mouth, digging his fingers into my cheeks. "Swallow."

His saliva slides down my throat and he smiles cruelly when I open my mouth again to show him. "Good little angel whore. You'll let us all fuck this mouth and paint your pretty little face with our cum, won't you?"

Before I can nod again, he rises to his feet, picks up another beer, and walks out. So do the others, too. The door clicks shut behind them, locking me inside. I blink. *What just happened?*

CHAPTER 3

AURELIA

"Wake up, little angel."

Aching everywhere from sleeping on the uncomfortable couch, I blink my eyes open. Three sets of dark eyes peer down at me. I scramble back, my heart thundering to life.

"Did you sleep well?" Ronan asks, reaching out to slide my hair from my face. I bare my teeth, and they laugh at me as Ronan pats my cheek hard. "Feeling feisty this morning?"

I grind my teeth but don't offer a reply.

Daemon throws something at me, and it lands on my chest. "Put these on."

When I don't move, he sighs. "It's clothes. Like these." He points to the dark fabric he wears on his body. "This is a T-shirt, and these are jeans." Gesturing impatiently at the material in my hands, he looks at me expectantly. "Put them on."

I don't move. They exchange glances, and Ronan tries hard not to laugh, causing my cheeks to heat with embarrassment.

"Like these." Alaric flaps his T-shirt.

Losing patience, Daemon shoulders past him and grabs the lumps of fabric on my chest. He forcefully pulls one over my head, guiding my arms through the holes. It's long, falling mid-thigh. "It's a dress."

"A dress?" I ask, peering up at him.

"Yes, a fucking dress! And these are a pair of panties." He dangles a flimsy piece of fabric in front of me.

He's so attractive, he's hard to look at.

They all are.

"You told me not to hide from you."

His dark eyes collide with mine. "I don't want other men looking at you." Crouching down in front of me, he helps me put on the silk panties before rising to his feet. I follow him with my gaze as he walks out with his dark wings tucked behind him. They're so big that they almost trail the floor.

"Brush your hair," Alaric orders, handing me a hairbrush. At least this is something I'm familiar with. I accept it and set to work on the tangly knots.

"You're coming to school with us today." Ronan lights a cigarette and blows a cloud of smoke at the ceiling.

"It's dark outside," I point out.

"You're in the underworld. It's always dark here."

"Oh."

"Yes, oh."

The embers spark bright orange as he takes a deep drag, peering at me with his curious dark eyes. "You're a virgin, but have you ever had a boyfriend?"

"What's a boyfriend?" I ask, making them chuckle.

Alaric clasps my chin hard, bringing his face close to mine. "I bet you've never been kissed either."

My lips tingle at his words. I shouldn't like how rough he is. No one has ever touched me like this before, not before last night.

"I bet your pouty little lips have never tasted a man's." His cruel smile and the knowing glint in his eyes are my undoing. I try to squeeze my thighs together discreetly, but he notices.

Smirking, he brushes his thumb over my mouth. "We'll have so much fun with you."

Ronan continues smoking as Alaric walks out the door and shuts it with a soft click. I don't dare move off the couch while he watches me through the tendrils of smoke. I'm painfully aware of the fabric against my skin and how it has ridden up my thighs. His dark eyes drink me up, tracing my every curve and lingering in forbidden places.

When he's done smoking, he crushes the cigarette beneath his boot, clasps my arm, and drags me off the couch. "It's time to go."

"Where to?" I ask.

He hauls me into the hallway and down a set of stairs. The stone walls are lined with flickering torches that light our way, casting shadows along the walls. Beneath my feet, the steps are icy cold and I shiver.

"There are certain rules we expect you to adhere to when we leave here." His voice is deep and raspy as he digs his fingers into my neck. I fight the tingle that threatens. The others wait for us by the bottom of the stairs, their dark, hungry eyes tracking my every step.

Daemon moves forward. "You're ours now and we get to do with you as we fucking please, do you understand?"

A blush creeps up my neck as anger rises within me thick and fast. It's a feeling I've only ever read about, as mythical as the boys in front of me. I glare at him, and he glowers back.

"Do you understand?" he asks tersely again.

I close the small distance between us. Behind me, my wings ache to stretch out and show him I'm not scared. I follow that instinct, and the fire that flickers in his eyes burns brighter when my wings unfold.

"I am not yours!"

In one swift motion, his hand shoots out and grabs me by the throat.

My wings snap shut.

"I can still taste your sweet pussy on my lips, *little angel.* Let's not pretend you don't want me to taste you again."

Behind me, Ronan and Alaric chuckle darkly.

"I hate you!" I snarl, surprised by the violent emotion.

Hate...

It's unlike any other emotion. Volatile and destructive, like a tornado in a trailer park. I want to hurt him while he begs for more. I want to claw his eyes out. I also want to climb him like the tree I used to scale as a young girl to look over the wall at the forest beyond.

His eyes flicker with danger and his smile grows. "Never felt anger before, beautiful girl? Tell me," he taunts, breathing against my lips. "Are you wet? Greedy for cock? Want to feel your tight little virgin cunt stretched to its limit? Hate sex is the best."

My wings are out again, and his unfolds to match mine. His wide smile is taunting, knowing.

"You can't beat me," he whispers, squeezing my throat while skimming his fingers up my thigh, beneath my dress. The slide of his touch over my damp panties causes me to gasp into his mouth. Daemon snatches up my lip, sucking on it until my legs threaten to give out. "No looking at other boys," he warns, snaking his fingers inside my panties. "If I catch you flirting with another boy, I'll make you regret it, understood?"

My hips rock forward, seeking the reward building slowly inside me when he rubs my clit. The same warm, fuzzy feeling that stole my breath last night.

A hand behind me slides over my wing, tracing the curve. "They're so white."

Daemon doesn't look away from my face as he says,

"When we're done with her, the color of her wings won't matter. She'll be corrupt beyond repair. Her precious Heaven won't want her back."

My eyes roll to the back of my head, and just when I'm about to be swept out to sea and drowned in his magical touch, he steps away. I'm unsteady on my legs, swaying on the spot. Strong hands grip me from behind, and a set of soft lips whisper in my ear, "Watch."

Daemon looks me in the eye while licking me off his fingers. I shiver as they disappear into his mouth before slowly sliding back out. "So fucking delicious," he drawls, moving forward again, patting my cheek with his damp digits. "Be a good girl today, and we'll take care of that ache later."

He's right—my pussy throbs with need. I want to beg him to finish what he started and put me out of my misery with his forbidden touch and filthy words, but I clamp my mouth shut instead. I'm a goddamn angel. I am pure. *Or I was until last night,* a voice inside my head whispers.

"Let's get this show on the road." Ronan walks past and opens the door for us. He smiles at me on my way out. "Don't look so angry, little angel. Would you rather we keep our new toy locked away in the tower?"

"I can't believe we caught a fucking angel," Alaric drawls behind me as we set off down the gravel path.

Daemon walks ahead of us, the embers of his cigarette glowing orange in the darkness.

"I know," Ronan responds. "The others will be so fucking jealous."

"Hey, Daemon. What did your dad say when you told him about the angel?"

Daemon turns and walks backward, his muscles straining against his dark T-shirt. Lowering the cigarette from his lips, he blows out a thick cloud of smoke. "He wants to see her for himself when he returns."

"Uh-oh," laughs Alaric, shoving me forward a step with his hand on my back. "Do you hear that, sweet thing? You'll meet Daddy dearest soon. Daemon's father is not someone you want to upset."

I release a laugh. "You're so cliche!"

He side-eyes me with a smirk. "Why's that?"

"Well, think about it. Three bad boys abduct me in the woods late at night, and their fathers turn out to be these powerful men everyone fears." I roll my eyes. "It's cliche."

Daemon's low chuckle up ahead makes the hairs on my neck rise. "Your innocence is refreshing," he says, his breath dancing in the wind.

Why is there a nip in the air here when it's warm in Eden?

Ronan speaks up behind me, "Daemon's father is one of the most powerful fallen angels here. It's why Daemon's wings are so big."

"I know how wingspan works," I snark, earning me another shove from Alaric.

"Shut that pretty mouth of yours, or I'll put it to good use."

The scary part is that my heart picks up speed at his threat. These boys make me feel alive in a way I didn't know was possible. This exhilarating fear is the feeling I craved when I snuck out through the gates.

"You said *one* of the most powerful angels. Who else?"

Daemon plays with a fireball in his hand as we keep walking. It's Ronan who speaks. "Daemon's cousin Dmitriy. Their dads are both equally powerful."

"Right," I drawl, "just when I thought it couldn't get any more cliche, we climb to new heights."

The boys gather around me as we reach a break in the trees. "Why don't you fly in Eden?" Alaric asks me, slowly unfolding his wings behind him.

I turn in a circle, watching their impressive wings block out the forest. "I-I don't know. I've never flown."

"You'll soon learn," Daemon promises, stepping up to me and sliding his arm around my waist. We shoot up into the sky, and I gasp with surprise. The treetops spread out beneath me like a green blanket in the darkness.

I circle my arms around Daemon's neck and wrap my thighs around his waist, hanging on for dear life like a spider monkey with my nose buried in his neck. If I look down, I'll scream. His chest vibrates with chuckles, and his powerful wings slice through the air with every shift as we soar through the sky.

"You can look down. I won't let you fall."

I shake my head, clinging on tighter. I'm never looking down. If I do, I'll panic and lose my grip, despite his promise not to let me fall. The wind in my wings tickles, awakening something primal inside me, and the ache to spread them and have them carry me is overwhelming as they flutter open experimentally behind me.

"Have you never had the urge to fly?" Daemon asks. I like him like this: kind and curious. My response is a quick shake of my head against his neck. We don't fly in Eden. What would have stopped me from flying over the wall if we did?

"How is she coping?" Ronan asks to my left, his voice laced with amusement.

"Better you than me if she pukes," Alaric teases.

Daemon's neck smells amazing, masculine and wild. If I could bottle his smell and give it a name, I would call it Bad Decisions. That's what these fallen angels are—your mother's worst nightmare. They're the thief in the night that climbs in through your bedroom window to steal your innocence. What's worse? You give it up freely.

I don't know how long we fly before my feet finally touch solid ground. We're not alone anymore, there are other young angels everywhere, dark and tall like my captors. In front of us is a tall stone building that reminds me of the castles from the fairytales back home. Four high towers and awnings. Stained glass windows and sharp-toothed gargoyles.

Eden is relatively small, while everything here is big. I've never seen so many students in my life before. Girls and boys watch me curiously. I shrug Daemon off and brush my hands down my dress, grateful to be covered. Everyone is naked back home, so being aware of my body and its nakedness beneath the thin layer of this dress is a strange sensation.

"Remember," Daemon says, clasping the back of my neck, "you're ours."

A beautiful girl with long, raven hair saunters up to us, her hips swaying and her long hair moving in an imaginary breeze. Her eyes sweep down my body and her red-painted lips curl in disgust. "Who's she?"

"Little angel, meet Dariana. She's the resident bitch, so stay out of her way."

The girl, Dariana, sneers at Ronan.

"Dari, the little angel is our new toy, so be nice to her. We found her walking the woods by herself last night." Daemon sounds proud, his fangs gleaming in the moonlight when he flashes her a smile.

"She's so *bright.*" Her nose scrunches up as she looks at me. "She shimmers."

"That's because she's a true angel," Alaric points out, walking ahead toward the castle.

Dariana's dark eyes snap to me. "You stole an angel?"

Daemon shoves me forward with his hand on my neck. "What do you do when you find a shiny coin on the ground? You pick it up."

Stumbling forward, I try hard not to fall on my face. It's humiliating to be paraded around like this. I stand out with my white wings in a sea of black feathers and dark eyes. Next to Daemon's olive skin, mine looks translucent and pale as snow.

"What are you going to do with her?" Dariana asks. Her instant dislike for me is palpable in the cool air. She had these boys to herself before they snatched me, and she dislikes the competition now that they have a new and more exciting toy.

"What we do with any other girl. Fuck her every hole and leave her ruined." Daemon's grip on my neck turns painful. He leans close and breathes me in. "But we'll take our time with this one. Toy with her a bit before we discard her in the forest to fend for herself."

"In the forest," laughs Dariana. "They won't let her back into Eden when you're through with her. She'll have no home."

Daemon's eyes are on me as he replies, "Well, then she better convince me to keep her. Isn't that right, sweet angel?"

"Fuck you!" I hiss, tearing free from his grip. Dariana's trill laughter turns heads, and curious eyes follow me as I storm inside the building with no clue where I'm going or why I'm here. More girls, wearing black dresses with thin shoulder straps that fall mid-thigh, join their little clique. They eye me with disdain as if I'm an insect they want to squash beneath their feet.

"Where are you going?" Alaric asks, slinging his arm over my shoulders. His smile is infuriating.

Another boy joins their group, eyeing me curiously before an easy smile finds his lips. "I've never seen a girl turn you down before."

"That's because girls don't turn us down," Ronan replies behind me. We're in a large open hallway with a grand staircase leading up to the second and third floors. Students lean on the railing upstairs, looking down at us and whispering. I'm the fresh gossip, the splash of color in an otherwise bland existence.

An older man with a neatly trimmed beard descends the stairs. He does a double-take when he sees me. "Are my eyes deceiving me?"

Alaric's smile is easy, but Daemon is tense as he takes up position in front of me.

"My, my, I haven't seen an angel from Eden in a very long time," the man says, walking up to us. "Care to explain why she's here?"

"We found her in the forest."

"Interesting," the man says, drawing the word out. He drags his eyes down my body and then back up again. "Pray tell, why were you outside the gates?"

Is he talking to me? I look to the others for help, but they're intent on the man in front of us. "Err? I was curious."

His eyebrows shoot up. "Curious?"

"Who are you?" I ask.

Dariana sniggers behind me.

"Who am I?" the man asks me, giving Daemon a long sideways glance before clasping his shoulder. He smiles at me. "Daemon is my nephew." The boy in question is stiff as a rod, and I get the sense he doesn't care much for his uncle.

"What are you doing here?" Daemon questions the man, who chuckles and lets go of Daemon's shoulder. "I came to see my son and nephew. I've been away for a few days."

Daemon says nothing.

"Well, I better be going. It was lovely to meet you," the man says to me, his smile too wide and sugary to be genuine. Daemon and Alaric watch him leave while Ronan scrolls on his phone.

"I don't trust him," Daemon growls, and Alaric nods in agreement. "I didn't like how he looked at her." They exchange a glance, communicating silently. I wish I knew what was going on inside their heads. Something tells me I'll need to figure them out if I want a chance at escaping this place. Freya will be beside herself with worry by now.

Dariana shoots me a disgusted look as she walks past me with her friends. To the boys, she says, "See you in class."

I watch them leave, secretly admiring their black feathers. The girls' wings aren't as big as the boys', but the black feathers shine beneath the glow from the flickering torches on the walls.

A warm hand slides around the back of my neck, shoving me forward.

"I can walk without you pushing me everywhere," I growl at Daemon, but he ignores me. His grip hurts and his jaw is tense as we walk up the stairs, then down a hallway lined with doors. Some are propped open, revealing classrooms. In Eden, we do all our lessons out on the soft grass. It's warm back home, not chilly like here. Maybe that's why our teachers don't crowd us into cramped classrooms.

We enter one and find seats toward the back. Ronan pulls out a chair, sits down, and drags me onto his lap. His hand snakes beneath the table, possessively cupping my pussy through my dress. A whimper slips from my lips. His heated breath wafts over my ear when he chuckles. "Want me to touch you in front of everyone here?" The warmth of his hand leaves my pussy, only to slide over my skin as he inches my dress up my legs. My body lights up like fireworks, every nerve ending coming alive.

I try to wriggle off, but he bands his arm around my waist and continues his torturous journey toward my throbbing heat. The tips of his fingers ghost over my panties, and I jolt in his arms, my lips parting. I feel him smile against my ear. "Ignore everyone else. It's just you and me here."

It's a little difficult to ignore the students flooding through the door and walking past our desk. But he's right—I soon forget when his hand slides inside my panties.

"Ssshh!" he soothes. "Be quiet, beautiful. You don't want the other students to realize I'm defiling you in the classroom, do you?"

Alaric knows exactly what's going on as he snorts with amusement and shakes his head. "I thought I was cruel."

Ronan laughs in my ear, his skilled fingers rubbing my aching clit in slow, mind-blowing circles. "She likes it."

Before I stumbled upon these boys, I had never felt a sensation like it. I spread my legs beneath the table despite knowing this sinful act could see me banished from Eden.

"Feels good, huh?" he breathes, shoving a thick finger inside me. "Don't make a sound, or I'll stop."

The slide of him against my inner walls... The full feeling and the slight sting from the stretch. I'm falling apart.

"Just put her out of her misery," Daemon drawls, balancing on his chair's back legs with his phone in his hand, looking bored and busy at the same time.

"I think I'll torture her all through class," Ronan chuckles as the teacher—a middle-aged woman with curly, dark hair and a flowy dress—enters the room. The minute her eyes land on me, she halts, pressing a hand to her chest. Alaric hides a laugh behind his closed fist, and Daemon doesn't look up from his phone.

"What on Hell's earth is that? An angel? Oh, boys," she tuts, shaking her head tiredly, "you bring so much trouble to our lands."

Daemon finally looks up and says in a slow, bored voice, "She left Eden of her own free will. The elders won't lift a finger to get her back. Besides," a slow smile curves his lips, "she's already too defiled to be accepted back inside the pearly gates."

My head snaps in his direction. Is that true? Am I no longer pure? Even as the thought enters my mind, I know I'm not. The slide of Ronan's finger inside me and the flick of his thumb over my clit speaks the truth. But how can sin feel so good? I couldn't ask Ronan to stop even if I tried. Not when he grinds down with the heel of his palm, whispering dirty words in my ear. Words I shouldn't like so much. Words like, *"Your tight virgin cunt squeezes me so well."*

Exasperated, the teacher shakes her head and walks up to the blackboard. The scrape of the chalk cuts through the silence while she mutters under her breath. I'm flushed, and my cheeks are blotchy with desire. I squirm on Ronan's lap, in need of release. My core tenses and slowly melts as the pleasure builds between my legs.

"Good girl," he praises, his hot breath dancing over the sensitive skin below my ear. "Keep nice and quiet for me."

The teacher launches into a discussion about fire magic, but I can't hear her as I climb higher and higher.

"You torture the girl," Alaric says with a laugh.

"You know classes bore me, and this beats listening to Mrs. Avery."

Just when I'm about to come, Ronan slides his hand out from my panties, leaving me trembling on his lap. "Not yet."

What does he mean by '*not yet?*' I'm so aroused, it hurts. The look I give him when I turn on his lap makes Daemon chuckle and place his phone down on the desk.

"Come here, beautiful," he coaxes, leaning back in his chair, his legs spread wide, the bulge in his jeans visible. "I'll take care of you."

A boy at the front is conjuring a fireball or attempting to while Mrs. Avery instructs him. Daemon, Alaric, and Ronan make it look easy when they do it. My feet move on their own accord. I have no say in the matter. My body knows that the boy with the cruel smile and hellfire in his eyes can give me what I need. Daemon smirks, and Alaric stifles a laugh behind his hand when I slide onto Daemon's lap, spreading my legs beneath the table.

I don't care. All I can focus on is the heat of Daemon's hard chest against my back and his big hand as he slides my panties aside. I ache. Fuck, how I crave release.

"What will you offer me in exchange for taking care of your needs?" he asks, his touch a little too rough.

I don't reply, I'm too turned on to think straight. If I respond now, I'll agree to shit I shouldn't. His touch verges on pain. It's a fine line to balance, and I'm close to slipping off. I need more.

"Answer me, beautiful."

"No," I choke out, and he smiles as he slides his other hand up to my throat. His fingers wrap around me and he whispers in my ear, "Then I won't let you come. I'll keep you teetering on the edge until you beg me on your knees to fuck you so hard that you forget your own name."

"Oh, God," I moan under my breath. The other students are throwing us curious glances, but I don't think they're wise about what's going on. They're too distracted by a real-life angel. I'm as much of a mythological creature from their fairy-tales as they are mine.

"You won't want to leave Hell once I'm done with you." His warm lips press against my cheek, and his grip on my throat tightens. "You'll beg and moan on your knees for me to let you stay. I suggest you do as I say. Be a good girl, and I might consider it."

"Fuck you," I hiss through the drugging pleasure. "I'll never beg."

His hand disappears, and my eyes fly open. *No, no, no.* Why did he stop?

"Then I won't let you come. None of us will."

My swollen clit throbs with its own heartbeat, and my pussy feels empty. These feelings are new and foreign to me. I need the ache gone. I need to straddle Daemon and rub myself against the thick bulge in his jeans until the wave comes crashing against the shore.

"Daemon," Mrs. Avery says, slowly walking up to us, her wings fluttering behind her. "Why don't you show the angel how you conjure a fireball?"

I catch a whiff of my scent on his hand when he lifts it off my lap and clicks his fingers. A fireball sparks to life, and flickering flames dance in front of me, making me gasp. Daemon shifts his hand, and the fireball takes on the shape of a wolf howling at the moon.

Mrs. Avery glows with pride. "Well done, Daemon. Your powers are coming in nicely.

Powers?

She walks back toward her desk, her hands clasped behind her back. "Your powers all come in at different times. There's no right or wrong. Some of you will be more powerful than others, and that's okay. By now, you should all have the ability to conjure up hellfire at the click of a finger. This Friday, I'll test you on it." Her eyes find mine. "Well, *almost* every one of you will have the ability to manipulate hellfire."

"You're not born of Hell," Alaric whispers, leaning in from across the aisle.

"Stating the obvious," I comment drily, making the three of them chuckle.

When the class ends, they drag me out of the room and down a long, carpeted hallway. The walls are lined with lit torches and framed paintings of fallen angels, all with large, black wings that spread out behind them. Students whisper and snigger as we walk past. I duck my head, feeling embarrassed. Daemon's grip on my arm doesn't ease up. I'm sure I'll bruise.

"What are you doing?" I ask when he pushes me into the bathroom.

He ignores me, roaring at girls by the sinks, "Get out!"

They scatter like a sea of cockroaches, and then we're alone. Ronan checks that the toilet stalls are empty while Alaric flips the lock. Scanning my eyes around the spacious bathroom, I back away. There's a large stained-glass window to my left and a small couch pressed up against the wall beneath it. The air smells citrusy. My lower back connects with the sinks, and I let out a small gasp. They stalk me, three predators sizing up their prey. There's no escape. I would have to run past them to get out, but how far would I get before they caught up? Would I make it past the first corner?

"You look frightened," Alaric says with a knowing smirk.

They're in front of me now. Ronan reaches out to drag his thumb over my bottom lip. He pulls it away from my teeth, his eyes darkening. His touch is not gentle, and I realize I don't want it to be. I want rough hands and the promise of hell that flickers in the boys' eyes. My breath hitches and my nipples peak, straining against the thin fabric of my dress.

"What shall we do with her?" Ronan asks.

Daemon shoulders past him, grabs my hips, and lifts me up on the sink. He steps between my legs, sliding my dress up my thighs until it's pooled around my waist and my damp panties are on display. His finger hooks the fabric, pulling them roughly aside. My heart trips over itself, my breath catching in my throat when the cool air hits my sensitive slit.

"Let's torment her."

He fists my hair at the same time he shoves his thick finger inside me. It hurts, but I want more. "Let's steal the very last of her innocence."

My body rocks on the sink as he rams his finger inside my pussy hard and fast. The burn soon shifts into pleasure, becoming something wild and untamed.

"I want to see her crawl on her fucking knees for us."

My head falls back on a moan when he pulls my hair to expose my neck to his hungry lips and sharp fangs.

"When we're done with her, she'll be ruined for other angels. Isn't that right, sweet angel?" he taunts, grabbing my chin and forcing my mouth back to his. He kisses me hard, drugging me with his scent and the punishing sweeps of his tongue.

Alaric nudges him out of the way and then takes his place, teasing my throbbing clit with his fingers. He flicks it once, twice, then thrusts his digit inside me until he's knuckle-deep. "Look down," he whispers. "See that?" He slides his finger back out, and I gasp at the slick arousal glistening in the soft glow from the torches on the walls. "That's what we do to you." He shoves back in, much rougher this time. "We dirty you up."

"Oh, God," I whimper, clutching his T-shirt. I'm burning up. Slowly but fucking surely, the flames of Hell crawl up my skin, torching my sanity.

"You're in Hell now, little angel. There's no God here. There's only pleasure and sin, all the things your creator denied you of to keep you *pure*." He chuckles, and the dirty sound sends tingles straight to my pussy. "Fuck pure! We want you on your back, moaning with your legs spread, ready to take our cocks like a good little angel whore."

I don't even notice him leave, but then, when a moment of clarity resurfaces, I gasp into Ronan's mouth as he grips the back of my neck, crushing his mouth against mine. His fangs elongate, grazing up against my lip. I taste blood on my tongue, a rich coppery taste that makes him groan and lean back to slap my cheek—not hard, but with enough power behind the blow to stun me. I blink up at him, dazed. His lips come back down, and he fucks me with his fingers until all I can see and taste is him. His scent, his power, and his whispered, filthy words against my lips.

"That's enough!" Daemon orders and Ronan steps back,

leaving me wanting and breathing hard. They watch me with hungry eyes.

As I lower my gaze, I realize the top of my black dress is pushed down to reveal my small breasts. My nipples are hard points that beg for a warm mouth and a skilled tongue. My daze slowly evaporates like the morning mist. I flick my gaze between the fallen angels. "What's happening?"

They take their sweet time answering. Daemon steps forward, sliding my dress back up to cover my breasts. "We're teaching you a lesson, little angel."

"A lesson?" I ask, trying to close my legs, but he pries them open and slides his fingers through my wetness. Holding his glistening finger up in front of me, he says, "If you want to come, you have to beg." He prods my mouth with his slick digit, forcing me to taste myself on him. "You don't get to come unless we let you. It's a privilege you earn when you're a good girl. Please us," he whispers, watching me suck on his finger, "and we'll reward you."

As soon as his finger slides out, I bare my teeth and snap my legs shut. "You'll never get me to beg."

They don't look surprised by my response. If anything, they look pleased, as if they enjoy the chase.

"As you wish," Daemon replies with a smirk. They file out, and I stare after them, wondering what just happened.

Are they coming back? Am I free to go?

Is this a test?

My pulsing clit is momentarily forgotten as I slide my ass off the sink before padding softly over to the door. I ease it open and peer outside. There's no sign of them anywhere, so I shut the door again and consider my options. This is too good to be true—they're not letting me go this easily. It's a test to see what I'll do. But there's no other way out unless I smash the stained glass. My only choice is to step into the hallway and see what happens, so that's what I do.

Inching the door open, I join the other students on their way to class. I'm the only splash of white in a sea of black. Students stop to stare at me with a mixture of awe, curiosity, and weariness. The crowd parts, revealing Daemon and his friends leaning against the lockers that line the wall.

I bolt.

My feet thunder on the stone floor as I turn the corner and run down the next hallway. I don't know which way is out, and I don't know how I'll ever find my way back home if I do make it out. It doesn't matter. There's only one thought going through my mind on loop: I need to escape the three fallen angels tormenting me.

As I round another corner, I collide with a hard chest and stumble back. Warm hands steady me. I look up into a set of chocolate-brown eyes.

"Hello there," the boy says, his eyes sparkling with amusement as I jump back, looking behind me like a spooked rabbit on the run from the fox. Or in this case, foxes.

When I try to step past him, he stops me.

"Where are you off to in such a hurry?" He looks familiar, but my mind could be playing tricks on me. All the fallen angels look similar, with dark features and black clothing.

I try to escape past him again, but he circles his fingers around my wrist and pulls me closer to him. "Are you okay?"

I'm not okay. Three dark-winged angels are trying to capture me. I quickly shake my head, looking nervously behind me.

"Who are you running from?" he asks, drawing my attention back to him.

"Daemon, Alaric, and Ronan," I reply, figuring everyone here knows who they are. His jaw hardens and he slides his hand into mine, then steers me into an empty classroom. The door shuts with a soft click. Nerves lock me in place as he places his finger over his lips, telling me without words to be quiet. Soon after, heavy feet thunder on the floor outside. Alaric's deep voice drifts through, "Where the fuck did she go?"

Their footsteps fade away until the only sound is my pounding heartbeat. The boy's concerned eyes come to mine, and it dawns on me that I'm locked in an empty classroom with a stranger.

"Are you okay?" he asks. "They didn't hurt you, did they?"

"No," I reply, relaxing somewhat. He seems kind, unlike everyone else I've met in my short time here.

"Are you sure you're okay?"

"I need to escape this place. I don't know how to find my way out. All the hallways look the same," I admit, feeling foolish.

He slowly walks up to me, his hands in his pockets. His broad shoulders and strong arms draw my eyes. Heat rises to my cheeks. Since I got here, I have noticed things about boys that I never did before.

"I'll show you the way out," he promises.

I light up with hope. "Really?"

He smiles. "Sure."

My cheeks blaze red. I avert my gaze, fighting the urge to fidget. My body feels strange. Nervous and trembling.

"But we need to wait a while until they're in class. They'll find you if we leave now."

"Oh, okay."

"What's Eden like?" he asks curiously, and a smile finds its way to my lips.

"It's warm, and the sun is always shining. The colors.... So many flowers and greenery, you wouldn't believe." It saddens me to think I might never feel the sun warm my cheeks unless I make my escape and find my way back home. Even if flowers grew here, you wouldn't see their varying shades of color because of the perpetual night.

"I've never seen the sun," the boy admits.

"You haven't?"

"No. It's always night in the underworld."

Curious about him, I inch closer, scanning my inquisitive eyes over the wings visible behind his shoulders. They're big, which makes me think he's not just any boy. Big wings are a sign of power and ability. He's studying my wings too, and I suddenly feel insecure about my white feathers.

"After the fall, our wings turned as black as night to symbolize the true nature of our souls. Yours is still in its purest form."

I don't know about that, I think, sinking down on a desk next to him. My three tormentors are on a mission to corrupt me, and they've done a fine job of it in the short time I've been here. Why else would my eyes linger on the muscles in his arms or the sharp line of his jaw when he turns his head to scan the darkness outside the window?

"Is it true that you don't know how to fly?"

"I don't."

His eyes collide with mine, and he studies me for a long moment before he says, "Unfold your wings."

"Excuse me?" I blush harder.

"You don't have to."

My wings slowly unfold until I feel them stretch to their full length behind me. The boy's eyes widen with curiosity. He rises to his feet and circles me. "Are your parents of high standing?"

"I don't know who my parents are."

The boy stops in front of me and frowns. "How is that possible?"

My wings slowly come down behind me, and I shrug. "No one knows their parents in Eden. We're born of the Light."

His eyes bug out and he makes a weird sound deep in his throat, like a cough or a choked laugh. "The Light?"

It sounds so stupid—I'm aware of that. I duck my head to hide my blush. "Can we talk about something else, please?"

Sensing my discomfort, he doesn't push me for answers. His shoes appear in my vision, and he tips my chin up with his fingers. "Don't hide."

"Why are you being nice to me?"

His smile is soft, teasing. "Don't you want me to be?"

"Things are different here. The people are... different."

He nods as if that makes sense while I peer up at him from beneath my dark lashes.

"What's your name?"

Just then, the door flies open.

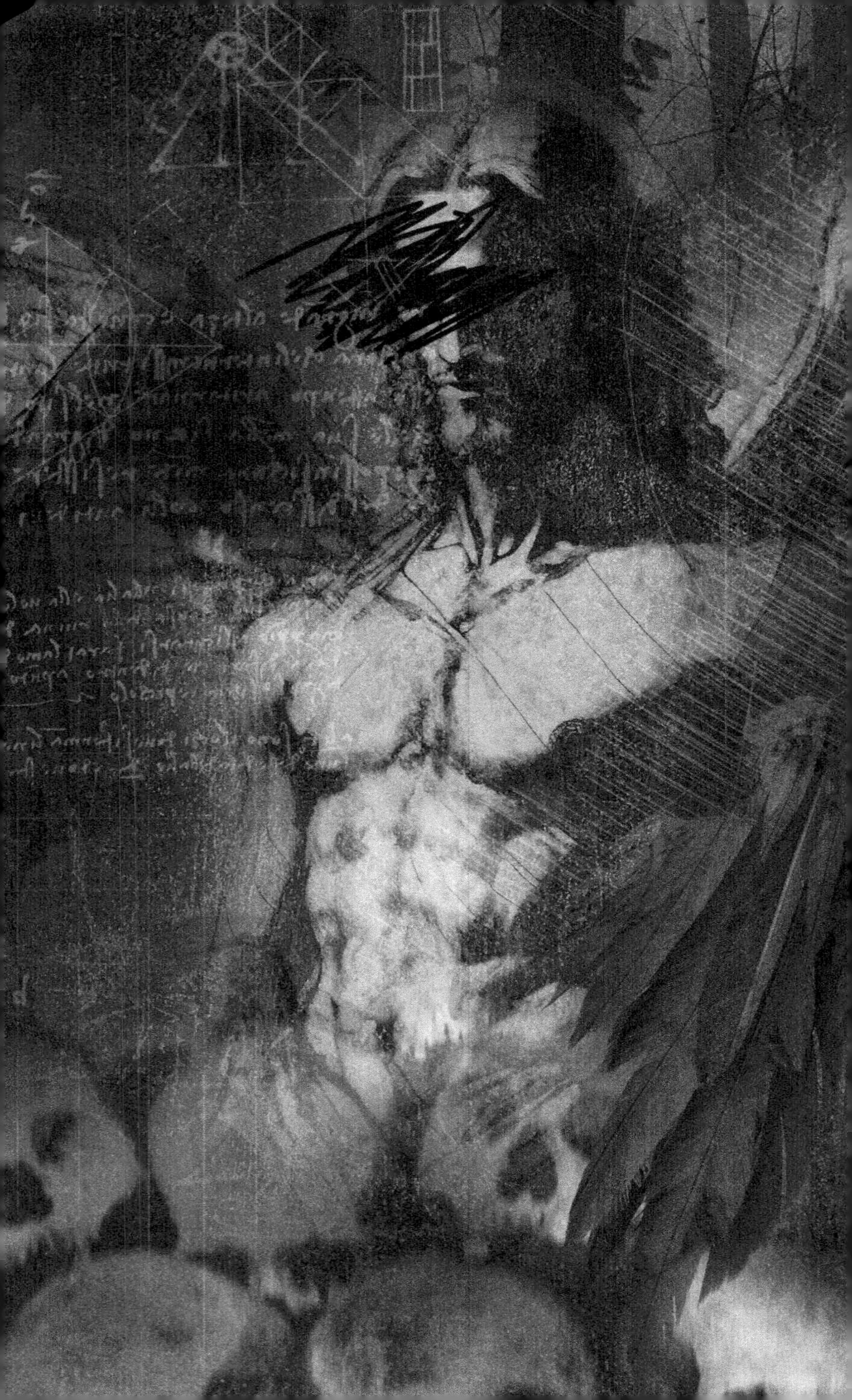

CHAPTER 4

DAEMON

Fury rises thick and fast inside me when we come to a halt inside the classroom. There she is, sitting on a desk and peering up at my fucking cousin with stars in her eyes. The fucker is up to no good. I can see it in the glint in his eyes when he turns to look at me. "Hi, cousin."

I tell him with one glare to back the fuck off. Not that he takes any notice. I shove him away and grip the little angel's chin. "Did he touch you?"

"Chill, man," my cousin laughs, his ridiculous pimples popping. I'm not stupid, I've been a piece on his playing board my whole life.

"Did. He. Touch. You?"

My little angel whimpers, and I almost give in to the ridiculous urge to be gentler with her.

Almost...

"No," she finally admits, and I release a breath I didn't know I was holding. Alaric is already up in my cousin's face, making him laugh even more. It's grating on my fucking nerves. Who does he think he is, moving in on our angel? This one belongs to us. I'll kill anyone who touches her.

"Leave, Dmitriy, before we make you regret even so much as looking at our angel."

His amused chuckle is low and deep, causing me to fist my hands at my sides. "Your angel? You don't even know her name!"

"We don't need to know her fucking name. Now, piss off!"

Dmitriy shrugs, then says to the little angel, "I'm sorry I couldn't help you escape."

She tries to look at him, but I dig my fingers into her jaw to keep her eyes on mine. No way is she looking at that fucker. The door shuts softly. Angel blinks up at me with her big, crystal-blue eyes that could bring a grown man to his knees. Why does she have to be so beautiful? Are all angels from Eden as breathtaking as her? I could stare at her all day, but I'm not in the fucking mood to be soppy. Not when she defied us by trying to escape.

"Did you think you could run away from us and not pay the consequences?"

The boys crowd in on either side of me. Our little angel bounces her eyes between us, unsure who to focus on. I make the choice simple for her by wrapping my hand around her throat. The urge to dominate her and make her bend to our will is an itch that demands to be scratched. I want to mount her like a fucking animal and possess her in every way possible while watching her squirm with pleasure beneath me. Hell, I want to *own* her. It's not enough to simply play with her. Alaric and Ronan are equally restless next to me. We all want a piece of her, like a cake you cut into tiny slices and feast on.

"Answer him!" Ronan demands on my left.

Her fiery eyes burn with defiance and her lips remain closed. She doesn't know who she's playing with. It's hot as fuck to have stumbled upon a girl who fights back. Here, in Hell, we can have anyone we want. If I click my fingers, the girls line up. But Angel is different. She doesn't take shit. She's scared, but she won't let us break her spirit. We'll see about that. I like to break pretty little things, and I won't rest until our little angel lies in a thousand broken pieces on my bedroom floor.

I reach out and slide my fingers into her hair, pulling sharply on the silky strands. I love her like this with her neck bared, the rise and fall of her soft tits as her breaths come quicker.

"You think you're so strong, little angel?" I taunt, stepping closer. My cock strains against the confines of my jeans, and when I begin to unclasp my belt buckle, she whimpers. It's a submissive sound I could get used to.

Just as I go to slide my zipper down, the door opens, and the headmistress walks in. Her dark eyes scan over Angel. Gossip spreads fast here at the academy, so she already knows we have acquired a new plaything. I'm disappointed; there isn't even the barest flicker of surprise in her eyes.

The left side of the little angel's mouth curves up in a smirk, like she has somehow won this round. I suck on my teeth while buckling my jeans before treating the headmistress to my most charming smile. "We lost track of time, mistress."

The lady in question waves her hand impatiently, and we part like the sea. Our little angel's smirk falls when Headmistress walks up to her. Now it's my turn to smile. Headmistress makes grown men shake in their boots with her cold eyes.

"What's your name, child?"

"Aurelia," she replies timidly.

Aurelia...

I exchange a look with Ronan and Alaric.

"How did you find yourself outside of Eden? Were you banished?"

Headmistress's black velvet dress hugs her curves like a second skin. I catch Ronan checking out her ass and give him a subtle shake of my head. If she spots him checking her out, she'll pluck out his eyes with her blood-red nails. True story—it has happened before.

"I wasn't banished. I was..." she looks at me, "...curious."

"A curious little angel?" Headmistress purrs, her voice soft as silk. "Tell me, child, has your curiosity been sated?"

Aurelia swallows, her eyes flicking back to the woman in front of her. "No, it has not."

"Oh?" Now Headmistress sounds genuinely surprised. So am I.

Alaric looks at me, his eyes wide and intrigued. *What is she doing?*

I frown. *Beats me.*

"You're a brave young girl," Headmistress says, flashing fangs as she smiles. "Either that or foolish."

Aurelia stays quiet.

Smart girl.

"So, what will it take to satiate your curiosity?"

"My powers."

Headmistress grows eerily still. "Your powers?"

"The fallen angels have powers, so why wouldn't I? I want to learn."

"Child, you're from Heav—"

"Why would that stop me from having powers? The fallen angels originate from heaven too, but they were banished. My elders don't teach us or encourage us to discover our powers. You do. I want to learn."

Headmistress is silent for a long moment before she turns halfway and looks at us. "She starts classes tomorrow. I want you boys to personally oversee her learning."

My mouth falls open. "But, Headmistress, she's an angel from Ede—"

"You heard her, Daemon. She wants to discover her powers. I'm holding you personally responsible to teach her."

"But Headmistress—"

"Do we have a problem here? Do I need to contact your father?"

My mouth snaps shut. My father is away for the week and wouldn't take kindly to being interrupted. I do a lot of stupid shit, but this is up there with the worst. He won't be pleased when he returns and spots our new toy. He already chewed me out when I told him about her on the phone after he called me in a rage.

"Good," she says, dragging the word out with a triumphant, slow-to-form, dark smile.

Alaric narrows his eyes at her as she walks out. As soon as the door shuts behind her, he turns to me. "What is she up to?"

Good question. Why would she want us to help *Aurelia* discover her powers unless she's curious? Headmistress doesn't have a kind bone in her body. She's not ordering us to oversee Aurelia out of the goodness of her heart. No, she's curious and eager to find out what powers—if any—Aurelia possesses.

Aurelia... I study the angel while she peers up at us. Her soft curves rise and fall with her every inhale, and her long, blonde hair falls down her back and shoulders like a cascading waterfall.

"So, you want to discover your powers?" I ask, wetting my lips. "You surprised me. I thought for a moment that you would beg Headmistress to let you go home. Not stay here with us."

"Don't flatter yourself," she hisses, sliding off the bench.

I'm a head taller than her. She reaches my collarbone, but the height difference doesn't faze her as she cranes her neck to glare at me. "I didn't ask to stay so I could be with you or your friends."

Struck with the urge to shut her up with my fingers in her mouth or my cock, I fist my hands to stop myself from reaching for her. I want her rage and fire.

"If I go back, I won't learn my true potential. Besides, we all know the gates won't open for me anymore. You, *Daemon*," she pokes me in the chest, "made sure of that."

The fire in her eyes burns brighter when I smirk.

"So I will learn everything I can." She steps even closer, her breath fanning my neck. "You better watch out, angel boy. I'm coming for you. I don't know how and I don't know when, but I'll reduce you to a pile of fucking ashes. You think I'll beg on my knees for you?" She gives a breathy laugh that stirs my cock in its denim prison. I definitely want to shut her up with it now—ram it so far down her tight throat that she chokes while clawing my thighs for reprieve.

"I'll have you crawling to me like a leashed pet. You and your friends picked the wrong angel to mess with. And by the time I'm done with you three, you'll wish you left me in the woods."

I'm rock-hard. Didn't her elders teach her why you should never poke the slumbering beast? This time, it's her who walks out and us who stare after her like puppies waiting for the command to please their mistress.

CHAPTER 5

AURELIA

Dariana sneers at me from her perch on Ronan's lap on the armchair, and two more girls giggle over by the window where they stand with Alaric. As soon as we returned to their house, Daemon dragged me up here and lit the fireplace with a click of his fingers.

I've since sat on the couch, trying not to kill someone with the poison dripping from my veins. My stomach churns every time the girls' laughter drifts over.

Since my arrival in Hell, I've experienced a range of emotions I can't place. This thick, clogging emotion that makes me feel nauseous is wholly unwelcome. I don't even know what it means—I just know the girls are the reason for it, and I don't like it.

Daemon sits in the armchair across from Ronan with his elbow on the armrest and his chin in his hand. His eyes burn into me, and my skin crawls every time his lips quirk. It's as if he knows how uncomfortable I am. Maybe he does. I keep my eyes trained on the flames in the fireplace, so I don't have to look at him or any of them.

"Headmistress is letting her attend classes?" Dariana asks Ronan. The distaste in her voice is unmistakable. She wants me gone.

"Yeah," Ronan drawls, too distracted by Dariana's cleavage as he dips a finger inside her low neckline. My teeth grind, and Daemon's lips twitch.

"But why? She should just send her back."

"That wouldn't be fun," Ronan replies, wiggling his finger. "We want to toy with her first."

Dariana looks displeased. Where's the fly swatter when she needs one?

I don't blame her. I could do with one too, so I could swat away the two girls hanging off Alaric's arms like he's God's gift to women everywhere.

Ronan slides down her thin shoulder strap, and the fabric follows, slipping off her full breast to reveal her rosy nipple. Ronan palms her breast, diving down to suck on the hard point. Dariana's eyes flick up to mine, and her lips curve to the left in a smug smile while Ronan laps at her nipple. It's all I can do not to shoot up from my chair and launch myself at her. The force of the emotion takes me by surprise.

I press my palm to my mouth, my trembling breaths gusting through my fingers while Dariana drags her fingers through his raven hair before guiding him to her other breast.

Sliding that strap down too, he slowly drags his tongue over her breast. I can't look away, mesmerized by their show. I've never seen a boy pleasure a girl before. These things don't take place in Eden.

Flames flicker in Daemon's eyes while he watches me squirm on the couch, then, "Dariana, make our little angel come."

What? I freeze, snapping my gaze toward him. What is he

doing? Dariana slowly rises from Ronan's lap and saunters up to me. Her full breasts sway with every step, and her dark hair moves over her skin, teasing her nipples.

"Ever been with a girl, little angel?" she breathes out, coming to stand between my legs. Her soft touch brushes my hair away from my eyes as I hold my breath, my skin tingling with anticipation.

I shake my head.

"You really don't have any fun in Heaven, do you?"

A small sound of surprise slips past my lips when she drops to her knees and shoves my dress up to my waist. Her hands slide back down with my panties. "I can make you feel things these boys can't."

Ronan snorts behind her, and Daemon hides a chuckle behind his hand.

"You'll never want to return to your precious Eden when I'm done with you. Let's give the boys a show."

My hands fly up to grip her silky hair when her hot mouth descends on my pussy. I moan, shuddering, unable to look away from her long lashes and red-painted lips on my clit. She sucks it into her mouth, digging her nails into my hips. The sensation is too much, and liquid desire shoots sparks down to my core as I fall back against the couch. God, I need this. After the agony the boys put me through today, my body trembles at her touch. I need a release. I need it so badly that it drives me insane.

"Little angel!" Daemon's voice rings out, sharp and commanding.

I lift my head, trying to focus on him through this haze of desire that threatens to obliterate me.

"Don't close your eyes. Look at Dari when she steals your purity."

"Please," I moan, unsure why I'm pleading. I want more friction, more pressure. More of everything.

"Look. At. Dari." His voice is deep, clipped, and drips with sex.

My body sings to his tune. I slide my gaze down and my lips part at what I see: Dariana gazing up at me, her tongue lapping at the desire that soaks my tight entrance. Daemon snaps his fingers, and the other girls walk up to us and stop on either side of Dariana. Their hands squeeze my breasts and slide my dress up and over my head.

It lands on the floor, and the cool air licks at my skin before their warm hands burn me up with firm strokes. My nipples are tweaked and pinched. Fingers slide into my mouth and I'm ordered to suck. They praise me and call me a good girl. I'm sensation, want, and need. The fingers in my mouth slide down my throat, causing me to gag.

"Do you like it, boys? Do you like seeing her come apart at our touch?" Dariana sucks on my pussy lips, slapping my cunt with her hand. The sharp sting is so sudden and unexpected that my back arches off the couch.

"You'll never see home again," one of the girls whispers tauntingly in my ear. "Never feel the sun on your face again, and you'll never know the approval of your God." The next pinch on my nipple hurts. "You're just a dirty little slut—a whore to discard when the boys grow bored. You'll never last." Her warm breath teases my ear. She grabs my face and brings my lips to hers. Then she darts her tongue out, sliding it over my bottom lip. Her cruelty barely registers.

How can it, when I'm melting into a puddle of want? My pussy pulses and my nipples tingle and ache. This is the highest fall and the sweetest death. Dariana pushes her fingers into me and laps at my clit faster and harder, her pace quickening. The fight is lost. I can't win against them and their torturous assault on my body. The many hands, intent on shoving me underwater and drowning me in this sea of pleasure.

The air leaves my lungs, and I fall apart with a silent scream as the orgasm rips through me with such force that I'll never again see the light shimmer on the surface. I'm not sorry; let me be tossed on stormy seas for a taste of this.

"Leave her," Daemon orders.

Rough hands slap my cheek and grip my jaw, ordering me to open my eyes. Daemon stares down at me, his eyes burning with something dark and nefarious. "Do you still wish to return to your precious Eden?"

What's the point of fighting him? I'm too satiated from the receding orgasm. "No," I reply honestly. My lips are dry. I wet them, reaching for his belt buckle, but he grabs my wrist in a tight, painful grip.

"If you want my cock, you'll have to beg for it."

Ripping my hand free, I crane my neck, looking him in the eye. "You'll never hear me beg."

"Then you'll never have my cock." He walks back to the armchair, sits down, and pats his thigh. "Dariana."

One tap on his leg—that's all it takes for her to hurry over like she's waited all night for the chance to fuck him. The jealousy inside churns my stomach, and I snap my gaze to the fire but soon look back when he grabs her ass and spreads her over his lap. His eyes are on me while he kisses her deeply and thoroughly, tasting *me* on her tongue. The fire in his eye—the sparkle of a challenge—stirs something dark inside me. I don't look away. Not when he wants to see me break. I keep watching as she unbuckles him.

Rising up on her knees, she lowers herself back down on his length. And I don't look away, even when I taste something foul on my tongue. My heart could tear into a million shredded pieces, and I still won't let him see me hurt. Or so I tell myself until it becomes too much to watch her bounce on him.

My body shoots off the couch without my permission, his dark eyes following me as I flee the room.

"YOU LOOK ROUGH," Ronan says the next morning when he enters the kitchen to find me sitting at the island with a plate of fruit in front of me. I ignore his comment and say, "How come I haven't seen you eat?"

He's shirtless, his pants hanging low on his hips. His tattoos draw my attention. They stand out against his skin, complementing the sharp lines of his rippling muscles. When he turns, I scan my eyes over his black wings.

"We don't eat food like you do. There's fruit in the cupboard because Daemon ordered the staff to pick you some yesterday."

There's so much to digest in that one sentence. "The staff?"

He turns back around and leans against the counter, watching me bite into a juicy green apple. "Daemon's father has servants. You don't see them because they keep out of our way."

I consider this as I scan my eyes over the kitchen. It's a big, luxurious house, and he has servants, too? His father must be a powerful man.

"What do you eat if you don't eat fruit?"

Ronan's smile takes on a darker edge, and he pushes off the counter, slowly walking toward me. "Why do you think we have fangs?"

I stop chewing, sensing a shift in the air.

"We don't have fangs for aesthetic reasons." He plants his hands on the island and leans in close. "We feed on blood."

My eyes widen and I open my mouth to respond, but

Alaric enters the kitchen. Dressed in nothing but boxers, he looks delicious. There's too much skin on display for me to think straight. I never noticed boys like this back home. We swooned over wings, not bodies. My cheeks burn bright red.

"Our little angel here is curious about what we eat," Ronan says to Alaric.

The man in question joins us at the island, leaning forward on his elbows. "Yeah? What do you think we eat, little angel? Besides pussy."

I blush even harder. They were up all night, pleasuring the girls. I could hear them through the walls, and it's why I look like a train wreck this morning. Lack of sleep tends to do that to you.

"Ronan says you drink blood."

Alaric laughs and his sharp fangs draw my eyes. "We do. Does that scare you?"

Sliding my finger over my plate, I swipe up the juice from the sliced strawberries, bringing my finger to my mouth. They watch me suck it clean. I take my time, teasing them. "No, it doesn't scare me."

"So it wouldn't scare you if we said we wanted to feed on you?" Alaric is amused. I can see it in the glint in his eye.

"I would tell you to fuck off."

"No," a voice behind them drawls. It's Daemon, leaning against the doorframe. "You would bare your neck and spread your legs like a seasoned whore while begging for our teeth and cocks."

"You think too highly of yourself," I tell him as I pick up a slice of melon. "I would sooner let your cousin drink my blood than you."

It's the wrong thing to say—or the right thing, depending on how you look at it. Daemon pushes off the doorframe, striding toward me. He turns my chair to face him and then he's in my face, growling, "If I see you so much as look in his direction, I'll make you regret it, understood?"

Placing the slice of melon back down, I fold my arms over my chest, refusing to let him see his effect on me. My heart is racing in my chest, and an ache starts up between my legs the longer he pins me in place with those dark, angry eyes that promise untold pleasure and pain. "The double standards boggle the mind. So you can look at—no, let me rephrase—you can *fuck* Dariana, but I can't look at your cousin?"

He doesn't reply, but the tic in his cheek makes me suppress a smile.

He's so tense.

"What if I told you I don't play by your rules?"

"Defy me, and let's see what happens."

I ease myself off the chair, shoving his chest to make him move. "I think I will. While you were fucking those girls last night, I touched myself to thoughts of Dmitriy's wings. God, I bet they look magnificent spread ou—"

Daemon grasps my throat and snarls, "Shut your mouth!"

"Or what?!" I snap. "What are you going to do? Have your girls touch me? Or will you torment me yourself and leave me hanging because I won't beg? It must be hell for you, big boy, to crave me to beg. Tell me, did you think of me when you fucked her last night?"

Daemon is seconds away from blowing up on me. He's strung so tightly that it's a miracle he hasn't killed someone.

"Meanwhile, I was thinking of someone else. Someone who would gladly feed me his cock, if only to watch *you* squirm."

He slaps me. I don't think he means to do it, but his hand flies out before he can stop himself. It's sexy as hell to watch him lose control. I want to poke the bear again.

Grabbing my hair, he pulls it. "Let's get one thing perfectly clear. You belong to us, and you're ours to do with as we fucking please. You don't have a fucking say in what we do. I saw you last night when you ran out. You were jealous. You wanted to scream at me to stop, but your pride kept you from voicing the hurt inside you. Until you beg, I'll fuck a different girl every night. You will break, Angel, sooner or later." He grabs my hand, flattening it over the hard bulge inside his jeans. "Beg, and it's yours. Beg, and no other girl gets to enjoy it."

I bare my teeth and snatch my hand back, cursing my tingling fingers that burn with the vibrant memory of the outline of his hard cock. "Go to hell!"

He simply shrugs and steps back. "I'm already in Hell, remember? And so are you now."

Alaric and Ronan follow him with amusement in their eyes as he walks out. Then they look at me. The handprint on my cheek. "You had to anger him, didn't you?"

Rounding the island, I smile sweetly at Ronan. "It's so much fun."

They gaze down at me as I stop in front of them and walk my fingers up their chests. "You shouldn't have taken me that night. Not all angels are good."

"We're catching on quick," Alaric responds huskily.

"Yeah?" I graze my fingers over his hard dick inside his boxers. Daemon is the leader. To get to him, I must go through these boys. His loyal minions.

"You're playing with fire," Alaric warns, but he doesn't stop me.

Humming, I squeeze his length through the thin fabric. "I think I would like to get burned."

"You're a virgin." Ronan steps behind me, brushing my hair from my shoulder. "We'd ruin you."

His hot breath on my ear and his hands grabbing my hips stir the rising darkness inside me. I want more. "So ruin me."

"You don't know what you're asking," he whispers, sliding

his hand to the front of my neck. He grabs it hard and nips my ear with his teeth. "We wouldn't be gentle with you. We'd tear through your cunt and feast on your virginity like a pack of starving lions."

I'm so aroused, the inside of my thighs are sticky with desire.

Alaric smirks at me, his fingers trailing over my throbbing cheek. "You heard Daemon. Beg and you can have us all."

They step back, then disappear out the door.

"Fuck," I growl.

My body hums with need.

Somewhere in the house, girls giggle.

CHAPTER 6

AURELIA

The clouds part, and the silvery moonlight casts the boys' faces in an ethereal glow as they stand with their legs planted and arms crossed. I scan my eyes around the open field, lined by trees, at the back of the academy. My breath is visible as I ask, "What are we doing here?"

"Headmistress wants us to teach you to fly. It's the first skill to master before we do anything else," Daemon responds.

I drag my gaze away from the blanket of stars overhead and frown. "You brought me here to teach me to fly?"

They don't respond, and the longer they stare at me, the more nervous I become. I clear my throat. "Now what?"

"Spread your wings," Daemon orders, and my ears heat.

It feels intimate to unfold my wings in front of these three boys, who watch me expectantly. I'm acutely aware of how I differ from them with my white feathers and pale skin. The air shifts behind me, and I chance a look at the guys as my wings stretch out fully. Neither of them says a word. They just stare.

"Move them." Daemon's deep voice licks at my skin,

causing heat to sink to my clit. I love how the breeze shifts his hair and how his dark eyes drink me up. I experimentally flex my wings, moving them in upward and downward movements. Nothing happens.

"You weren't lying when you said you've never flown," he says, circling me while I continue moving my wings.

"No." The admission is embarrassing, especially when everyone here is such a skilled flyer. Why didn't they teach it to us back home? Did they worry we would fly over the wall and discover this place of darkness for ourselves?

Daemon rounds on me again, towering over me while his fingers trail over my jaw in a surprisingly gentle touch. "Flying is in your head. It's a mental state. You were born with the ability to fly, but you need to believe it. If you doubt, your wings won't carry you."

I gaze up at him, mesmerized by the shadows on his face. "What if I can't believe it? What if the doubt is always there?"

"Then you won't fly."

He makes it sound so simple: believe, and you will.

"Look at me," he says, cupping my chin. "I believe in you."

My heart jolts. I can't let myself feel these emotions inside me. Not for him, Ronan, or Alaric. If I fall for them, I'll never see Freya again.

"Now fly," he whispers, his thumb brushing over my lips. "Give a sharp flap and shoot up."

I try, but nothing happens when I move my wings. My bare feet stay planted on the ground, and disappointment weighs heavily on me.

"It will come," he says. "When you're ready, it will."

"Show me how you do it."

Stepping back, his wings erupt behind him in a display of power and magnificence. It happens so fast, so suddenly that I gasp. My reaction makes him smirk. "More impressive than the boys' wings back home, huh?"

I hate to admit it, but yes. I never reacted like that when the boys back home flexed their white wings. This is different. Daemon oozes danger, bad intentions, and trouble. How can I not feel drawn to him when his muscles move beneath his T-shirt and his dark hair falls into his eyes? How can I not want to burn myself in his flames despite being warned about the dangers of playing with fire? It doesn't matter that I hate him at the best of times. I want to prick myself on his thorns, and I want to slice him open on mine.

I let my eyes fall closed while my wings move behind me. The breeze rustles my feathers, and my shoulders ache from the weight of using them like this. They're heavy but powerful. Warm hands brush my hair off my shoulders and slide down my arms. It's not just Daemon anymore but Ronan and Alaric, too.

"Bigger sweeps of your wings, Angel."

Fingers dig into my jaw and soft lips brush up against mine. It's not Daemon. This boy's scent is different—more earthy and spicy. "That's it, beautiful. Just like that."

It's Ronan.

His tongue dives into my mouth to taste, ravage, and feast on me until he's satiated. I'm drunk on them and their roaming hands on my body. The feeling of the air shifting behind me. Then it happens—my feet slowly leave the ground and my heart speeds up with excitement. It's so overwhelming that I lose concentration and drop back down.

"Dammit!" I hiss, breathing hard, angry with my inability to use my wings how they were designed to be used.

"How's it going?" Dariana asks as she joins us. She's breathtaking as always in her short, black silk dress that leaves very little to the imagination.

"It's going shit!" I growl at the same time the boys say, "She left the ground."

Dariana blinks, looking between us. "She left the ground? Really?"

Alaric slings his arm around my shoulder. "You should have seen it. It was amazing."

I wish I could share his excitement. I have seen them fly multiple times, and what I achieved today is nothing close to what they can do. I'm a newborn lamb who can barely stand, never mind balance.

Dariana rolls her eyes. "Stop swooning over her wings."

"Have you seen them?" Alaric questions. "There's not a single angel here who won't sprout a hard-on."

"Come on," Daemon says, nudging his head toward the academy. "Let's get to class."

As they walk away, I stretch my wings out and try to peer at them over my shoulder but fail. Why is it so hard to fly? It's what wings were made for. What did Ronan say? They weren't created for aesthetic reasons. Sure, he meant his fangs, but it's the same for my wings. It makes my stomach churn with bitterness to think that my elders didn't teach us to fly or allow the thought to blossom in our minds.

"You'll get the hang of it soon."

I jump, spinning around.

Dariana is still here, her brown eyes scanning over my wings with a guarded expression. "I can see why Daemon is so taken with you."

"Yet he fucked you last night," I snap, immediately regretting my words. It's not fair to take my anger out on her because she took what she wanted last night. Daemon doesn't belong to me. Hell, I don't even want him to. I prove as much every time I push him away. Still, Dariana has felt the power of him inside her, filling her up.

"But he thought of you the entire time," she replies,

closing the distance between us. She smells of midnight and shadows that lure you closer to certain death. "Daemon and the others are not used to girls who turn them down. You're uncharted territory to them. This isn't Heaven," she whispers, tucking my hair behind my ear. "Morals and compassion don't have a home here in our world. Daemon will hurt you to get a piece of you, and if you don't offer it up freely, he'll carve it out of you."

My breath stutters when she slides her fingers down the side of my neck. Her movements are slow, a ghost of a touch.

"Why are you fighting him?" she whispers, her breath fanning over my lips. "Let him in, and he'll make you feel things you never knew possible."

"Shouldn't you want to get rid of me? Am I not a threat to the empty seat by his side on the throne?"

She hums, trailing her touch lower over my dress until her fingers brush against my bare thighs. Snaking her hand beneath my skirt, she smiles when my lips part. "I should, but I'm strangely curious." She drags her fingers over my damp panties and hooks the fabric. Moving them aside, she slides her hand inside.

"Dariana..." I whimper, but she silences my soft sound of pleasure with her lips on mine. Sucking on my bottom lip, she bites down and dips a finger inside me. I cry out as a spark of pleasure trickles down my stomach to my aching pussy, and she moves in again, kissing me deeper.

When we come up for air, she whispers, "Ever heard of the saying *curiosity killed the cat?*"

I quickly shake my head, seeking her touch with rolls of my hips while gripping her shoulders. I'm about to combust. Her hungry mouth sucks, nips, and nibbles a path down my jaw and neck. "Nothing good will come from me touching you like this, but I can't stop." Then she snarls, and I cry out when a sharp pain sears the skin on my neck.

She's drinking from me.

Deep pulls that draw the blood from my trembling body. She's taking without permission, subduing me with her skilled fingers that rub and tease and slide.

"Sshh!" she soothes, licking the wound and flicking my clit with her thumb. "Don't tell the boys."

Seeing her sharp teeth coated in my blood and the drops of deep red on her chin sends me over the edge. I come hard, spasming on her fingers while she whispers in my ear, "That's it, little angel whore, come on your queen's fingers."

The wave soon recedes, and she slides her fingers out from beneath my skirt and sucks my desire off them. Her eyes hold mine, a hint of something dangerous glinting in their pits, reminding me I'm out of my depth.

She cups my chin and cradles it softly. "Drop to your knees."

My throat jumps when I slowly lower myself onto the damp, cold grass beneath my knees. I stare up at her face, framed by the moonlight.

"Lift my skirt."

I place my hands on her smooth legs and slide them up her thighs and around her ass, palming her soft skin. Her wet pussy is in my face. I can smell her.

Her nails scrape my scalp before she applies pressure to the back of my head and guides me to her. "Look at me. I want to see those big eyes gaze up at me while you worship my cunt."

She's so close to my hungry mouth, her thighs glistening with arousal.

"Do you know how pretty you are on your knees, awaiting instructions with your lips parted and your big, innocent eyes staring up at me? Look down, little angel. Look at my pussy."

I do. My hungry eyes take in her wet cunt and the soft landing strip of curls above her slit. I want to breathe her in, taste the drop of arousal trailing a path down her thigh.

"You're dripping," I whisper, when she gives my hair a sharp yank.

"You do that to me, little angel. You make me want to defile you and watch you sin."

I gulp.

"Now, stick your tongue out and taste me."

"What if they come looking for me?"

"Shut up and do as you're told," she replies, pulling on my hair. The fresh smell of the grass beneath my knees mixes with the heady scent of her desire as I lean in to bury my tongue in her soaking folds. Her sweet flavor fills my mouth and coats my chin. Moaning out loud, I lap at her, my nails digging into her ass.

"Fuck," she moans, staring down at me while I circle her clit with the tip of my tongue before sucking it into my mouth. She tastes so fucking good, and I can't get enough of her scent and soft, feminine sounds of pleasure. The sharp scrape of her nails.

"Hell, just like that, little angel."

I hold her gaze while lapping at her entrance and tasting her sweetness on my tongue, feeling it coat my lips. My knees ache and my wings unfold behind me to shield us from prying eyes. Ronan mentioned lions tearing into a kill. This is like that—I'm protective of Dariana and her throbbing cunt. If anyone tried to take my feast away from me now, I would snarl and bare my teeth. I won't let anyone have her until I'm satisfied. Her body and addictive moans are mine.

"Such a good girl," she praises, riding my mouth with expert rolls of her hips. "Lick me just like that."

Her soft breasts sway inside her dress, and she bites down on her plump bottom lip when I fill her up with my tongue.

She's so warm, wet, and tight. My shoulders ache from the weight of my wings. I'm not used to keeping them extended this long, but the instinct to keep prying eyes away from my catch is too strong. If they see her, they might try to take her from me, and I would sooner kill than let that happen. Not now when she's so close to falling apart in my arms.

"Oh, Devil," she moans, her head thrown back as I gaze up at her, framed by my white wings. Her raven hair falls down her back in a thick waterfall. I would pull on it if I didn't have my hands full of her perfect ass. Two more licks and she lets out a loud moan as she stiffens in my hands. I hold her through her orgasm, eagerly licking up her cum. She tastes so fucking good.

When her breathing returns to normal, she lowers her leg and steps back. Her dress slides back down to cover her swollen pussy from my hungry eyes, and I mourn the loss of her sweet moans in the air. At least I can still taste her on my tongue. She's on my chin, my cheeks, and the damp strands of my hair.

"Remember," she says as I lower my wings, "not a word to the boys."

CHAPTER 7

AURELIA

I find them outside one of the classrooms, surrounded by throngs of girls. Jealously instantly grabs me by the throat and shakes me, growling, *"Just fucking beg!"*

I won't.

I don't care what it takes.

"Look who it is." Alaric grins, both arms wrapped around a set of twin girls, with tits that nearly spill out of their minuscule dresses. "You found us."

"Yeah, well, it wasn't easy. This place is a maze and every corridor looks the same."

Ronan has his tongue down a girl's throat, but it's Daemon who narrows his eyes and says, "What's that on your neck?"

I stiffen but keep my mask in place. "I don't know what you're talking about."

He shoves the girl hanging off his arm, and she stumbles back with a shriek. The satisfaction I feel when he strides up to me and clasps my jaw in a bruising grip should worry me. But it's quickly becoming evident that I want his undivided attention, and I'll act like a child if it gets him to hurt me sweetly like this.

"Who fed on you?" His voice drips with delicious danger as his angry eyes flash with a warning.

I'm skating on thin ice, and when he leans close and breathes me in, it cracks.

"You smell of pussy."

Alaric laughs behind us. A drawn-out, lazy sound that goes on and on.

"Not just any pussy—Dari's."

I glare up at him but keep my lips shut.

"I've licked that cunt enough times to know her scent like the back of my hand."

His words evoke the reaction he wanted as I bare my teeth.

A blinding smile spreads over his lips and he flicks his eyes behind me. "Thought you could get one on me?"

Dariana shrugs as she walks past us into the classroom. "It was worth a try."

The amused glint in his eyes annoys me enough to huff a breath and shoulder past him, but he seizes my arm and pulls me back. "Thought you could outsmart me, little angel?"

"You think too highly of yourself. You didn't once enter my mind while I was tongue deep in her cunt."

His eyebrows fly up. I thought my comment would make him angry, but he laughs instead, which transforms his face and steals my breath.

"Your rebellious side gets me hard."

"Or mad. Next time, it'll be someone else."

Now *that* gets me the reaction *I* want. His rough touch is back, marking and hurting me.

"You love to push my buttons, don't you?" he growls, wrapping his fingers around my neck. Students watch us curiously. I finally have his fire burning into me, and it gets me high.

"One day, you'll push the wrong one, and then you'll have to deal with the consequences."

"Is that supposed to scare me?" I whisper, unfolding my wings in a display of defiance.

Gasps ring out around us, and Daemon tightens his grip on my throat. "Close your wings!"

"Or what?!"

Leaning down, he brushes his lips over my ear, eliciting shivers and a zap of pleasure that shoots straight to my core. "Your wings—like you—belong to me. Close them!"

It's so tempting to give in to him and be the good little girl he wants me to be. I'm not a good girl. I'm a very, very bad girl who doesn't listen to Daddy. He'll need to spank the defiance out of me if he wants me to do as he says. Until then, I'll continue behaving like a little brat.

The air shifts behind me as my wings move in long, powerful sweeps. There's no denying I have big wings, especially for a female angel. I don't know why or what it means, but the urge to unfold them when I feel threatened is as instinctual as the need to fight back when I'm cornered.

"Do you think my wings turn them on? The boys watching?"

A fierce, animalistic snarl sounds deep in his chest. He's just about to react and give me what I need when someone clears their throat next to us.

"It's strictly prohibited to spread your wings in the hallway, miss. Close them at once!"

I blink and look at the teacher beside us. When I don't immediately listen, his mustache twitches with annoyance. Daemon still has his hand on my throat. We must look like quite the pair. My wings snap shut, and I shoulder past Daemon into the classroom.

Ronan chuckles behind me. "Couldn't help yourself, could you?"

"Nope."

"He'll hurt you one day."

I pull out a chair. "I'm counting on it."

Sitting down beside me, Ronan balances on the back legs of his chair, leaning so far that it's a miracle he doesn't fall. "I like you, little angel."

It's a strange feeling to blossom like a flower in spring when a boy praises you.

"You don't know me," I point out, and Ronan sits forward with his elbows on the desk.

"I know you better than you think."

"Yeah? How so? Tell me one thing about me."

"You're an angel with a dark side."

"It's an observation and doesn't count."

Daemon and Alaric plop down onto the seats in front of us. I try not to drag my eyes over their broad shoulders and the dark curls at the nape of their necks between their large wings.

"Your name is Aurelia."

With an eye roll, I turn in my seat to face him. "Tell me something real."

His lips twitch. "Something real?"

"What are my dreams, Ronan? What scares me? Why did I venture into the woods that night? You must be curious. Why did an angel sneak out of Eden to venture into the deep, dark woods where dangers lurk? I knew the risks."

His eyes linger on mine for a long moment, searching my blue depths. "You never felt at home in Eden. You were an outcast, smiling when you were supposed to, but your heart always yearned for something outside of those tall gates. A craving you couldn't place. You were the good little angel who would sit down for class but crane her neck to look back at the gates and listen to the whisper of the woods."

I've stopped breathing.

Ronan leans in and whispers, "Only a few hear the calling of the woods. Did you know that? It coaxes them home. You never belonged in Eden. Your wings are white like God's blinding light, but the woods know you. From the moment of your birth, the moment you took your first steps, your feet have led you to the gates." He leans back and spreads his arms. "Is that real enough?"

I swallow, unable to look away from his dark eyes that glimmer with a hint of masculine pride and amusement. My heart aches in my chest at the truth in his words. "If I don't belong in Eden, where do I belong? Here? In Hell?"

"Hell is only a name invented by your elders. Your fairy-tales were designed to keep you shackled. If not for them, what would stop you from escaping Eden? As to where you belong, that's for you to find out."

Surprised by the wisdom behind his words, I flick my eyes between his, and he laughs.

"Don't look so shocked. I'm not just a pretty face."

Alaric snorts, throwing a crumpled-up piece of paper at Ronan. "You smooth fucker."

"Watch and learn. I'll get her to beg me first."

This time, it's me who snorts. "You think a few smooth words will have me begging?"

Leaning in close, he places a kiss on the corner of my lips, then smirks. "I think it's only a matter of time."

My heart is beating with a staccato rhythm in my chest. It's difficult to breathe when he drugs me with his spicy scent and the desire he stirs in me. How do they get anything done here in the underworld? I've been horny since the moment I arrived. It hasn't stopped.

His lips brush mine and his smile grows. "Pretty girls like you always beg, sooner or later. Just think, *Aurelia,* how I could make you feel. Imagine me driving into you hard and fast, claiming your virgin cunt, while you claw your nails down my back."

His warm breath fans my lips, heating my insides, and I gasp when he skims his nose over my neck. The sensation he evokes in me is so overwhelming and powerful that I sink below his waves.

"Students, eyes forward," the teacher, Mr. Kozlov, with the mustache, orders us.

I resurface, gasping for air. Ronan laughs when I shove him away before facing forward in my seat.

"Today, we'll dive deep into ourselves to find our center. Can anyone tell me what resides in our core?"

A girl with a dark bob lifts her hand in the air, waving eagerly.

Mr. Mustache doesn't look her way when he says, "Yes, Liliya."

"Your powers reside in your center."

I sit up straighter, ignoring Ronan's chuckle next to me.

"That's right. Very good, Liliya. I would appreciate it if everyone else bothered to do their homework too," Mr. Mustache grumbles as he walks down the aisle.

"She wants his dick," Alaric coughs under his breath, and Ronan shakes with laughter next to me.

"Who knew you were so immature?" I whisper.

Alaric winks at me and nudges Daemon's shoulder with his.

Looking up from the phone in his hand, Daemon frowns. "What?"

"Didn't you fuck her once?"

"Who?"

Alaric lifts his chin toward Liliya. "Her, the teacher's pet."

Daemon follows his line of sight. I don't like him looking at her. Not with those eyes that flash with memories I wish he didn't have.

"Yeah." He doesn't elaborate, and I fight the urge to strike the back of his head. I'm so sick of being a virgin while they've fucked every girl in the vicinity. It leaves a bad taste on my tongue to think the girls in here have had them when I haven't. Not fully.

"Close your eyes," Mr. Mustache says in a soft, soothing voice, unlike the sharp tone he used outside in the hallway earlier. "Imagine yourself walking through the forest. The damp moss beneath your feet, the bird song in the trees, the smell of earth in your nostrils. Somewhere in the distance, a twig snaps."

I sink back in my chair and let his soothing voice carry me away, deeper into myself. My muscles relax and my wings slump, grazing the stone floor.

"There's an old and weathered red door suspended in the air. It hovers just above the ground, slightly ajar, as if to urge you to peek inside. Twigs snap and damp leaves stick to the soles of your bare feet as you move closer. Whatever is beyond that door wants you to see it. It wants you to interact with it."

Silence reigns inside me, supreme and powerful. I inch closer to the door. Whispers urge me to look inside, to see what it hides.

Come, child. Come closer.

Branches cut my skin, but the sting barely registers.

So close.

My hand lands on the door and I apply pressure to the weathered wood. It slowly creaks open, inch by inch, while I hold my breath.

Just then, the bell rings, causing me to startle and open my eyes.

The door is gone.

Mr. Kozlov's voice rings out over the sound of chairs scraping on the floor. "Now you've had a taste of guided meditation. We'll continue exploring your center next time."

It takes me a moment to realize that I'm supposed to move. It doesn't register until Ronan slaps me on the back of the head. It's only gentle, but I whirl in my seat and bare my teeth like a feral animal. The boys laugh, but I don't. I was seconds away from finding out what hid behind that door. It was something big and powerful, and it had waited a long time for me to find it.

"Come on, little angel. Let's go."

As I scoot my chair back, Daemon seizes my arm and hauls me to my feet.

"What the fuck is this?"

Confused, I look down.

Scratches line my arms. Fresh cuts that ooze with droplets of blood.

"I-I cut myself on the branches as I approached the door."

"What?"

"The trees," I start, but he shakes his head.

"The meditation wasn't real. There's no way your vision could harm you like this."

"Well, it did," I say, wrenching my arm free. Now that I've seen the cuts, they sting as I walk away, leaving the boys to exchange worried glances.

CHAPTER 8

ALARIC

I flip another page in the book in front of me on Daemon's bed and rub my face before blowing out a tired breath. "I can't find anything."

Ronan, lying on his stomach, is on a mission after he picked up every single book he could find on angels in the library. Now they're stacked in a precarious pile next to him on the floor.

Daemon throws his book against the wall, leans back in his desk chair, and lets out a string of curse words. "I don't like this!"

Ronan doesn't look up from the page in front of him. "No, you don't like not being in control."

"Did you not fucking see her scratches?"

"I did. They were impossible to miss."

Daemon sits forward with his elbows on his knees and rubs his face. "Fuck this shit."

Blowing out a breath, I turn another page and scan my eyes over the drawings of angels with halos. "Have these authors ever met an angel?" I comment, closing the book. "Aurelia glows, but she doesn't have a fucking halo over her head."

"The fall was so long ago. How can we even know what's true anymore?" Ronan asks, scratching his head while he reads over the page in front of him. Out of the three of us, he has the most patience.

"What I don't get," Daemon says, hands steepled and forming a point over his mouth, "is why she would leave Eden in the first place. She must have known she would never return, right? She can't be that naive to think the gates would magically let her back inside after her first taste of darkness. Her odds of finding her way back in the first place were slim. Once you enter those woods..."

We fall silent, each lost in our own thoughts.

"I'm starving," I comment, rubbing my tired eyes. "It's been too long since we fed."

"Think our little angel is up for watching? She's curious about this world, right?" Daemon asks.

Ronan finally looks up, amusement shining in his dark eyes. "Do I think our little angel is up for watching you fuck and drain a human girl? No, I don't—at all."

He considers this.

"But it's not like you care about her feelings, right?"

Daemon leans back, spreading his legs. "No, I fucking don't."

Liar.

"Okay, then," Ronan replies, and it's obvious by his tone of voice that he doesn't believe Daemon for a second. We both know Daemon is lying to himself.

"Let's go hunt."

We follow him out into the hallway. Daemon lights up a cigarette, then walks ahead with determined steps to Aurelia's bedroom. As he bangs on her door, he gives us a brief glance while taking a deep pull on the cigarette. Smoke leaks out past his lips before he sucks it back in and bangs on her door again, harder this time. "Open up, little angel!"

The door slowly creaks open, and her blue eyes widen as she takes us in—three testosterone-filled men with hungry eyes and aching fangs. After inching the door open, she slides out and sinks back against the mahogany wood.

"You're coming with us," Daemon orders, bringing the cigarette up to his mouth. Smoke curls in the air, and the flames from the torches on the walls flicker in her blue eyes.

"Where?"

"I wasn't fucking asking." Daemon crushes the cigarette under his boot. "Get moving."

She yelps when he grasps her neck, forcing her to walk. He's rough with her, more so than I've seen with any girl.

He likes her but won't admit it.

CROSSING the border to the human lands is something we're so used to that we don't bat an eyelid, but our little angel's eyes are wide and curious as she takes in the back alley. Spinning in a circle, her skirt flares around her thighs. The fog is dense tonight; steam comes out of the sewers nearby, and it reeks of piss and garbage.

"Welcome to the city," I drawl, walking ahead.

"Where are you going?" Her bare feet pad on the concrete. We should have made her put on her shoes, but it's too late now. "The humans will see your wings."

"Not true," Ronan comments. "Humans only see what their minds are capable of perceiving. They live in a world where they're taught from childhood that nothing exists outside of their scientific articles. What others tell them is 'true,' and it makes them blind to that which can't be explained with logic. God could stare them in the face and they wouldn't see him. Instead, they explain away his existence with some theory about how their brain interprets reality based on some traumatic event in their childhood, thus creating visions that aren't real. They could walk past a shifter in the street and think it's a weird-looking dog. If it transformed into its human shape, they'd blame what they saw on schizophrenia. Me and my brothers could fly in the sky, and they would explain it as some weird reflection of light."

"You're saying they won't see your wings?"

"Not until they believe. And they won't believe until their lives are in mortal danger. Then they're ready to believe in almost anything to save their skin."

She follows us out of the alley. The streets are almost empty at this hour of the night, except for groups of partygoers hanging around outside the bars. My little angel takes it all in, her bright, blue eyes shining with awe. She's stunning beneath the soft glow of the streetlights.

We enter a nightclub, then weave through bodies until we reach a spacious dance floor. The walls pulse with the heavy beat of the music, and the air is thick with the smell of sweat and alcohol. Women in short dresses and high heels dance provocatively while men eye them up like meals.

"What are we doing here?" Angel shouts over the music.

Daemon already has his eyes set on someone—a girl with fiery hair and pale, freckled skin. The red dress she wears fits her like a second skin, conforming to her soft curves while she moves in time with the sultry beat. Daemon steps up behind the human girl, and Angel grits her jaw when he pulls her back against his chest. They move fluently together. Daemon works his magic right before our eyes, priming his prey and subduing her with his scent and strong hands.

Our little angel, driven by the instinct to protect her territory, tries to stride past. I pull her back, banding my arm around her waist. She can't see it yet, but her primal desires are at the forefront, clouding her vision.

"Now is not the time. I can't let you interrupt the hunt."

Stiffening, she cranes her neck to look up at me. "What do you mean by that?"

It's cute how naive she is sometimes. "Look," I order, tipping my chin toward the scene in front of us. I can practically hear the little angel grind her teeth when Daemon buries his nose in the girl's neck. She can't see the bigger picture yet.

"Let me go," she orders, extracting herself from my arm, and I stare after her as she storms off in the opposite direction.

"Should we follow after her?" Ronan asks.

"Leave her be. She needs us to get back."

Ronan looks at me uncertainly. He's the soft one in the group, and the thought of a true angel alone in the human world with so little knowledge of the dangers here is bound to pull on his heartstrings. The thoughts flee my head when Daemon snakes his hand beneath the woman's skirt. We've hit the jackpot. We move in as one, following Daemon hot on his heels as he steers the girl outside into the back alley.

The light above the door is broken, and it's dark except for the soft glow from a streetlight further down the passage, where it opens up to the main street. Daemon steers the girl deeper into the dark alley, away from the light. Hidden by the steam from a sewer, he corners her against the brick wall, hiking her skirt up above her waist.

A fragment of clarity enters her mind when she spots us behind him. Her eyes widen and she gasps, but Daemon muffles the sound with his hand. My fangs ache with the need to feast. Daemon, the fucker, knows this, but he takes his time, toying with his food like a cat with a mouse. He holds back, though.

Ronan notices it, too. The look he gives me is one of equal

curiosity and confusion. So maybe Daemon won't fuck her despite his threats to the little angel? This is the first time I've seen him shy away from an easy fuck before a feast.

"Fuck," he growls, shoving her off when she reaches for his belt, then he releases a frustrated roar and says to Ronan on his way past, "You deal with her."

It's impossible to hold back my amused smirk while we watch Ronan lift the woman up against the wall and settle between her legs. Why are we doing this? Because the blood tastes sweeter after she has come. We could drain her without seducing her first, but it doesn't offer the same high. All fallen angels know this.

"Pussy whipped, huh?" I tease.

Daemon snaps his head to me. "Fuck you. I'm not pussy whipped."

"No? Is that why you're not balls deep in her right now? Why you let Ronan do the dirty work?"

Daemon, who hates showing weakness, sucks on his teeth in annoyance. The very idea that a girl could control him like this makes his skin crawl. Ronan teases the girl, stroking her over her panties, but he doesn't take it any further and his fingers never slip beneath the fabric. Daemon soon loses patience, shoving me forward. "Sort her out."

Chuckling, I raise my hands. "Fine, I'll do it since you motherfuckers became pussy whipped overnight."

Ronan looks relieved when I take his place. How fucking difficult can it be to fuck this woman? They behave like it's an enormous struggle to spread her legs and sink into her heat. But when I hook my fingers into her panties, I can't do it. Something stops me. I try again, but my hand slides back out. What the hell? I palm her creamy neck, rest my forehead against hers, and summon the strength to do what's needed. The woman's long hair brushes against her flushed cheeks, and her plump lips look inviting enough that only a fool would turn down the opportunity to taste them. Turns out, I am that fool.

Daemon loses patience, shoving me out of the way. In one swift motion, he tears into her throat, growling when she cries out. It's our cue to move in, too. We surge forward on silent feet. Falling to my knees, I sink my teeth into the femoral artery in her thigh while Ronan brings her wrist up to his lips. Her subdued struggle soon ends. She falls limp against the brick wall as her heart slows to a stop. We drain her of every last drop before stepping away, blending with the shadows. Her slumped body falls to the ground, and her lifeless eyes stare up at the dark sky.

Daemon, who is breathing hard, wipes his mouth. "We won't talk about this again."

"I think we should," Ronan replies, toeing the girl's thigh. "Why couldn't any one of us fuck this girl?"

Confounded, I shake my head. "I thought I could, but then when I tried to slide her panties aside, something stopped me."

A loud crash startles me, and I turn to see Daemon let loose on a trash can. He kicks it, not once, but three times.

"The angel is just a fucking girl," he growls. "She's not that fucking special."

Ronan waits for him to calm down before speaking, "Then why didn't you fuck the human?"

"Why didn't you?" Daemon counters, his forehead coated in a thin layer of sweat. He wipes it off with the back of his hand, then stiffens. "Where the fuck is Angel?"

"Inside somewhere," I say, sucking a bead of blood off my thumb from the corner of my lips.

Daemon walks back inside and we follow behind, coated in blood and death. It's not the best idea to re-enter the bar after a feed. While the humans might struggle to see the wings, they're no strangers to blood. They part like the sea when they spot us making a beeline for our angel across the dance floor, where she sits on a couch, straddling the lap of a human man. I don't have a short fuse like Daemon, but fury still boils my blood. She's a fucking brat when she wants to be. She knew we would find her, and she made sure to lash out at Daemon the best way she knew how—by awakening his jealous side.

He seizes her arm, tearing her off the man. Angel falls on her ass and shoots back up to her feet, staring in disbelief and horror.

"Think you can fucking touch my girl?" Daemon growls at the unsuspecting stranger who was at the wrong place at the wrong time. Before the man can respond, Daemon rips out his windpipe, and blood gushes from the wound. The sounds of gurgling, choking, and gasping make me smirk. Daemon is teaching the little angel a very important lesson: defy us, and someone has to pay the consequences.

After climbing off the man, Daemon throws the fleshy lump on the floor and then storms off without another word. Angel, with her wide eyes and stricken expression, has her hands pressed over her mouth, unable to believe what just happened. I have to admit that it was a bit extreme. I've never seen Daemon rip out a man's trachea for flirting with his girl. That would require Daemon to care—something he has never done before.

Very interesting.

Angel storms out after him, uncaring about the shocked, crying humans. As soon as we step outside, she shoves Daemon's back. "What was that back there?! What the actual fuck, Daemon? You killed that man!"

He whirls on her, his eyes flashing with lethal danger. Covered head to toe in blood, he looks like the devil himself. "I warned you what would happen if you so much as looked at another man. He deserved it. That fucker thought he was halfway in your panties."

She shoves his chest hard, but he doesn't budge. "You're sick, Daemon! You're fucking sick!"

"Guys, we need to leave unless we want to explain to your father why we ended up in human jail," Ronan says. It's meant as a joke, but he has a point. We've already created a mess. Sirens wail in the distance. We've never caused a scene like this before. Usually, the girls disappear into the silent night to be found by some poor homeless person. Our angel made a spectacle tonight with her little show that let loose the monster in Daemon.

"What the fuck are you doing?!" she growls when he bands his bloody arm around her waist and launches them into the air.

My wings spring out and I take off after them, soaring high above the rooftops. "Your father has quite the mess to sort out."

Daemon barely acknowledges me, and poor Angel clings to him like a spider monkey, her legs wrapped around his waist and her arms circling his neck.

"Two dead bodies. Three flying angels," chuckles Ronan on Daemon's other side.

His dad will soon sort it out, but he might not be too happy.

We cross over to the underworld. The temperature immediately drops, and the night seems darker as we fly over the treetops.

Our little angel keeps arguing. "I can't believe you did that. You're such a psycho!"

If she's not careful, he might drop her.

CHAPTER 9

AURELIA

When we finally land outside Daemon's house, I'm covered in blood from clinging to him. My black dress is stained crimson; strands of blonde hair stick to the blood smeared on my cheeks. I also reek of copper mixed with Daemon's masculine scent.

No sooner have his feet touched the ground, than I shove him off, storming inside. He's hot on my heels, a dark storm cloud about to collide with mine. The lightning show we put on when he pulls me to a stop inside the front door is spectacular.

"Where the fuck do you think you're going?!"

I slap his cheek hard and feel a smug sense of satisfaction when his face whips to the side. But the feeling doesn't last long. Daemon shoves me back and I stumble into the hallway desk pushed up against the wall, sending a vase of black roses crashing to the ground.

Lifting me up, he sets me down on top and covers my mouth with his hand, silencing the angry string of poison spewing from my lips. "You think you can defy me, little angel? You think I will silently brood in the shadows while you roll your hips against another man's crotch? Wrong, so fucking wrong. I will slaughter every single male who dares put their filthy hands on you. So don't try me again."

My voice is muffled behind his hand. Despite that, I don't stop hurling abuse at him. I call him a 'motherfucker' and an 'asshole.' Words that would make my elders blush and throw me out of the gates so fast that my head would spin. How the fuck does he dare tell me what I should do?

Ripping my panties off, Daemon shoves a thick finger inside me. I'm not ready and it hurts, but it also feels so fucking good. I spread my legs wider, daring him to fingerfuck me like he means it. And he does. He soon has two fingers buried deep inside me, spreading and hurting me in the best way possible. Behind him, Alaric and Ronan watch with matching smirks. I might misbehave more often if their leader rewards me like this.

"You think that *human,*" he spits the word, "could make you feel like this?"

I love this angry Daemon. I love how he hurts me before soothing the pain with filthy words and flicks of his thumb over my swollen clit.

When he lowers his hand from my mouth to grab my throat, I release a crazed bubble of laughter. "I think his cock would have felt amazing inside me."

Say hi to the angel with the stick in her hand, which she uses to poke the hornets' nest every time she gets the chance —that's me.

"Shut up!" Daemon growls, removing his fingers and plunging them into my mouth. I gag, but he doesn't let up. "You think you can disrespect me like this? I'm not someone you want to mess with."

"But it's so much fun," I taunt when his fingers slide back out.

I'm hauled off the hallway table, and anger radiates off him as he drags me upstairs to his bedroom. I should probably be scared, but a thrill of excitement runs through me at the thought of what he might do to me. Ronan opens the door and Daemon shoves me inside, causing me to stumble and fall to the floor. The icy stone bites into my skin and my bleeding knees sting deliciously.

Daemon fists my hair, pulling me up to kneeling while using his other hand to unbuckle his belt. They all do. "It's time to teach your filthy mouth a lesson." He undoes his buttons, shoving down the front of his jeans and boxers. His cock pops out, hard and big—so fucking big. My mouth instantly waters in anticipation.

"You were a little brat tonight." He slaps his veiny dick over my lips, then chuckles when I eagerly stick my tongue out. I flatten it, peering up at him through a haze of lust as my scalp burns and my bloodied knees ache. *Use me.* Alaric and Ronan join Daemon, stroking their dicks and taunting me with their thick lengths.

"You want a taste?" Alaric asks.

I crave to lean in and take him in my mouth, but Daemon's tight grip on my hair prevents me.

"You want us to choke you, sweetheart? Make you cry?"

I nod eagerly, moaning when Daemon rubs the thick head of his cock over my tongue.

"Beg!"

I grow cold. *No, no, no.*

Anything but that.

They pick up their pace, pleasuring themselves with long, expert strokes, their masculine, veiny hands pulling, tugging, and jerking.

"We'll fulfill your every fantasy if you beg. You can have us all," Ronan promises.

I set my jaw. "I will never beg."

"What a shame," Daemon drawls, letting go of my hair to grip a handful of strands at the nape of my neck. He wrenches my head back and strokes his cock over my face.

"Keep looking at me like that," he says in a breathy voice as my clit aches and throbs. "You can have my cock anytime you want if you just say the word."

"I hate you. You're a monster."

"Yes, I am. I'm *your* monster." His warm cum hits my face in quick spurts that rain over my lashes, cheeks, and lips.

I eagerly stick my tongue back out to catch the last squirt. I'm gazing up at him, covered in his release, when Ronan takes his place and orders me to flatten my tongue. I would like to pretend I put up a fight, but I don't. My clit aches almost painfully when I taste his salty release as it coats my cheeks and lips.

"Fuck," he groans, smearing the sticky cum over my skin with the crown of his cock. Over and over he rubs, circling my tingling lips with the thick, bulbous head, and I try to snatch it up, eager to taste him and feel his veiny length fill my mouth. "So fucking pretty!"

"My turn," Alaric demands in a husky voice, and Ronan steps back. "If you behave like a brat, we'll treat you like one," he says, jerking his length hard and fast. "You can't win against us, so don't even fucking try because we'll bring you to your knees every time."

I smile up at him. "Bring me your worst."

His answering chuckle is low and husky. "Careful what you wish for. Now open your mouth like a good whore."

I do. My pussy drips with desire, and the urge to rub my thighs together is overwhelming. Unable to look away from the fire in his eyes, I whimper.

His warm cum beads on my tongue, trickling down my chin. I'm ruined, marked by three men. Alaric zips himself away and claps Daemon's shoulder on his way out of the room. Ronan leaves, too.

We're alone. Daemon towers over me, dark eyes blazing with hellfire. "Look at you," he drawls with a dangerous edge to his voice. "On your knees, covered in us."

I don't hide. I meet his stare and let him see the darkness residing inside me—the darkness he placed there.

Stepping closer, he presses down on my lip with his thumb and pulls it away from my teeth. "There's such fire in you, yet you're so eager to please on your knees."

I tear away from his touch, snarling like an animal. The sudden movement hurts my bleeding knees.

"You can stay here since you're so fucking ungrateful that I killed for you," Daemon says, fisting my hair. Anger radiates off him in waves. With a sharp yank, he bares my neck. "You can stay on your knees, covered in our cum like a whore, until we come and find you again. If you move, I'll punish you."

I spit on him, and he slaps me. It only arouses me more.

"Do not defy me!" he orders, gripping my jaw hard. "Understood?"

The flaring of my nostrils is the only reply he'll get from me. He lets go, then walks out without another word. The door slams shut behind him, and I glare at it as if it's Daemon himself. Fucking asshole! Who is he to tell me what to do? Ordering me to kneel here like some slave. But I don't move. I kneel like a good girl. Because somewhere deep inside, I'm grateful he killed that man. And some sick, twisted part of me loved the monster that bared its teeth and ripped out that man's windpipe without a second thought. I have that effect on Daemon. He'll kill for me, not any other girl.

CHAPTER 10

DAEMON

"How long are you letting her wait?" Alaric asks, bringing the glass of scotch up to his lips. We're spread out on the couches in the living room, drinking my father's expensive alcohol. It's not like he's here to tell us off. I take a deep pull on my cigarette, letting the smoke leak out before breathing it back in. The chandelier on the roof looks older than Hell—the curse of old wealth. Everything is fucking antique around here.

Alaric is watching me expectantly.

I blow out a cloud of smoke, rolling my head. "She can fucking wait until I'm good and ready."

"It's been three hours," Ronan comments. Knowing that fucker, he probably feels sorry for her.

"And she can wait for three more." I bring the cigarette to my lips, letting my eyes fall closed. The embers spark. I'm so fucking relaxed. More so than I have been in a long time. I like thinking of her kneeling in my bedroom while she awaits my return. Her pretty face covered in my brothers and me. I bet her clit throbs.

A small part of me hopes she has moved so I can hurt her. The thought of putting her on my knee and spanking some fucking gratitude into her is an itch I need to scratch. Why is she so fucking stubborn? I know she wants my dick, so why is she refusing to say please?

I groan, rubbing my eyes, the cigarette pinched between my two fingers. I want her to beg so fucking badly. No, I *need* her to.

"What the fuck will it take to break her?" Alaric asks, echoing my thoughts.

I lower my hand and open my eyes. The firelight reflects off the chandelier. "I don't fucking know, but I'm determined to find out."

"We could just fuck her anyway. It's not like she doesn't want it," Ronan says.

"No," I reply, "she'll beg."

"And when she does, we'll ruin her."

My smile is slow to form. Alaric is as brutal as me; he knows we'll tear into her like a pack of ruthless, feral animals. When we're done with her, she won't know her own name anymore, and she certainly won't be dry-humping human men in bars. The mere thought has me fisting my hands. I take another pull on the cigarette to calm myself down before I do something I'll regret, like walk up there and fuck her ass raw. Smoke curls in the air while the burning wood crackles in the fireplace.

"What happened in the alleyway?" Alaric asks.

I don't want to think about it. "It was a glitch."

"A glitch?" laughs Ronan, then rolls his head on the back of the couch to look at me. "What do you think this is? A Super Mario game?"

I snort a laugh, but it's a tired sound. What is Aurelia

doing to me? I'm faulty. I failed to fuck a human girl, and then I killed a man. All because of an angel with blonde hair and blue doe eyes.

"Fuck, man," I groan, rubbing my face. "We'll have to invite Dari and her friends over. Set this shit right."

"Don't act like such a dick," Alaric says with a laugh. "You don't want to fuck Dari."

"I also don't want to be pussy whipped. No woman gets to have that power over me."

Ronan sits forward and snatches the cigarette from between my lips. He takes a deep drag, holds it in his lungs, then blows the smoke in my face. "Too late, brother. She's got you by your motherfucking balls."

I shove his face away, making him laugh. "Let's show her who's in charge."

We stand up and make our way upstairs. My dick stirs with anticipation. What will we find? Is she still kneeling like a good girl, or did she disobey me? I win either way.

The hallway is quiet except for our heavy footsteps and the rain pattering on the window. I feel fantastic now that I've fed —strong and alive. It also helps to have my little angel where I want her: on her knees and submitting to me.

I exchange a smirk with my brothers as I place my hand on the door handle.

Alaric lifts his chin. *Open it.*

Pushing down on the handle, I inch open the door like a kid at Christmas. The little angel is the wrapped toy, and I can't wait to tear into her packaging.

"Well, well," I say smugly when I walk in and find her kneeling like I ordered her to.

The fire still burns in her eyes, threatening to incinerate anything that steps too close. Behind me, Ronan chuckles cruelly, the sound dripping with darkness.

"Our little whore can be a good girl after all."

Her wings spring open, knocking over the candleholder and books on the nightstand as she bares her teeth. I fucking love it when she does that.

"Whoa!" Ronan exclaims behind me. "Someone is feeling threatened."

"What are we going to do with her?" Alaric taunts, circling her like prey. "Should we punish her?"

Her blue eyes follow us, tracking our every move. I step up to her and lift her chin with a finger. The cum on her cheeks has long since dried, and I almost feel sorry for her, but she looks so pretty like this: ruined and used.

"She's been a very good girl. I think she deserves a reward for kneeling here like an eager slut all night." I stroke my thumb over her lips, back and forth. "Don't you think you deserve a reward, little angel?"

"Yes," she breathes out, and my cock takes notice of the submissive tone in her voice.

"Rise."

She slowly stands up. Her knees hurt, but she tries hard to disguise the discomfort she feels. Before she can say a word, I grab her hips and lift her cunt up to my mouth, her thighs on either side of my head. Angel releases a squeal, which soon morphs into a strangled moan when I suck on her pussy through her damp panties.

With my arm banded around her ass, I slide the fabric aside to lap at her delicious pussy. Her taste is so fucking addictive. My little angel pulls on my hair while I walk us the four steps to my bed. I drop her down, watching her bounce on the sheets.

Climbing on after her, Ronan spreads her smooth legs. "Such a pretty pussy." Then he looks over his shoulder at us and asks, "Doesn't she have a fucking pretty pussy, guys?"

I fold my arms over my chest and say to Angel, "Keep your eyes open the whole time. If you close them, we stop."

Walking past me, Alaric puts his knee on the bed. He's rough as fuck when he yanks down her dress to expose her tits. Ronan drags his nose over her pussy and breathes her in while Alaric rolls her nipples into hard points.

Her heavy blue eyes stay glued to mine, and I hide my smirk behind my hand when her lips part. Ronan eats her out like he's waited a lifetime to taste her. It's not every day he gets to feast on one of God's angels. Our little plaything is a first-class meal, the finest dessert you can get your hands on. Ronan knows it. We all know it.

Alaric takes her nipple into his mouth, kneading the other breast. Meanwhile, I stand with my arms crossed and my feet planted, watching Angel fall apart at my brothers' hands. They drag it out, bringing her to the edge and keeping her there, suspended between pleasure and desperation. Her grip on Ronan's hair looks painful, her soft moans escalating in volume until I'm sure even the dead can hear her. Alaric and Ronan won't let her come until I give the command, and I won't give her respite until she fucking begs. I don't care if it takes all night.

"Oh, God," she moans. "Oh, God. Oh, God. Oh, God!"

Ronan slaps her clit and shoves his fingers inside her. "Your God can't help you now, little angel."

Alaric chuckles before biting down on the skin next to her rosy nipple, soothing the bitemark with his tongue. I need a fucking taste myself. Nudging Ronan out of the way, I flip her over on her front. "Are you a good girl for us, Angel?" I ask, bunching her dress around her waist.

"Yes, I'm such a good girl."

"Lies!" My hand comes down on her ass with a satisfying thwack. I knead the reddening flesh, then strike her again. "Good girls beg, Angel."

"Fuck you!"

Her response makes Ronan and Alaric laugh. I'd lie if I

said I wasn't amused, too. I raise her hips until she's on her shaky knees with her creamy ass in the air. Her puffy cunt glistens in the soft light from my bedside lamp, and the inside of her thighs are sticky with her arousal.

My dick throbs as my mouth waters. "I always get my way, sooner or later, beautiful. You will bend to me."

She cries out when I grab her hips and lick her tight exit. My tongue swirls and teases until she trembles on all fours, moaning my name. She still doesn't beg, though. Stubborn, fucking woman.

Kneeling in front of her, Alaric unbuckles his belt and slides his zipper down. Trust him to take advantage of the situation. Not that I blame him. Who wouldn't want to fuck her pretty mouth at every opportunity?

"Do you like being our plaything?" he asks her, pulling down the front of his jeans and letting his dick spring free. I could lick her ass all night. She's so fucking responsive, mewling like a cat and arching her back against me.

"Yes," she breathes out, wetting her lips in anticipation.

"Nu-uh," Alaric taunts, stroking his dick just out of reach. "You can't have this, baby. Not until you beg. Only good girls get to choke on my cock. And you, little angel, are a brat."

"Fuck, this ass," I groan, leaning back and giving it a hard smack. My handprint blossoms on her skin.

Watching the scene unfold from the side to the bed, Ronan slides his big palm over her arched back, admiring the beautiful curve of her spine beneath her wings. "You're so fragile, little angel," he comments. "We could snap you in half." His cruel words have her moaning when he fists her hair, pulling her head back. "Daemon killed for you tonight. Say thank you, like a good girl."

"Thank you."

Smirking against her exit, I lean back to palm her creamy ass cheek. It molds perfectly in my hand.

"You can do better than that," Ronan says, tightening his grip on her hair.

"Thank you for killing that man, Daemon."

Fuck, the way she says it with so much desire in her feminine voice...

"I'll kill any man who looks at you, Angel," I tell her, sinking two fingers inside her cunt. She's so wet that I meet no resistance. "I won't feel regret for slaughtering them like pigs. You know why?" My fingers slide back out, slick with her desire. I taste them, licking her off me, then shove them back inside her warm heat. "Because this greedy cunt is mine and my brothers. No one gets to taste it, fuck it, or play with it but us."

"I need to come," she whimpers, thighs shaking.

"And I'll let you. If you beg."

"Fuck, Daemon. Just make me come!"

"I don't hear any begging."

Alaric strokes her hair away from her face while he runs his big hand over his cock. He's dying to ram it into her mouth and watch her gag on him, but he wants to hear her beg as much as I do. Climbing off the bed, I wipe my mouth. Ronan takes my place, and I admire the sight of her on all fours while he eats her out from behind. She can barely hold herself up.

"I can't... I need..."

Alaric fists her hair on top of her head. "Just fucking beg already so I can fuck your throat."

"Mmmh!"

Ronan grunts, not letting up on his torturous assault on her pussy.

His face is covered in her.

"Shit, okay, fuck!"

I stiffen. Is this it? Is she about to beg?

"Please, I need to come."

"I didn't hear you," Alaric says, shifting closer.

"Please, please, please."

It's music to my ears. The sweetest fucking symphony.

"Please what?"

"Please fuck my mouth. Make me come. Just please..."

"Good girls get rewarded." Alaric slowly sinks his dick inside her mouth, and her satisfied sound is cut off when he thrusts down her throat. She gags, causing my cock to twitch in my pants.

Fuck...

"That's it," Alaric growls, holding her in place. "Such a good girl. You can take it. Your throat feels so damn good. So fucking good. Relax for me, little angel, breathe through your nose."

She comes.

It's fucking spectacular to watch her climax with Alaric's dick stuffed in her mouth while Ronan feasts on her soaking folds. He doesn't stop until the pleasure becomes too much and she tries to wriggle away. Stuck between the two fallen angels, she's unable to escape.

"You can come again," Ronan orders, biting her ass cheek. "Give me one more. I want your cum in my mouth."

I take a seat in the armchair by the far wall and settle in to watch the show. If she thinks I'm giving in to her this easily, she has another thing coming. Angel chokes around Alaric's cock in her mouth as he picks up his pace, thrusting hard and fast, using her for his own pleasure. Our little angel isn't so pure anymore. She's corrupt, taking cock like she was created to please her fallen angels.

And she does it so well. Beautiful fucking tears trail down her cheeks. Alaric sweeps them up with his thumb and licks them off. Angel comes again, convulsing, moaning, and trembling. Her prone little body has never known pleasure like it. After this, she'll be ruined for all other angels, and I like the thought of that a little too much. I don't want her to look at other men ever again. We're the only gods she needs to worship.

Alaric stiffens and then grunts as he spills his release down her throat. Slapping her ass and climbing off the bed, Ronan kneels on it with one leg while unbuckling his belt. "My turn. Come here and suck my cock."

Angel wipes her mouth and crawls over on shaky limbs, her blue eyes briefly meeting mine, before Ronan fists her hair and proceeds to make her wish she hadn't begged.

"Don't you want to join in?" Alaric asks me, walking over.

With my elbow on the armrest, I rub my lips. My cock is hard as a rock in my pants. "No, when I finally fuck her, I want her to be so desperate for it that she'll crawl through the house after me on her hands and knees."

"She's stubborn. You might wait a long time."

"I'll wait as long as it takes."

"You're as bad as each other."

"Fuck, that feels so fucking good," Ronan groans. It must do; his wings unfold behind him.

I roll my eyes. *What a show-off.*

"Yeah, like that, beautiful."

"Just finish off already," I call out, and Ronan laughs but keeps his eyes trained on the little angel, watching her suck on his dick. "I'm making it last."

Alaric digs in his pockets for his pack of cigarettes. He hands me one and lights his with a click of his fingers. After lighting mine, I extinguish the hellfire in my hand and take a deep inhale, relishing in the sweet burn.

"That's it, angel. Relax your throat for me."

Smoke curls in the air as the rain comes down harder on the window. The cleaner left it open this morning, and now my room smells of fresh rain, sex, and cigarettes. I'm almost down to the filter when Angel finally swallows his release. She does it so damn eagerly while moaning and arching her pert little ass up in the air.

As he steps away, she sits back on her heels and looks at me expectantly. She's flushed, her breasts painted with Alaric's bite marks, and her tangled hair sticks to the mascara streaks on her cheeks. How can I not want to walk over there and add my own marks to her smooth skin?

I flick my cigarette away and pat my thigh. "Come here."

She slowly slides off the bed and goes to stand but pauses when I shake my head.

"Crawl to me. Ass in the air."

Ronan lies spent on the bed. It'll be a long time before he moves again. Our little angel sucked his soul out of his body.

She sets her jaw but follows orders, and the moment her hands land on the stone floor, I hold my breath. Angel crawls to me. Her beautiful tits sway and her white wings move on her back as she arches her ass in the air like I asked her to. Fuck, she's dangerous. If I'm not careful, she'll rip my heart out of my body and sink her teeth into that, too. It's enough that she has me by my balls.

Settling between my legs and gazing up at me, she slides her hands up my thighs. I watch her set to work on my belt with eager hands. I feel like a king—a royal on his throne—while she pulls down my zipper. Lowering the front of my jeans, she hesitates. Her beautiful eyes stay glued to my weeping length as precum beads on the tip. I'm so hard, it's uncomfortable. As she leans in to lick it off, I fist the hair on top of her head to hold her off. "What do you say?"

Her tongue is out, her blue eyes peering up at me. Hell, I'm torturing myself. Warring with herself, her eyes flick down to my length. "Please, Daemon, may I suck your dick?"

"You want this?" I tease her, stroking my veiny length from root to tip and then back down. "All you have to do is beg again, and I might just let you."

Alaric chuckles next to me. "You have the self-control of a saint. Are you sure you didn't sneak out of Eden, too?"

"What's it going to be, little angel? Are you going to please your master, or should I give Dari a call? She'll do more than beg."

"Master?" Ronan chuckles. He's not dead after all.

"I think I would quite like her calling me that," I reply with a smirk, letting go of her hair to cup her chin. "Want to suck your master's dick?"

The beautiful flames in her eyes burn brighter when she sits back and hisses, "Fuck you! You're not my master!"

Such sweet foreplay.

"Suit yourself," I reply, tucking my dick away, but she's on me, yanking my jeans down. My cock is in her hot mouth in the next second. She sucks me down, moaning deep in her throat. *Holy shit.* She feels so fucking good. I let her bob on me for all of two seconds before shoving her off with enough force to make her stumble back onto the floor. "You're not having my dick until you beg me for it. Your sucking is mediocre at best, so you won't convince me by taking without permission."

It's a lie—she sucks like a motherfucking queen, and it was a damn struggle to push her away and not lose myself in her warm mouth, but it was worth offending her to see the fire in her eyes. She's positively fuming.

"I. Hate. You!"

My dick throbs.

Lifting my chin, I give a silent command to Alaric, who slides his hand inside his pocket, takes out his cell, and swipes the screen. Then he puts it to his ear and asks, "Want Dari to bring a couple of friends too?"

I nod, palming my length. "Yeah, at least two."

Angel snaps her eyes to Alaric, but she's too angry to call us out on our bluff. Her breaths are coming hard and fast, causing her beautiful tits to rise and fall. I want her ass in my hands and her nipples in my mouth.

"Please, Daemon, may I suck your cock?" she bites out.

I nearly come. My balls tighten at the fury in her eyes. "Daemon?"

"Master."

"Good girl." I place my hands on the armrests, spreading my thighs wider. "I'm all yours. Worship at your king's feet."

Alaric lowers his phone, and we share an amused glance. We toppled her queen this time, and the sweet victory tastes delicious on my tongue.

Her warm mouth covers me again, and I don't stop her this time. I let her taste and suck on me like she's waited a lifetime for my dick. The urge to ram my cock down her throat is strong, but it would defeat the purpose. I'm the one in control here, not her.

"Deeper, beautiful. I want to hear you gag."

Her throat constricts around my length, and I bite down on my tongue to stop myself from coming. "Spread your wings. Let me see them while you suck me."

They slowly unfurl, large and majestic. My hand lands in her hair, holding her down on my length while I begin to fuck her throat. I said I wouldn't take control, but the primal need to make an angel with such large wings—almost as big as mine—submit is overwhelming. I'm her king; she bows to me. "Hell, your throat, little angel. I could listen to you gag all fucking night."

Her wings threaten to close, so I give another deep thrust, feeling her throat constrict around me. "Keep them open. I want to see them when I stuff your mouth with my cum."

Her nails dig into my thighs, drawing blood through the rips in my jeans. It hurts, but I welcome the pain. She wants it, but she also doesn't want it. It's a heady mix. I'm an asshole, and I don't pretend otherwise. She still comes crawling back for more.

"Fuck," I groan, sliding out of her mouth. "Stick your tongue out and flatten it."

Hell, the sight of her with her mouth open, tongue out, ready and eager to take my release, pushes me over the edge and I paint her with my desire. With her wings spread out behind her, she looks up at me as my cum showers over her face, beading on her lashes and lips. I always want her like this. Bruised, ruined, and spent. She looks like she let three insatiable fallen angels have their way with her, and there's no way back now.

She's ours.

CHAPTER 11

AURELIA

I couldn't sleep last night, tossing and turning in bed. It stopped raining in the early hours, so I tiptoed out of bed and snuck outside into the yard at the back of the property while the boys were asleep. Daemon is in his bedroom, and Ronan and Alaric are spread out on the couches in the living room. The air smells of damp grass and failure. I've tried to fly for the last two hours, but it's impossible.

I don't know what I'm doing wrong. I'm an angel with wings. If I can't fly, then who am I, and what's the purpose of my wings? I feel like a fucking failure.

The birds are slowly waking up, singing their songs in the trees. It amazes me that they still know the hour of the day despite the perpetual night. Life finds a way to flourish even in the darkness.

Closing my eyes, I breathe in deeply in an attempt to wrangle my frustration. My shoulders ache from the weight of my wings. It's a pain I'm quickly growing used to, and until my muscles strengthen, it'll keep hurting.

I give an experimental flap, but nothing happens. Nothing at all. My bare feet stay planted on the ground.

"Dammit!" I growl.

"Do angels curse in Eden?"

My heart trips over itself and I whirl around. Daemon is slowly walking toward me, his hands in his pockets and shirtless. My mouth goes dry.

"Not trying to escape, are you?"

"No," I croak as he stops in front of me, towering like a demon.

"Good. Because I would find you."

My throat is sore from his rough treatment earlier, and bruises litter my body from Alaric's rough touch. I still can't believe I begged for his cock and called him Master. It must have been a temporary lapse of judgment because I was drunk on dick and not thinking clearly. Daemon might be the sexiest asshole I've ever had the misfortune of stumbling across, but I refuse to be one of his regular groupies. Just because I begged once doesn't mean I'll do it again. Not willingly.

"Why are you out here?" he asks, his fingers trailing down my arm.

My skin swells with goosebumps that spread across my arms like a forest fire.

"I'm trying to learn how to fly."

As he grabs my waist and pulls me to him, our chests collide, knocking the wind out of me. I try to take a breath, but his masculine, earthy scent is everywhere, weakening my resolve.

"Close your eyes."

"I don't trust you," I whisper.

My hard nipples chafe against the thin fabric of my dress while his other hand slides over my hip to my lower back.

"Good. I'm not someone you should trust."

Despite his warning, my eyes fall closed and my breath catches in my throat when his lips brush my ear.

"You need to believe."

"You make it sound so easy," I reply, hyperaware of his possessive touch and his heated breath on my lips.

"Spread your wings again."

My shoulders strain as I feel the shift in the air behind me. Daemon is standing close, his heat seeping through my thin dress.

"Imagine yourself back in Eden. Your bare feet sink into the grass, and the sun warms your cheeks. Birds sing in the trees as the bushes rustle nearby. A rabbit jumps out, with its twitchy nose and long ears. Everything is peaceful. Tranquil. Up ahead are the tall, golden gates."

"Daemon," I whisper, gripping his strong upper arms. "Shut up!"

His chest vibrates against mine with a chuckle.

As I step closer to the gates, my eyes widen. I crane my neck, looking up, up, up into the clouds. "What's on the other side?"

Freya drops her skipping rope to the grass and scrunches up her freckled nose as she follows my line of sight. "Bad things."

I snap my eyes to hers. "Bad things? What bad things?"

Freya lost her front baby tooth the other day, and her adult one is peeking out, but it'll be a while before the gap fills. If the elders knew we were out here, we would be in trouble, but Freya is a good friend. She follows me everywhere.

"I don't know," she says. "But the elders say we should stay in here where it's safe so that no one can steal our light."

I scan the nearby area until my eyes land on a tall tree with thick branches nearby. It disappears into the clouds. Running over to it, I heave myself up on the first branch.

"What are you doing?" Freya asks curiously.

The green leaves are in full bloom, like they always are here. In the human world, they have seasons. We don't.

I pull myself up on the second branch, my small legs dangling in the air. "I want to see what's on the other side."

"But you'll fall."

The next branch is just out of reach. Jumping up and swinging my legs over, I smile down at her. "You'll catch me."

Freya shields her eyes from the sun with her hand. "They'll come looking for us soon."

"I know. I won't be long." My piggy tails are ruined. I have a scraped knee and leaves stuck to my hair. I'll be in trouble when I get back, but I don't care.

It takes me a while to reach the top, and by the time I finally heave myself up on the thin branch, I'm breathing hard and my muscles ache. I creep forward, careful not to fall, and move the leaves aside. Beyond the tall gates is a forest—a deep, dark forest lined with fir and birch trees. Low-lying mist hovers above the treetops, seeping into their branches and spilling out on the forest floor. It's so dark that I can sense the supreme silence from my perch on this branch.

"What can you see?"

Aurelia...

I drag my eyes away. "Err, a forest."

"A forest? Is that it?" Freya asks, disappointed.

I swallow thickly, and my eyes slowly return to the darkness that seems to be calling out to me.

Aurelia...

I lose my balance, letting out a shriek as I fall. Branches catch my skin, my hair, and my feathers. The pain barely registers.

"Aurelia!" Freya cries, her voice thick with fear.

My wings erupt, knocking into branches, but then the most miraculous thing happens. My downward fall stops. Suspended in midair, I stare wide-eyed while my wings disturb the air with big, powerful sweeps.

Freya gasps and breathes out, "Oh, my God."

The fear in her voice startles me and I fall the rest of the way, landing with a hard thud.

"Are you okay?" Freya asks, kneeling beside me.

Blinded by the sun, I push up to sitting. There's not a cloud in the sky. What happened just now? Why did I stop falling?

"Please don't tell anyone," I beg, gazing into Freya's blue eyes.

"I won't," she promises.

My eyes fly open, and I blink at Daemon. "I flew!"

He looks adorably confused, if you could ever call anything about Daemon adorable.

"I fell from a tree when I was eight years old." I hurry to add, "I flew."

"You flew?"

Nodding eagerly, I continue, "Yes. My wings erupted from my back when I fell, and I hovered in the air for a brief moment. I didn't even realize I was flying at the time. My best friend was there, and I made her promise never to breathe a word to anyone."

He starts to speak, but I interrupt him as I step back and place my hands on my head. "I didn't understand it at the time. It was instinct, Daemon."

His brows knit together. "So, are you telling me we should shove you off a cliff and see if you fly?"

I stop pacing and roll my eyes at his ridiculous remark. "Very funny. No, my point is that I wasn't thinking about anything. I wasn't even trying to make anything happen. It *just* did."

"Because you were in danger," he confirms.

"I can fly, Daemon." I release a surprised laugh. "I can fly!"

Daemon peers back at the dark house before looking at me. "Then try again."

"What? Right now?"

He walks toward me with such intention in his dark eyes that I stumble back a step. Damp leaves stick to my bare feet as I retreat, and my heart starts racing in my chest. He doesn't stop until my back connects with a tree.

Placing his hand on either side of my face on the trunk, he whispers, "Show me your power, little angel."

My chest rises and falls with each quick breath. He's so close that his heat burns me everywhere we connect. "I can't fly if you're crowding me like this."

He strokes the backs of his fingers over my collarbone, my pulse point, where my heartbeat flutters against my skin. "So push me away. Tell me to stop."

I can't think when he's this close. Why does he affect me like this? He's an asshole underneath the smirk and all that delicious muscle.

Sliding my hands up his stomach, I feel each groove contract. My intention is to shove him away—to assert my freedom—but then his lips descend on mine, and his kiss is so sweet and toe-curling that I sink into him.

"Angel," he whispers, braiding his fingers in my hair and tasting my lips softly, hungrily. There's nothing rough about his touch now. Is this the same Daemon who licked my ass last night before ordering me to crawl to him?

He steps back, looking dazed. And if I'm surprised by his gentle kiss, he looks even more confounded. "I'm sure you'll figure it out," he says, rubbing at the back of his neck. "Just err.. just spread your wings and trust. Let yourself be guided."

I stare at him unblinkingly while he walks back to the house. I've never met a more confusing man. First, he steals me away to the underworld, and now he trusts me not to run away. There must be a catch.

CHAPTER 12

AURELIA

The lady behind the reception staples a stack of papers together, her eyes falling up and down my body, before she hands me the paperwork. "Sign these. Your class schedule is there, too. You have been assigned a locker, which Dariana kindly offered to show you."

As if summoned by magic, Dariana's high heels click on the floor. Her black dress is short and hugs her curves to perfection. It's hard not to gawk and even harder not to blush. She takes the paperwork from the lady behind the counter and walks off, calling out over her shoulder, "Are you coming or not?"

I shake myself off and hurry after her. Students stare as we pass. I don't blame them; we look like an odd pair. Yin and Yang.

"Where are your keepers?" she asks, barely sparing me a glance.

It's hard to keep up with her. She's too fast, weaving

through bodies like she knows that everyone will step aside for her.

And they do.

"I don't know," I reply.

This morning, they took off and left me alone at the reception. I think I stood there blinking for ten minutes before the lady behind the reception cleared her throat. I feel lost. I'm so used to them hovering over me at every turn.

"They trust you not to run away now."

"I guess so," I reply.

They have something I want, and they know it. I won't leave here until I have mastered flying—a chance I know I won't get offered in Eden.

"Why are you volunteering to show me to my locker?"

Her eyes briefly meet mine before she focuses her gaze forward. "Why not?"

"You're being kind. It's weird."

She snorts.

"It is!"

We pass a corner, and she pulls me to a stop next to a set of lockers. "This is yours. And these here," she gestures to the lockers surrounding it, "belong to Daemon, Alaric, and Ronan. Your leash is stretchy, but make no mistake, you're still leashed."

"Oh."

She gives me a bemused look, leaning her shoulder on the locker next to mine while I open it to peek inside. "What do I do with it?"

Her eyebrows fly up. "You put things in it."

My ears heat. "I'm sorry. Things are different here in Hell."

Dariana eyes me for a moment before slamming my locker shut. "Follow me."

I try, but it's not easy. She knows these hallways like the back of her hand, and I don't.

"Where are we going?"

"Away from here."

"But the lesson?"

"Can wait." Her small hand finds mine as we step outside into the dark.

Lanterns light the path, their flames surrounded by countless moths. We cut across the damp grass, and she guides me deep into the surrounding woods. Somewhere in the distance, a wolf howls as sticks break beneath my bare feet.

Dariana soon grows fed up with her tall heels sinking into the ground, so she removes them and carries them in one hand. There's a break in the trees, and I gasp as we step out into an open field. The sky is lit up with stars. Too many to count.

"It's beautiful here," I whisper, turning in a circle, eyes on the sky.

"Yes," she says, and something dark and delicious in her voice makes me pause.

I tear my gaze away from the blanket of burning lights above.

Discarding her shoes, her feet sink into the grass, carrying her closer. "Spread your wings."

I gulp, trapped in her gaze.

"Do it."

"Why?"

"Trust me."

"I don't trust anyone," I admit, slowly letting my wings unfold behind me.

Dariana's eyes follow their movement, trailing over my white feathers before settling on my face. Her own wings spread out behind her, black as night. "You're wise. The moment you trust, you'll get your heart torn out."

"I've been kidnapped and stolen away to another realm. How much worse can it get?"

She steps closer, the air thickening with something electric and dangerous. "You left Eden, little angel. Monsters lurk in the woods. Don't tell me the elders didn't warn you."

They did, but it only made me more curious. Dariana sees the truth in my eyes, and the smirk on her lips steals the breath from my lungs. "Monsters are dangerous. You should have listened to your elders."

"What are you doing?" I whisper when she slides her fingers over my eyes to close them.

"It's time to fly."

"I don't know how."

"Yes, you do," she replies softly, tapping my temple. "It's in here." The warmth of her smooth palm seeps into my skin when she places her hand over my heart. "And it's in here. The color of your wings doesn't matter. You were created to fly. All you need to do is trust."

"You told me not to trust."

"In others. You can always trust in yourself."

I can't think when she's this close. The memory of how she made my body sing lingers in my mind like an expensive perfume. I open my eyes.

"Follow my lead." She moves her wings slowly up and down in long sweeps that shift the cool air. "What are you waiting for?" Her warm hands slide lower, over my breasts, before gripping my waist.

Locked in her gaze, I move my wings while drowning in her brown mocha.

"Faster," she coaxes, her breath dancing over my lips. "That's it, good girl. Feel the wind and the freedom."

She gives a powerful flap of her wings, and I follow her lead, despite the ache in my shoulders from the weight.

Leaning in, she brushes her lips over mine. "Don't stop. Keep moving them no matter what.

"I'm scared," I admit.

Scared of her, of how she makes me feel, and of the confusing mix of emotions inside me.

"Fear is good. It's how you know you're alive. If you didn't fear, it wouldn't feel this good."

"What wouldn't?"

"This," she replies, plunging her hot tongue into my mouth. We're a clash of lips and teeth, roaming hands, and wings that slice through the air. My fingers tangle in her soft, silky hair, and hers in mine. Our chests touch with every rapid breath, every soft whimper, and bite of teeth. Dariana tastes of all the things my elders warned me about. Before her, I had never looked at a woman this way, and now I can't imagine never touching one again. She's so soft and smooth.

"Open your eyes."

I blink them open and gasp.

Below us, the school sits nestled amongst the trees. Above us, billions of stars flicker, guiding the way. My eyes come back to Dariana's, and I couldn't look away if I tried.

"I'm flying."

"You are," she confirms before letting go. When I begin to panic, her head shakes. "Stop thinking."

I drop. Not by much. But enough to make my heart leap to my throat. "I can't just stop thinking."

"Let me show you something." She entwines her fingers with mine, and we fly higher and higher. Up here, the air is cooler.

She's beside me now, holding her hand over my eyes. "Are you ready?"

I'll never be ready. Not for her, not for this world, but I whisper yes. She removes her hand. Far away in the distance, tall walls rise up into the sky, and the golden gates shimmer in the sunlight. It pours from the heavens like a sunbeam and lights up Eden and everyone within it.

My home.

Freya...

"Just like you gazed out over the walls, curious about what lay on the other side, we fly up here and look back at your world, wondering what lies behind those tall walls. Why God's light shines upon your lands but not ours."

Homesickness clogs my chest and throat as tears well in my eyes. The urge to fly back and beg for forgiveness is overwhelming. Deep down, I know they'll never let me back in. I'm tainted, spoiled by desire, and no longer pure. My white wings will never fool anyone in their world. Not now, when they're dipped in ink.

"What did we do to deserve to dwell in the dark?" She's behind me now, her voice thick with envy and bitterness. Emotions I couldn't place before now.

"Is it so bad to feel pleasure?" she asks, blocking out the view of my home. The soft brush of her thumb over my lips makes my lashes flutter and my breath hitch as my body comes alive.

We slowly descend and our feet sink into the damp grass. Dariana guides me down on the ground, shielding me from the world with her dark hair. It falls around us like a curtain as she says, "Tell me, little angel, did you ever feel pleasure behind those gates? Did anyone ever touch your pale skin or whisper sweet nothings in your ear?" Sliding my skirt up my thighs, she snakes her hand beneath the fabric. "Did anyone ever make you sigh their name in pleasure and beg for more?" Her plump lips skim over my jaw and then down my neck, chasing my racing pulse. I'm drunk on her and the smell of damp grass.

"Did you ever," she whispers seductively, hooking her fingers in the thin fabric of my panties and pulling them aside, "get taken so completely that you would die a thousand deaths to feel their touch again?" She shoves two fingers inside me and steals my surprised cry from my lips with her hungry mouth. "You won't look at that place with such longing in your eyes by the time we're done with you." Her words are a promise and a threat. "You won't shimmer in the fucking darkness at the thought of returning." Diving down, she sinks her teeth into my neck while snarling like an animal. The pain is so sharp that I cry out. She fucks me through it, her thumb flicking my swollen clit as she thrusts and thrusts and thrusts.

"Dariana," I moan, arching my neck to give her better access while she drinks from me in long pulls, rubbing her fingers against my inner walls.

And when she's done, she grabs my jaw, snarling like an animal, "I get to feed on you whenever I want, understood?"

I nod, spreading my legs wider as her sweet assault on my pussy takes me higher and higher.

Pleased with my response, she presses down on my clit with her thumb. Her blood-stained teeth and her dark eyes are all I can see. "Don't get any ideas, little angel. We will come for you if you try to fly back home to your precious little Eden."

She's so rough. Almost as much as the boys.

"And we won't be so nice."

"Oh, fuck," I whimper, hovering right at the edge. All it will take is one more flick, and the world will fall away.

"Tell me you understand!"

"Dariana, please," I whimper. "I need to come."

"And you will," she says with a dark smile. "When you deserve it."

My lips part on a soundless cry. It's hell to hover so close but not be allowed to jump when I want nothing more than to free fall into her depths.

Taking pity on me, she flicks my clit and clamps her hand over my mouth to muffle my loud cries as I come. "That's it," she breathes, rubbing me through my orgasm and ignoring my attempts to close my legs when the pleasure becomes too much. "That's my innocent little angel. Keep those pretty thighs spread for me."

Before I can regain my breath, she slides her skirt up and straddles my face. She's not wearing underwear, so when she sits down and orders me to lick, her sweet taste explodes on my tongue. It's too late anyway—I'm drugged on her scent as she rolls her hips and grinds herself against me.

"Fuck, Angel," she moans, biting down on her plump lip. "Hell, that feels so good!"

My own skirt lies pooled around my waist, my panties hanging off my ankle as the cool night air licks at my damp, puffy cunt. Twigs snap underfoot, and deep, masculine chuckles announce their arrival before I see them.

"Fuck, Dari. I should have known we would find you here, riding the little angel's face."

Unbothered, she flips Daemon off and orders me to continue. Hard boots kick my ankles apart, baring me to their hungry eyes while they circle us like vultures that lie in wait for the lion to finish feasting so they can move in.

"Do you like her taste, little angel?" Alaric asks. "I bet she tastes fucking sweet, huh?"

"I know she does," chuckles Daemon. "Pussy is addictive, Angel. Once you've had a taste of those sweet juices, you'll come to crave it."

I pump my tongue in and out of her tight heat, my cheeks smeared with her desire. Daemon is right, this is a drug.

"Shut up," Dari snarls, "I'm trying to get off here."

Someone pries my legs open, and then a warm mouth descends on my slick folds, making me see fucking stars.

"Hell..." Dariana moans, shuddering. "Fuck, I'm so close..."

Boots appear on either side of my head. Daemon tips Dari's chin up. "You fed on her again."

She bares her teeth when he grips her harder, growling, "Don't you fucking dare hiss at me. I'm more powerful than you!"

Skilled fingers fill me up, and I gasp beneath Dariana's dripping pussy.

"Did I say you could feed on her?"

I moan, rocking back against the mouth on my cunt.

"No, you didn't."

Daemon drags her off, tossing her to the ground. "If you want to use *our* Angel—*our* belonging—you ask for permission first. Understood?"

She's up on her knees, glaring at him, her cheeks flushed with anger and arousal. "Fuck you!"

Daemon's deep chuckle could make a grown man fear for his life, but Dariana bares her teeth again, earning her a hair pull.

Daemon is a dick.

A delicious, fucking dick.

"Defy me again, and I'll make you regret it."

As he strides over to me, he orders Alaric to hold her down. Ronan retreats, and then Daemon flips me over on my belly and smacks my ass before unbuckling his belt. "I know you like her, Dari, but you'll have to find your own toy. This one is mine." With a fierce hold on my blonde hair, he yanks my head back, leaning down and whispering against my temple, "This will hurt."

Daemon takes me with one powerful thrust, burying himself to the hilt. My shrill, pained cry bounces off the nearby trees.

It hurts.

Oh, God, it hurts.

He's so big!

"Your virginity, like you, is mine, little angel. I want your blood smeared over my dick."

He doesn't wait for me to adjust. There are no candles, no rose petals, and no sweet touches. My hands slide in the damp grass, dirt clogs my nails, and my scalp burns with pain. Tears pour freely down my cheeks and my soft cries turn him on more. My pussy stings like it's on fire, but I don't beg him to stop. Despite this fucked up mess, I don't want him to.

Dari's eyes hold mine while Daemon stakes his claim beneath the star-filled sky.

"So fucking tight, sweet angel."

"You're fucking ruthless," I bite back.

He slides all the way out, then slams back in. "You wouldn't have it any other way."

Ronan crouches down in front of me and cups my chin with a sinful smirk on his lips. "Don't feel sorry for Dari. This is Hell. Morals have no place here. You take what you want, little angel. Right now, you want Daemon to hurt you with his dick."

I snarl at him, and Daemon yanks my head back further. "Teach her a lesson, Ronan."

Shifting up on his knees, Ronan unbuckles his jeans, lowers his zipper, and slides his fingers into my hair, then pulls on the strands until I wince. "You've been a bad girl tonight."

My mouth waters when he pushes his jeans and boxers down.

"A very fucking bad girl."

Daemon slaps my ass again. "Don't be so upset, Dari. I'll let you play with her again if you ask nicely."

"Go to hell, Daemon."

"Look around you," he says on a powerful thrust. "We're already here."

The pain is slowly dissipating, transforming into something mind-blowing. As Ronan slides his dick into my mouth, I arch back against Daemon, silently begging for more.

"Such a good little whore," he praises, grabbing hold of

my wings in an entirely possessive and demeaning way. "If I ever find you pleasuring someone else without my permission again, I won't be so fucking nice to you, my little angel. Understood? You belong to us, not anyone else. Don't think you strolled in here of your own free will. No, we saw you, we took you, and until we grow bored of you, little angel, you'll do as we say."

Tears stream down my cheeks while Ronan fucks my throat. It's brutal but, at the same time, worshipping. They want me to know I belong to them, but they also want to get me off. Every slap, every stroke of their fingers, and every hair pull is designed to bring pleasure and soothe the sting of their brutality.

"Fuck, you take our cocks so well," Ronan praises me, staring down at my face while I gag on him. "I can't wait until Alaric gets in on the act too, and we take you at the same time."

"She's not ready yet," Daemon states behind me. I want to argue with him, but Ronan's grip on my hair holds me in place, his cock buried deep in my throat.

Snaking his hand beneath me, Daemon rubs my swollen clit hard and fast until I hurtle over the precipice. My body tenses when every muscle in my body contracts.

"That's it, baby. Come on my cock. Let me feel you squeeze me."

These boys will be the death of me. It's so intense.

They pull out and step behind me as I fight to catch my breath.

Daemon slaps my wings. "Spread them."

My chest heaves as I do as I'm told. I'm spent and exhausted, tingly and achy everywhere. Daemon's grip on my hair hurts while they pleasure themselves behind me.

"Are you watching Dari?" Daemon pants, his grip tightening on my hair. "You might think twice next time you're a bitch and want to steal our angel." To me, he says, "Keep your wings spread like that, beautiful."

Then it happens—their release showers over my wings in quick spurts, defiling the pure white feathers. It's degrading, but the throbbing ache between my legs tells a different story. Strings of white cum coat my wings, beading and trailing down toward my shoulder blades. Daemon tucks himself away before stepping around me and grabbing my chin with his bloodied hand.

My virginity...

"Don't go behind my back again. It will never end well for you."

Something dark unfurls inside me. As I peel my lips back, I feel an ache in my incisors. I snarl like an animal, but the sound dies in my throat when he pulls my hair and spreads his wings behind him in a show of dominance.

"Retract your fangs now!"

Fangs? I don't know how to fucking retract them. All I know is that my thighs are smeared with blood, my wings are covered in cum, and the scent of Dari's needy pussy tantalizes my senses. I need to get to her so I can finish what I started. I need to taste her cum on my tongue and sink my teeth into her olive skin until my mouth fills with coppery blood. The urge is so fucking sudden that I snap my teeth at him.

It's the wrong thing to do.

He slaps me before gripping my jaw again and glaring down at me. "Apologize!"

My eyes dance over his raven wings, stretching out behind him. He's a powerful fallen angel, there's no doubt about it. But I don't yield to anyone, especially not him. Not when he stands in my way of the sweetest fucking pussy on this planet.

I unfold my wings behind me, drawing a gasp from Dari's lips. No one challenges Daemon in this neck of the woods. He's the ultimate alpha, and I'm lucky to have caught his attention. He likes my defiance as much as he hates it. The urge to dominate me is what drives him to fill my mouth with his bloody fingers until I choke. The games we play are so fucking twisted. But fuck, I never want to lose and I never want to win. If he wants to get to my queen, he's got a lot of fucking pieces to knock out first. I'm safely guarded in my tower.

"You like it," he observes, sliding his fingers back out and then thrusting them back in. "Interesting."

I bite down on him hard enough to notice the tic in his jaw. As soon as I let up, he removes his fingers and pulls me to my feet by my hair.

He towers over me, dark and delicious. "You can fight me all you want. You'll never win."

I spit on him and he flicks his gaze down, watching the saliva slide down his black T-shirt. Then he chuckles darkly before grabbing my arm and dragging me toward the school. "Oh, I look forward to breaking you like a wild horse."

Dariana runs after us. "What are you doing, Daemon?"

"You know fucking well what I'm doing."

"I should have asked for permission to play with her, okay? It was wrong of me to go behind your back."

He ignores her, shoving me in front of him. Branches scratch the bare skin on my pale arms and legs, the hem of my dress is dirty, and wet leaves stick to the fabric. My scarlet virginity trails a slow path down my legs. It's on Daemon's hands. There's a streak on his forehead from when he ran the back of his hand over it to wipe off the sweat.

"Daemon, think about this. She's an angel. She's not strong like the rest of the girls here."

"You're wrong," he says, pushing me again, and my hair snags on a branch. "She's stronger than anyone here. We've only tapped her potential."

Alaric chuckles next to me as we emerge from the trees and

cut across the grass toward the lit-up lanterns that line the path to the academy. "You're in deep shit now."

We ascend the stone steps to the academy, and as we enter, students turn and stare, their eyes widening.

"Move!" Daemon orders me, his fingers circling my arm.

"Let go of me," I hiss, slapping him, but he doesn't even notice.

We walk down numerous corridors before entering a spacious room littered with seating areas; plush couches pushed up against damask wallpaper, an open space in the middle with numerous wooden poles, and a pool table off to the side. I can't look away from the poles. Shackled to them are human girls and boys, their terrified eyes darting around the room.

"See that?" Daemon growls in my ear, steering me over to the nearest pole. "Welcome to the cafeteria."

I try to fight him off, but he bends down and picks me up, carrying me fireman-style. It's humiliating. Laughter rings out around me, and he dumps me to my feet beside a human girl and grabs a handful of hair at the nape of my neck. "You want to bare your incisors at me like a fucking brat?! Then put them to good fucking use!"

When I refuse to reply, he jostles me. "Feed on her!"

The loud sounds around me fade into the distance as his words sink in. Beside us, the girl cries quietly. My heart breaks for her. Never have I seen such cruelty before. Hunger didn't exist behind the gates. In that world, we ate for pleasure, not sustenance. We were always fulfilled. But things are different here.

"You've let Dari feed on you twice. You need to rebuild your strength and fruit isn't going to cut it. Not anymore."

Confused, I shove him off and say, "You can't live on angel blood, so why does your kind feed on angels?"

Ronan and Alaric laugh behind me; my naivety is refreshing to them.

Meanwhile, Daemon levels Dariana with a glare. "Want to explain to our clueless little angel here why you've fed on her twice?"

Dariana looks sheepish but covers it well by raising her chin. "You're too serious, Daemon. Lighten up. I was only playing with her."

With a snort, he brings his attention to me and grabs me by the throat. "Dominance, sweet angel. Power. She gets off on asserting her power over you. Even more so because her wings are smaller than yours. And you let her play with you like a cat plays with a mouse."

"You do it too," I sneer.

He gets in my face. "I *am* more powerful than you."

My smile is sugary, laced with poison. I enjoy these games as much as he does. "No, pretty boy, *I* am more powerful than you."

"Yeah?" he breathes. "Prove it. Drain the girl."

I pale, my eyes flicking between his. Do I have it within me to kill a human girl? Sex may be a sin in my world, but killing someone? Taking a life?

His other hand shoots out to grab my chin, his fingers sliding between my lips. He prods my incisor. "Let them out to play."

It's instinct to snarl at him. There's a she-wolf inside me who doesn't like it when the alpha forces her to submit.

"Don't touch me," I growl, batting him away, but he wraps his fingers around the back of my neck. Then he dives down and sinks his teeth into the pulse point at my throat. The sharp sting steals my breath. Daemon isn't gentle as he tears into me, holding me immobile with his tight grip. There's nothing sweet or romantic about it. He steals my life essence with deep pulls that leave me weak and trembling. Blood pours down my front, staining my dress. His big hand slides through the warm liquid when he moves his fingers to the front of my throat.

He laps at the incisor wounds before biting down again, causing me to cry out in pain and shame. Daemon was right; this is dominance play. Everyone in here is witness to his power over me. I don't stand a chance against him.

"Now," he says, smiling at me through bloodied teeth, chin smeared with scarlet, "drink her dry, or I'll continue feeding on you for everyone to see."

"Then you'll have to kill me," I hiss, feeling lightheaded. "I refuse to hurt a human girl."

"The thing is," he whispers, hooking his finger in the collar of my dress and pulling it away from my skin to peer down at my naked breasts and hard nipples, "I wouldn't kill you quickly. I'd drag it out, make you beg for death."

My skin tingles beneath his gaze. I want him to touch me. How fucked up is that?

"I'm not scared of you, Daemon," I whisper back. I'm so fucking weak.

He hums, steadying me with his hands. "You should be. How about this? I'll make you a deal. If you feed on her so you can regain your strength, I'll let her live. If you refuse, I'll have Dari here kill her. How does that sound?"

"I thought you traveled to the human world to feed."

"We do," he confirms, his thumb stroking the side of my throat. "But it's not always possible to feed that way. The humans here don't taste as nice because they're scared and anemic, but they suffice when we can't get away to hunt. Besides, some angels don't like to visit the human world to feed. They prefer to do it here."

"I want to go home," I whisper. The horror I've witnessed here today is a slap in the face. Pain doesn't exist in Eden. We don't shackle humans to wooden poles and feed on them. We don't hurt others.

"That's a fucking shame," he growls, grabbing my hair. "You're not going home, so you better stop that thought."

"I hate you!" I hiss with the last of my strength. "I wish I had never left Eden."

He grinds his teeth before stepping back and lifting his chin at Alaric behind me in a silent command. Then he walks away without a backward glance. There's a weird pang in my chest, which I snuff out as soon as it makes itself known. I refuse to feel bad for spewing poison at him.

I'm too weak, my knees buckling beneath me. Alaric is there to catch me in his arms as the darkness overtakes me.

The last thing I hear is Dariana's voice. "I told you she wasn't strong enough."

CHAPTER 13

DAEMON

Cigarette smoke fills the room, and the patio door is slightly ajar to let in the smell of fresh rain outside. We're in the living room downstairs. Dark, gray walls and large leather sofas spread out messily. On the back wall behind me is a bookshelf lined with human skulls. The coffee table in front of me is only there to rest your feet on—no other reason.

The human girl between my spread legs blinks up at me. Unlike the humans tied to the poles, she's not scared, although she should be. If all goes according to plan, she'll awaken the monster I know slumbers inside of my little angel.

"What's your name?" I ask her to put her at ease more than anything. I don't give a shit what her name is as long as she serves a purpose here tonight. I need Angel to feed after I almost drained her and if she doesn't feed willingly, I'll force her hand.

"Natalia."

Ronan smirks at me through the cloud of smoke and takes

another deep pull on the joint pinched between his fingers. This human girl is one of the academy's pets. She's here because she hopes to gain immortality, and her foolish heart believes one of the fallen angels will grant it to her one day. We're not fucking vampires.

"Just drain a human and feed the blood to the little angel in a glass, like mulled wine," Alaric suggests, taking the joint from Ronan.

I twirl the girl's dark hair around my finger, shaking my head. "I want to topple her queen. She thinks she's so fucking pure. I *know* she's not. I don't care what it takes." I cup the girl's jaw, bringing her brown eyes to mine. "I will break her if it's the last thing I do."

Alaric squints at me through the cloud of smoke, a smile tugging at the corners of his lips. "You're both as fucking stubborn as each other."

I tsk. "She'll dance to my tune by the end of the night."

"She's weak," Ronan comments, sinking down further on the couch, his legs spread obnoxiously wide.

"No thanks to you, Daemon," laughs Alaric.

Smirking, I stare down at the girl's face. "What can I say? I like to break pretty things." I jostle the girl's chin. "Or, in this case, I like to watch pretty things destroy weakness."

It's the first time I've had anything to do with a human pet. The other angels play with them, but I have no interest in humans besides draining them dry. But for what I have planned tonight, this girl will do just fine. Jealousy is a dragon everyone here has had years to learn how to ride. My sweet angel has not. She's far off becoming a dragon slayer, and I count on it to get my way tonight.

"There's only one problem with your plan." Ronan chuckles amusedly.

"Yeah, what's that?"

He gestures to the girl. "Last time you tried to fuck a

human girl, you failed. How do you plan on making Angel jealous when you can't even touch the human sexually?"

"Who says I have to touch her?"

Ronan and Alaric exchange an amused look. They think I'm full of shit. That this won't work.

"You saw her incisors elongate. The monster inside her is slowly awakening from its slumber. I intend to poke it with a stick."

"Poke it with a stick." Ronan shakes his head, but he's laughing, too. "What's taking her so long anyway?"

I trail my fingers over the girl's mouth. Her lips are soft and plump, but the blue tinge at their corners tells the true story. Like all humans in our world, subjected to regular feedings, she's anemic and not the ideal food for our angel. But short of snatching a human from the human world, she's the next best thing. If she's crying and screaming, this won't work. No, I need her to be a willing participant. And right now—on her knees between my legs—she has stars in her eyes. She knows who I am and will do anything to please me.

"Let's see if we can tempt our angel's monster to come out and play."

AURELIA

I wake up alone in my bed with a pounding headache, and when I try to sit up, the room spins. I'm still weak after Daemon almost drained me last night in his bid to dominate me and force me to feed on that poor girl.

As I recall the humans shackled to the wooden poles, I shiver. At first, I couldn't make sense of why they call this Hell. Now I'm slowly starting to understand. Desire and hunger are rampant here. Lust and longing. Jealousy and bitterness.

It's raining outside, and the soft patter on the window

draws my attention. I slowly climb out of bed and walk over. I'm in a clean dress. This one is a shimmering black and falls halfway down my thighs. I've never worn anything this short or revealing before. I've also never seen rain.

I stand there, watching the raindrops on the window slide down the glass in a race toward the bottom. Curiosity has me reaching out to open it. Before I can unlatch the hook and slide it open, I hear voices downstairs. The beat of base, and deep muffled laughter.

I pad barefoot down the stairs, careful not to step where it creaks, and pause outside the door to the living room. Ronan chuckles. Alaric is in there too, but I can't make out what he's saying.

Swaying on my feet, I grip the handle. The door creaks open and I peer inside. The air is thick with marijuana smoke, a black fabric L-shaped sofa sits pushed up against the back wall, and large windows line the left side of the room. Tall doors open up to a patio area.

Beside the sofa, on a second settee to the right, Alaric and Ronan sit spread out. Their dark eyes spark with humor when I walk in. I get the sense they've been expecting me.

"Good morning, sleepyhead."

I pad deeper into the room, unable to look away from Daemon, who is seated like a king in front of me on the L-shaped couch. Between his legs, on her knees, is a human girl with stars in her eyes. Daemon doesn't look up at me as he tips her chin with his fingers and brings the joint to his lips with his other hand.

Ronan explains, "Don't worry, little angel. This young girl is here in our world of her own free will. She hopes to be offered immortality."

I gnash my teeth as something dark and ugly stirs inside me.

"She's pretty, isn't she?" Daemon asks, watching me

through lowered lashes, before tipping his head back and blowing out a cloud of smoke. Nausea swirls inside me. I'm not sure if it's because I'm so lightheaded and weak or if it's the girl between his legs.

"Why don't you join us?" Ronan suggests, patting his thigh. The smirk on his lips is cruel.

I struggle to think coherently. Everything is a haze, but I get the distinct feeling they're toying with me. The human girl in the room is not the prey the lions lie in wait to attack.

I am.

I rub a hand over my face and blink to clear the haze, but nothing seems to work.

"Have a seat," Daemon orders, sounding far away. To the girl, he says, "Unzip me."

She must be excited, because she sets to work on his belt with eager fingers. On the other sofa, Alaric and Ronan chuckle. I don't know what they find so amusing.

Ronan asks, "Struggling there, brother?"

Daemon shoots him a glare while grinding his teeth so hard that it looks like they might pulverize. The sound of a zipper being undone somewhat clears the haze. My heart is racing too fast. Beside me, the rain comes down harder on the window, soaking the floor where the patio door is ajar to let in the damp air.

The human girl slides her hand over his impressive length and something inside me breaks. Daemon looks tortured behind the mask he wears so well. His eyes stay glued to mine when she leans in and takes him in her mouth.

"Are you comfortable sitting on your hands?" laughs Alaric, his body shaking with chuckles.

"Shut the fuck up," Daemon barks, his forehead damp with sweat. He closes his eyes, breathing deeply through his nose as he leans back against the couch. Meanwhile, pain lances through my chest at the sight of the girl pleasuring him so fucking willingly. My skin crawls with unfamiliar emotions. I feel territorial. My incisors ache and throb as my wings unfold behind me.

As if he can sense the shift in the air, Daemon slowly opens his eyes and smirks at me. *What are you going to do?*

The girl moans and something inside me snaps. I'm on her before I know what's happening, tearing into her flesh with my sharp teeth. Her loud screams only spur me on more. Coaxing the beast with glowing eyes, to step out from the shadows. I snarl like an animal and sink my teeth in further. I drink and drink and keep drinking until her heart slows before ceasing to beat.

As silence falls over the room, I throw her off and wipe my bloodied mouth with the back of my hand. Energy surges through me. My veins tingle and spark with a strength I've never felt before. The world is a red haze as I look back at Daemon, who chuckles when I bare my teeth and flare my white wings. Then he shoots up in a blur of movement and fists my hair. It hurts so fucking good.

"What have I said about baring your teeth at me, little angel? You're not in charge here. I am."

A fierce snarl rips from my lips, and I shove him with such force that he flies back and collides with the back wall. On the couch, Alaric and Ronan stare with their mouths hanging open before collapsing into laughter. "Well, I'll be damned."

There's a dent in the wall and the couch is upturned. But Daemon, he's in front of me with my throat clasped tightly in his big hand. "You're in big fucking trouble now."

"Fuck you," I hiss, then knee him in the balls and throw myself at him. I should run in the opposite direction, but something inside me—something dark and dangerous—is set on dominating him.

"Fuck," he growls when I sink my teeth into his neck.

We collide with the upturned couch, toppling to the floor.

Alaric and Ronan continue laughing as Daemon tries to fight me off.

"You fucking..." he grunts, getting the upper hand. Tossing me onto my back, he straddles me and pins my arms to the floor with his knees. Blood trickles from bite wounds on his neck, soaking the front of his T-shirt. He's so angry that his sharp incisors sink into his bottom lip.

Daemon grabs me by the throat and squeezes. "You submit to me."

My pussy throbs with need. I've never felt more alive and more in my body than I do right now. Power thrums in my veins, heady and addictive. My wings push up against Ronan and Alaric's feet as I spread them beneath me. I refuse to submit to Daemon. He lifts his chin to Alaric, who jumps up and disappears from the room.

"You want to play games, sweetheart?" Daemon's voice is dark with promise. "I'll play."

Alaric returns with a knife and hands it to Daemon before walking back to Ronan, careful not to step on my wing. Cold, sharp metal presses up against my neck.

"If you don't retract your teeth and close your wings, I'll cut you."

The red haze is slowly fading, but I don't retract my teeth. Instead, I lift my head off the floor, snarling at him. His deep, cruel, and humorless chuckle makes me tingle between my thighs.

"Such a naughty girl," he purrs, nicking my pulse point with the knife. A single trail of blood runs down, soaking into the wooden floor. Daemon shifts on top of me and the heat of his warm mouth on my neck makes me arch my back. He holds himself just out of reach so I can't feel the press of his body on top of me. His tongue drags over my skin and he laps up the blood. It feels so fucking good.

"Now," he says, cutting my dress open down the middle to

free my swollen breasts. They spill out, heavy and achy. My pink nipples are hard peaks that beg for his warm mouth. He grants me no release, and when he grabs my chin and sinks his sharp teeth into my neck, I don't fight him. Heavy footsteps thud on the floor, and I hiss in pain when teeth pierce either wrist. Daemon grinds his hard cock against me, sending sparks of desire straight to my core. I cry out, yielding to them, offering myself up as a sacrifice. They don't drink me dry. They take only enough to make their point. I'm their submissive. Their plaything.

Theirs...

Then they rise to their feet, staring down at me with bloodied teeth, spread wings, and dark, bottomless eyes. My legs fall open and I slide my hand between my thighs to tease my wet opening.

"Please," I whimper, my pussy throbbing. It won't take much at all.

"Good girls get rewarded, but you, little angel, have been a very fucking bad girl again."

They sit down, Ronan and Alaric on the couch to the left. Daemon kicks the dead girl out of the way and rights the upturned armchair before dropping down onto it and putting his ankle on his knee. With a snap of his fingers, he brings a flame to life and plays with it while he watches me.

Shifting onto my knees, I skate my eyes between them as my nipples tingle in the breeze that's coming from the open patio door. "Okay, you win. You're the big, bad alpha, and I'm just the weak little angel."

Daemon's jeans are still unbuckled. I can see the outline of him straining against the fabric. "You're learning," he drawls, the flame dancing across his fingers. "You can fight me, but I'll always win."

My wings itch to unfold, but I keep them closed.

"Checkmate," he says with a smirk as his eyes travel down to my hard nipples.

My breaths come quicker.

"Remove your dress."

It hangs off me in tatters. I slide it down the rest of the way and it soon pools around my knees. Three hungry eyes fall to my bare pussy.

"What do you say?" Alaric lifts his chin toward Ronan and Daemon. "Shall we go and find us some *good girls* to fuck? Girls that don't behave like fucking brats?"

As one, they rise to their feet and walk out, leaving me kneeling.

Again.

But this time, I don't intend to wait here while they fuck other angels. They wanted my beast to come out to play. Well, she's out, ready to tear into hearts. It's true what they say—sometimes you should be careful what you wish for. I'm not one of their groupies. I have no intention of pleasing them. If they want to fuck other girls, I'll awaken the beast in them. I know just the person to help me.

CHAPTER 14

AURELIA

The boys stayed out all fucking night. I have no words to describe the fury coursing through my veins this morning at the thought of them with other girls. How fucking dare they think I'll behave when they disrespect me like that. If it's a taste of their own fucking medicine they want, I'll gladly give it to them.

I find Dmitriy the next day at school as he walks out of the cafeteria. It sickens me to think about what he did in there, but I better get used to it fast. I'm in their world now, and I must learn to play by their rules if I want to win against Daemon.

I follow behind, wishing I could blend in with the crowds. It's impossible with my pale skin, blonde hair, and white wings. The black dress isn't enough to make me pass for a fallen angel. Quickening my pace, I seize my opportunity. Dmitriy's eyes widen with surprise when I push him into an empty classroom and flip the lock. But rather than ask me what I'm doing, his lips quirk with an amused smile. He stays quiet, watching my slow approach.

"I am not a good girl," I grit out, circling him. "I'm so fucking fed up with such expectations." My fingers slide over his black wings, which are coarser than my downy feathers. "I snuck out of Eden, but that doesn't mean I'm good or pure," I spit.

"I'm starting to get that sense," he says with a smirk. He looks so much like Daemon, but he also doesn't.

"Why does Daemon hate you so much?" I continue circling him, trailing my eyes down his body and then back up.

Dmitriy shrugs, his hands in his pockets, his eyes on me. "Old family rivalry between our fathers."

I like that Daemon hates him. It's why he's perfect for what I want to achieve. None of the other angels here measure up.

"I'm not a virgin anymore."

His mask stays intact and he gives nothing away.

"Daemon stole it from me. Like he stole me from my home." I come to a stop in front of Dmitriy.

"You snuck out."

I don't like his response. Not one fucking bit. "I was near the gates. I could have snuck back in."

He steps closer, tall and imposing. "Once you enter the woods, you never find your way out."

"Do you always talk so much?" I ask him as I lean back against the door.

He follows, placing his hand on the dark wood. Beside us, the sconce on the wall blazes brighter, like the fire in his eyes.

"I'll hurt you."

"Maybe I want to be hurt."

His hand flies up and grips my jaw, forcing it to the side. Then he whispers in my ear, "You don't."

"I thought you were the kind one."

His nose descends on my neck, dragging over my skin as he breathes me in. "You're in Hell, sweetheart. There are only monsters in these woods. Kindness doesn't exist here."

I meet his dark gaze. "Maybe I'm the biggest monster of them all."

He regards me while twirling my silky hair around his finger before pulling sharply. "You're a pussycat."

I shove him away and let rip a snarl. "I'm no fucking pussycat!"

I'm a coiled snake in the grass, ready to strike.

"Then show me your lioness."

Laughter bubbles out of me, the kind that sets off alarm bells. "Lions are herd animals. They kill together, and they also seek the safety of the pack. I'm a tigress, roaming the woods by myself. I kill *alone* and I rely on no herd for safety."

"What am I? The unsuspecting antelope?"

I shake my head, my hand sliding behind his neck. "No, you're the appetizer before the main meal."

And the perfect weapon to get back at Daemon for treating me like I'm worthless.

I pull him down to my mouth, silencing his response with hungry, deep kisses. If sleeping with the enemy is what it'll take to break Daemon, I'll lay my cards out on the table. I'm all in.

Dmitriy lifts me against the door and groans into my mouth. "He'll kill you if you open your legs for me."

Heat sinks to my clit at his threat. I want Daemon's anger. I want him to hurt me and let his monster tear into me. I want to burn in his flames. After all, we're in Hell.

"Not before he kills you."

"You're wrong," he says, ripping my panties straight off and unbuckling his belt. "If I were anyone else, he would. But I'm his cousin and he can't kill me."

"Shut up and fuck me," I growl.

"Bad girl." He grins, taking his big, veiny dick out.

"I told you, I'm not a good girl."

"No, you're not," he agrees, lining himself up with my entrance. "And I intend on fucking you like the bad girl you are."

I cry out when he slams into me and clamps his hand over my mouth.

"Sshh!" he soothes, slowly inching back out, ensuring I feel the slide of his dick before he thrusts back in. "Such a bad little angel. Look at those beautiful tears trailing down your cheeks. I told you I would hurt you."

Speared against the door, I take his pounding as he pistons against me. I don't know what feels better. His big cock, hurting me in the most delicious way, or knowing Daemon will kill me for this?

"I want my cum seeping out of you when Daemon finds you," he whispers cruelly in my ear. "I want to see the fucking fury in his eyes."

His teeth pierce my flesh, and a hot, burning pain sears through my neck. If I thought Daemon was rough, this is on another level. Dmitriy wants to inflict damage on my pale skin so Daemon will see the masterpiece he carved on my body.

His teeth retract and he snarls in my face, making me whimper beneath his hand on my mouth. "Want to be a good girl yet?"

My head shakes. I never want to be a good girl again. I want to be fucked like a whore, and to be used and discarded. That's exactly what he does. He uses me to get off, treats me like a fuckable hole, and brings me to climax as a fuck you to Daemon.

And when I orgasm, his eyes spark with something dangerous. "That's it, let me see you come. Give me those heavy eyes."

He stills as soon as my muscles relax, spilling his release

deep inside me. Then he steps back, shoving me down on the cold stone floor. I stare up at him with my skirt bunched around my waist while he zips himself into his pants.

"I'd call him in here now, so he could see you on the floor, flushed and freshly fucked. But I don't want to spoil the fun just yet. It's only a matter of time before I'll hear his roar shake the foundation of this old academy." Leaning over me, he cups my chin and says, "You better run while you still can."

DARIANA FINDS me in the hallway as I walk toward my next class. I'm so sore that I wince with every step.

"Holy crap," she blurts, steering me over to a nearby alcove. "What the actual fuck, little angel?! Please tell me my eyes are deceiving me. You didn't fuck Dmitriy, did you?"

I wait for a group of students to walk past in their black clothing. "What's it to do with you?"

"What's it to do with me?" she asks incredulously. "Daemon is my friend for a start."

"Oh," I nod, "is that why you went behind his back and fucked me?"

She levels me with a look that tells me I'm naive. "That's not the same thing. We mess with each other all the time. But this," she gestures wildly at me, "is the worst betrayal."

The insides of my thighs are sticky with Dmitriy's cum, my chin burns from his scratchy beard, and my lips are still kiss-swollen.

I laugh bitterly. "They went out to fuck girls last night, so don't come talking to me about betrayal."

Much to my surprise, she bursts out laughing. "Is that what they told you?"

Confused, I open and close my mouth.

"They stayed at mine. There was no fucking involved." She soon sobers when she sees the stricken look on my face. "You believed they cheated on you."

"Why would they lie to me and make me believe they fucked other girls if they didn't?"

"To make you jealous." The way she says it is so matter-of-fact. "And it worked. Not only did they make you jealous, but you went out and detonated the bomb of all fucking bombs."

I swallow past the thick lump of shame in my throat. "What I do with my body is my choice." Even if Daemon didn't fuck anyone last night, he still let that human girl touch him and taste him in front of me.

"Oh, Hell..." Dariana starts pacing in front of me. "When Daemon finds out... shit..."

"What?"

She whirls on me. "He'll kill you, for starters."

I walk off and tears prick my eyes now that the anger is settling down. So what if Dmitriy's sticky cum is trailing a path down my thighs? What does it matter? It was just sex.

Right?

The tears spill over, and I hurry to wipe them away. I don't know how to handle these types of situations and novel emotions. I'd never had sex before I came here, and I'd never felt these feelings. It's all so new and scary. And now I've acted irresponsibly because I was hurt and angry.

"Stop, Angel," Dariana says, rounding me. "Baby, it's okay. We all make mistakes. Some worse than others, admittedly."

Rolling my eyes, I push past her. Maybe Dmitriy is right? Maybe I should run while I can.

Dariana's heels click on the floor before she pulls me to a stop again, cornering me between two torches on the stone wall. "Let's take you home. You can have a shower and wash his scent off you. No one has to know."

"Dmitriy will tell him."

"What proof does he have? It'll be your word against his. And Daemon will think he's trying to hurt you."

Flicking my eyes between hers pitifully, I chew my lip. "Why are you being nice to me? This is your chance to get rid of me."

She steps closer, and our chests brush as she whispers, "Maybe I don't want to get rid of you."

It's hard to breathe when she's this close, smelling of midnight and late evenings. "Everyone looks out for themselves here, Dariana."

Her wings unfold behind her, shielding my tear-streaked cheeks from the other students. She slides her warm hand over my breast and up my chest, then wraps it around my throat. "I am looking out for myself, little angel."

A shiver runs through me when her thigh slides between my legs.

"Let's take you home and wash you. No one will ever know."

"Okay," I breathe out, drowning in her dark eyes and long lashes.

A brief smile graces her lips before she steps back and interlaces her fingers with mine. "Everything will be okay."

I want to believe her, but when I hear masculine, rowdy laughter followed by heavy footsteps turning the corner, my blood turns to ice.

Alaric notices us first. His laughter dies in his throat and he slaps Daemon's chest, who looks up. I instinctively back away as my fight or flight response kicks in. Daemon is faster. He catches up to me in four long strides and pulls me into his chest before slamming me against the stone wall.

As he moves my hair away from my neck, his eyes darken. "Who fed on you?!"

This is the moment I planned on squaring my shoulders

and telling him to piss off after he fucked those girls last night. Only, he didn't fuck anyone and I have screwed everything up. He scents the air, then stiffens. It scares me how still he is. I can't even look him in the eyes. Tears well up and I try to hold them back, but they fall.

"My fucking cousin?!"

"Daemon," Dariana tries, but he can't hear her. Not now.

"You fucked my damn cousin?!"

Wincing, I hug my arms around me to protect myself from the onslaught of his anger. I feel dirty. Used. The sick pleasure I experienced earlier fills me with shame now. It was a mistake to leave Eden. I don't belong here in their world. I don't belong anywhere anymore.

Daemon looks at me with such disgust that I want to disappear into myself. On either side of him, Ronan and Alaric exchange glances.

With an unnerving calm, the kind of calm that precedes a deadly storm, Daemon steps back and releases a roar so loud that the nearby students startle. Then he's back with his teeth bared, wings spread, and anger radiating from every pore. "I've played nice with you. I've given you every-fucking-thing. I even let you attend school here. And this is what I get? Tell me," he leans in close, sneering, "did he fuck you good?"

Flinching, I whimper.

He doesn't let up on me. "Answer the damn question. Did he fuck you good?"

"Daemon, please."

"ANSWER THE QUESTION!"

"Yes," I whisper, and he drops me like he's been burned, then stumbles back.

Without another word, he strides off, my eyes following his retreat. Guilt gnaws at my insides, turning my stomach and twisting my organs. Why did I act so fucking foolishly? What did I think would happen? Did I want revenge so fucking badly?

My arm is grabbed. Ronan drags me along without a backward glance.

"Don't be too hard on her." Dariana hurries to keep up. "She doesn't know the rules of this world yet. Fuck, she hasn't even experienced anger or jealousy before you brought her here. She acted out of spite. So what? Don't tell me you've never done the same?"

"Shut the fuck up, Dari," Alaric says tersely.

The moment we step outside, Ronan bands his arm around my waist and we set off flying toward their house. I could tell him I know how to fly. But I don't. I'm numb, focused on the steady heartbeat in his chest. I long for easier times when all I felt was a peaceful calm. Not this brewing storm of emotions. These highs and lows.

We soon land, and they lead me indoors, past the living room and up the creaky stairs. No one speaks. After locking me in my bedroom, they leave, and I sink down onto the bed. The ache inside my chest spreads, pressing against my sternum. How long will they keep me in here this time?

My feet carry me over to the window. I unlock the hatch, sliding the glass panel up. It's a mild evening, warmer than usual. The night air is alive with the sound of crickets in the tall grass and animals in the woods.

I look back at the door. It's still locked. They're not coming back anytime soon. Climbing out on the thin ledge, I heave myself up on the roof, my wings flapping behind me when I feel like I might fall. I don't.

The wind moves my hair around my face as I straighten up and turn in a slow circle, scanning the trees that surround the house. If I want to see my home again, I'll need to fly.

I gaze up at the thick clouds, contemplating my options. Can I actually do it? Dariana distracted me last time, but now it's different—it's just me. There's no one here to distract me with soft touches and soothing words of encouragement.

"I can do it," I tell myself, slowly unfolding my wings. They're heavy, stretching out behind me, but I'm slowly growing used to them. My shoulders don't ache as much. I try to flap them like a bird, but nothing happens. Discouraged, I flop down, my wings drooping behind me. What will it take for me to learn how to do such a basic task?

My gaze snags on the trees to my left. When I was young, I fell from one and that's how I learned to fly. I shoot to my feet, smoothing my hands down my dress while building up my courage. It's time to fly or fall. After inhaling a steadying breath, I run for the edge, leap off, and for one brief moment, panic overtakes me as I feel myself falling. But then my wings erupt from my back, carrying me higher and higher.

I stare down at the house below. "I'm doing it. I'm flying."

The wind feels fantastic in my feathers and hair. Cool and refreshing, like a cold shower in a heatwave. I fly in a circle before directing my gaze toward the distance, where the sunbeam lights up my old home like a floodlight. A pang of homesickness makes itself known inside my chest, but something stops me from escaping. There's a strange tug on my heartstrings. If I had a pair of scissors, I would slice right through them and free myself from the men below.

With that thought in mind, I soar off into the night, ignoring the pull to fly back. I don't belong to anyone. No one owns me, and no one gets to control me.

I fly for hours until my wings burn with exhaustion and my limbs ache. Still, I carry on. When my feet finally slide into the tall grass outside the gates, I collapse to the ground, weeping with relief.

The golden gates shimmer, tall and opposing, as I slowly rise to my feet. I step forward, my soles sinking into the soft grass. The sound of crickets falls silent at my approach. In fact, *everything* falls silent, as if the world itself is holding its breath. I'm right in front of the gates, gazing up.

"Hi," I whisper as a tear trails down my cheek. I feel different now that I'm here, and I know even before I place my hand on the door that it won't open. The sense of peace and non-judgment I experienced behind those gates is a far cry from the emotions swirling inside me now. But I try anyway as I place my trembling hand on the gate with bated breath. The absolute silence leans in too, waiting.

"Please," I whimper, pressing my forehead against the gate. "Let me in."

When nothing happens, I release a sob. "I want to go home."

Nothing.

Not a bird singing in the trees. Not a cricket chirping in the grass. I taste tears on my lips as I continue crying silently. Then something else happens: anger rises inside me thick and fast. Anger at the fucking unfairness of it all. Curiosity is what led me out here in the first place. The gates *let* me out. It's not my fucking fault the wolf steered me off the path to Grandma's cottage.

"Let me in," I cry, banging on the shimmering gate. "Let me the fuck in! You can't let me out if you're not going to let me back in. Fuck you! It's not my fault those boys stole me away and introduced me to sin." I kick it too, for good measure, before collapsing to the ground in a heap of pathetic tears. I can't stop crying. I just want to go home. I never asked for any of this.

My head snaps up and I grit my jaw. I will find a fucking way in—somehow. Ignoring the pain in my shoulders, I let my wings erupt to their full glory. This time, I don't doubt myself. I let them carry me higher and higher until I'm flying above the walls, staring down at my home. Everything is so light and colorful. The deer munches on the grass. The hare is there too, just the way I remember it. If I squint, I can make out the houses in the distance. Freya is in there somewhere. I've missed her so much.

As I fly closer, I hit an invisible wall. Surprised, I flatten my palm over it and slide it over the barrier. Was it always there?

"Please, no," I whisper as my hand slams down. The wall doesn't budge. There's no way in other than through the gates. I don't know how long I fly, watching the deer munch and the rabbit hop, before I let my wings carry me down to the soft grass.

Aurelia...

Ronan was right that time in class. The woods call my name. Even now, as I stare blankly at nothing, it whispers, urging me to disappear into its shadows.

Something snaps inside me. I launch myself at my wings and tear into them, ignoring the sharp bite of pain while I rip my feathers out. "Stupid, fucking white feathers." I rip, tear, pull, and yank, smearing my wings with red blood.

When the strength finally leaves me, I sit in a cloud of floating, swirling feathers. They land around me, decorating the ground in white, like a sheet of snow. The pain is excruciating and my tears won't stop falling. It's hard to breathe through this sadness inside me. It holds me in its grip and refuses to let me resurface for air.

My head shakes in denial. I've not been banished from my home. I'm not sitting here in a fucking torn-up, feather pillow of confetti because Eden spat me out and refused me re-entry. As if that's not enough, I can't fly anymore now that my wings are plucked. The pain is too much. I release an almighty scream, and I don't stop until my lungs burn with something other than despair.

Silence descends again, thick and heavy. Now I understand why they call this Hell. I've killed a girl, and now I sit here, covered in blood, after plucking my own fucking feathers like a distressed, caged animal. My throbbing incisor teeth sink into my bottom lip. I didn't even know I had those until recently. I'm a monster with white wings. A terrible deception.

That's how the boys find me—broken and curled up in a pile of my own destruction outside the gates of my former home.

"Holy fuck," Ronan exclaims, staring down at me and the sea of feathers. Daemon doesn't say a word. He simply scoops me up and cradles me against his chest. Then we're off, flying back toward my caged prison.

CHAPTER 15

AURELIA

Life moves on whether we want it to or not. The sun rises and sets. Only here, it's always dark. A week has passed since my escape. Daemon won't speak to me, and Alaric and Ronan keep close as if they worry I might try to escape again. Though we all know it'll be a while before my feathers grow back in. In the meantime, I get to look even more like a freak in this world of black.

I can't seem to move past the fact that my home rejected me. I'm a shadow of my former self, walking the hallways with my gaze down. I should pay attention in class. Especially now that it's becoming abundantly clear that I won't ever return to Eden. I need to learn all there is about life in Hell, but it's hard. I don't even have the strength to feel jealous when Daemon brings girls home.

I sit on the couch, squashed between Ronan and Alaric, while a girl dances sultrily for Daemon in her panties and bra. My gaze burns a hole in the carpet. Is this my life now? Stuck here? In this world of despair, where we feed on others' suffering? Why else would he pull her down on his lap and spread out like a king while she rolls her hips against him?

Ronan nudges me. "Earth to Angel."

I drag my eyes away from the worn carpet and gaze up at him. His dark hair curls at the ends and his brown eyes, framed by dark lashes, search mine.

He snaps his fingers in front of my face and says, "She's about to fuck him. Aren't you going to do something? Launch yourself at her for the most epic catfight of the century? Stake your claim?"

My eyes wander over to Daemon, and I watch as she slides down the straps on her bra and bares her small, perfect breasts. "It's only fair, isn't it? I fucked his cousin." I rise to my feet and walk out. Daemon follows me with his eyes, but his attention soon gets drawn back to the girl when she throws her head back and bares her slender neck.

I've barely made it upstairs before Ronan grabs the back of my neck and shoves me into his bedroom. Alaric follows us in, kicking the door shut. A king-sized bed with gray silk sheets takes up most of the space. The window behind it is ajar, and sheer, black curtains move in the slight breeze. There's a large desk with a pile of books on it, one of which lies open. It smells of Ronan in here—woodsy and mysterious.

He drops down in his chair, reaching for a joint on his desk, while Alaric walks past me and sinks down on the edge of the bed.

Confused, I look between them. "Why am I here?"

Ronan lights up his joint, puts his feet on the desk, and crosses them at the ankles. "We're hanging out. The time for moping is fucking over. So they didn't let you back in, big fucking deal. Now you get to hang with us out here and have fun."

"Fun." I taste the word on my tongue as I walk to the bed and lower myself down next to Alaric, then lie back and stare at the ceiling.

"Yeah, fun," Ronan says while Alaric looks down at me.

"What do you miss the most about Eden?" Alaric asks, his tone curious instead of mocking, and Ronan groans.

"What?" Alaric questions. "It might help her to talk about it."

Ronan smokes his joint, waving a dismissive hand in the air. "Whatever."

"Go on." Alaric nudges my bare knee.

I keep my eyes on the ceiling as I think of what to say. "I miss not feeling."

They both give me a weird look, so I try to explain. "Everything is stable in Eden. We don't experience anger, jealousy, bitterness, or even high levels of joy. We're just *happy*."

"If that's the case, how did you end up outside of Eden?"

I shrug. "Curiosity mainly. I felt drawn to the gates."

"You couldn't have been happy all the time, or you wouldn't have defied your elders and snuck out."

He's right. I wasn't always happy in there, looking back, but I also didn't experience this rollercoaster ride of emotions. "I miss my best friend, Freya."

They're silent for a moment while we listen to the soft beat of the music that filters from Daemon's room. "What's she like?"

"Alaric," I breathe, wiping away a tear. "I try not to think about home when I'm here. It hurts too much."

He lies down on his back beside me and gazes into my eyes. His brown irises have specks of lighter hazel in them. "Talking about pain is good."

"What are you? Her fucking therapist?" Ronan asks with a snort.

Ignoring him, Alaric brushes the backs of his fingers over my cheek. "Change always hurts before it gets better. I know you can't see it now, but this will become your home. And one day you'll look back and think, 'I can't remember living anywhere else.'"

"This isn't my home," I argue. "You'll grow bored of me and throw me out. I'm at your mercy."

Alaric looks back up at the ceiling, and I trail the sharp line of his stubbly jaw. "Daemon is a dick, but he's fiercely loyal."

I chew my bottom lip in thought. "Yeah, that's why he's downstairs now with *her.*" I regret the words as soon as they leave my lips, but it's too late. "You said you planned on finding girls to fuck. I was angry. I wanted to fight back."

Alaric looks at me, his eyes skating between mine as smoke fills the room.

"You told me compassion and kindness have no place in this world, but you're being kind to me right now."

Amused, Ronan chuckles. "He hasn't got a kind bone in his body."

Alaric leans in to taste my lips with a soft kiss before palming my cheek and deepening our connection. His tongue sweeps against mine and he sucks my bottom lip between his teeth, then lets go and flops back on the bed. My chin burns from his day-old stubble.

"Maybe I don't want to see you mope anymore. Now that Daemon has stolen your virginity, you're fair game. Maybe I want to see you smile again so I can fuck you."

"You want to fuck me after I slept with Dmitriy?"

Alaric clenches his jaw and slowly rolls his head on the pillow. When our eyes clash, he says, "Dmitriy thought he could hurt us through you. I'm not Daemon. I won't let that piece of shit win."

"Why do you hate him so much? What's the rivalry about?"

Running a hand down his face, Alaric shakes his head. "It's always been there between their fathers. Daemon and Dmitriy inherited their rivalry. Everything is a competition to them. Who is the most powerful? Who has the biggest fortune?"

Ronan tosses his joint on the floor before straightening up in the chair and crushing it beneath his heel. Then he gets to his feet and walks up to us. "What's it going to take?"

I lift my head off the bed. "What are you talking about?"

In a swift move, his hand shoots out and grips my ankle. He drags me down the bed, drops to his knees, and sweeps his hands up my thighs before sliding them back down with my panties. "For you to stop moping and rediscover your fucking fire. You want Daemon to look at you again? Fight him!"

I start to argue, but he shuts me up when he spreads my legs and covers my pussy with his hot mouth. Beside me, Alaric smirks before getting up and helping himself to a joint. He lights it up and flops back down beside me, smoking lazily while my eyes roll back. God, I've missed this feeling. The sheer freedom of simply letting go.

Ronan takes his sweet time as he brings me to the edge and keeps me there. He blows on my sex, sucks my clit into his mouth, and swirls his tongue over the swollen nub.

"Ronan," I whimper, rocking against his mouth. "Oh, God..."

"There's no fucking God here. Your God kicked you out, remember?" Ronan growls as he slaps my clit hard.

Fisting the sheets, my heels slide on the bed. It's too much. It's too little. I want to crawl away and I want to push closer.

Alaric blows smoke in my face before shifting onto his elbow and placing the joint between my lips. He orders me to suck. The smoke that fills my lungs burns sweetly, and I begin to cough. Alaric's laugh is long and drawn out.

Placing the joint between his lips, he shoves my dress

down and kneads my naked breasts. He takes a deep pull on the joint, pinching it between his index and middle finger as he holds the smoke in his lungs while rolling my nipple between his fingers.

A dirty smirk curls the corner of his lips right before he grabs my chin and blows the smoke into my mouth. My soul floats, bobbing on the surface in a sea of pleasure and drugging touches. They bring me to life, only to kill me slowly with their destructive, possessive, and dominant natures as they steal the breath from my lungs.

With his fingers buried deep inside me, Ronan laps at my swollen clit until I'm begging him to let me come. He's merciless, keeping me right where he wants me. Toying with me like injured prey.

My moans grow in volume, and Alaric bites down on my bottom lip to shut me up. It's so sharp that I gasp as blood rushes to the surface.

"That's our beautiful angel," he whispers, his lips pressed against mine. "Let us make you feel good. Let us ravage your angel cunt. There's nothing to be ashamed of."

There's a thud downstairs.

Ronan laughs between my legs. "Hell is about to break loose."

Clarity threatens to clear this blissful haze, but Alaric grips my jaw, demanding my attention, and plunges his tongue into my mouth. He sucks on my tongue and bites my bottom lip. My kiss-swollen lips burn and tingle while he continues to devour me. I moan as he explores every inch of me with hard kisses. I need more, so much more…

The door flies open just as Ronan fills me up with his tongue. Daemon takes in the scene. His belt is unbuckled, his T-shirt is creased, and his hair stands on end. Not to mention the smeared lipstick on his mouth.

Alaric breaks away from my lips and takes another pull on

his joint, then holds it out. "Want some? There's plenty to go around."

The door slams shut, rattling on its hinges. Daemon snatches the joint from Alaric, tosses it to the floor, and crushes it beneath his boot. Then he grabs my arm and hauls me to my feet, ignoring my surprised shriek when he yanks me to his chest. "Did I say any of you assholes could touch her?"

Rising to his full height, Ronan makes a show of wiping his mouth. "You were otherwise occupied. I wasn't going to let good pussy go to waste."

Alaric covers his smirk with his fisted hand. They're amused. I'm not. I'm fucking angry.

Whirling on Daemon, I slap his cheek. "How fucking dare you come in here and tell them they can't touch me when your lips," I smack him again, "are smeared with lipstick."

The words have barely left my mouth when he wrestles me to the bed and flips my skirt up. He holds me down with his hand on the back of my neck, then smacks my ass hard. I yelp, and he smacks me again, harder this time.

"That's for fucking my cousin." The next resounding thwack makes me cry out. "That's for disobeying me at every fucking turn!" His hand slides between my legs, and he chuckles darkly as my cheeks blaze.

I'm dripping with desire.

"I forgot what a dirty little slut you are."

"Fuck you!"

Smack!

A treacherous moan slips from my lips, and he plunges two thick fingers inside me.

"You think I wouldn't punish you for opening your legs for my cousin?"

"I thought you would kill me," I admit, my voice muffled in the sheet.

"Tempting," he says, removing his fingers to smack me

again. My skin is on fire from his blows. "I fucking hate the thought that he's been inside you."

I shoot up, breathing hard, and shove him away. "How dare you make me seem like such a fucking whore when you were upstairs with a girl just now? Fuck you, Daemon!"

His wings sprout behind him, knocking over the tower of books on Ronan's desk. Then he's on me, forcing me down on the bed. Subduing me with his weight and power.

My body comes alive like a flower in spring.

"What the fuck do you want from me, little angel?"

His hand is on my throat and I claw his cheek, pleased to see blood rush to the surface.

"What the fuck do *you* want from me?" I counter.

"You!" he growls, his nose brushing up against mine, and then he jostles me. "I want you!"

My heart stops beating as his words register. Daemon wants me? What does that mean? He climbs off and walks to the door, but before he gets there, I scramble off the bed, run in front of him, and block the way out. His cold expression gives nothing away when I kneel down in front of him, gazing up at his devastatingly handsome face. "If you ever touch another girl again, I'll run away and never return."

Daemon grabs my chin, bruising me with his punishing grip. "Try it and see. I'll hunt you down." He steps around me and exits the room.

As the door shuts behind me, I blink back tears.

"Well, that went well," Ronan comments drily, seated beside Alaric on the bed.

My tears seep out, wetting my cheeks. I've lost him. I'm nothing more than a broken ornament he refuses to part with, but he doesn't like me enough to keep me on the mantelpiece anymore. I'm locked away in a dark cupboard somewhere. I'm the unwanted gift he feels obliged to keep.

"Why don't you come here?" Ronan says as they both unbuckle their belts. "We'll make you feel better."

With one last glance at the shut door, I squash the pain down along with the rest of my confusing emotions. Out of sight, out of mind. My feet carry me over to Alaric and Ronan.

Their veiny dicks glisten with precum as I kneel down and lose myself in their darkness.

CHAPTER 16

AURELIA

As I wait for Dariana outside her classroom, a warm hand slides around the back of my neck and drags me along.

"How's my favorite girl today? My cousin hasn't killed you yet."

"It was a fucking mistake."

Dmitriy tsks, leaning in close to my ear. "There's something I think you should see."

My heart hammers inside my chest as we push through bodies and head toward the cafeteria, the last place I want to be.

"If you need to feed, I can wait outside."

"Don't be ridiculous." He shoves me in, then pulls me over to one of the couches pushed up against the wall. My ass hits his lap, and he bands his arm around my waist. His lips brush up against the curve of my ear as he points across the room. I follow his line of sight and stiffen when I spot Daemon with a girl on his lap. Her black wings are small and cute, folded against her back while she toys with the hair at the nape of his neck.

"They look cozy, don't they?" Dmitriy whispers in my ear, then, "He's not loyal to you." He squeezes my chin between his finger and thumb, bringing my eyes to his. "Daemon doesn't deserve your loyalty. You're in Hell now, sweetheart. The pain in your chest has no room here."

I grit my teeth but don't reply. I'm so sick of being torn apart by fallen angels.

"Don't cry," he whispers, smiling against my lips. "I would never hurt you like he does. If you were mine, I would make sure everyone knew. There would be no lesser girls on my lap. Only you."

"You don't want me. Why are you d..." I start but fall silent when a shadow falls over us.

I look up, caught in Daemon's stormy eyes. His shoulders are tense and the knuckles on his fisted hands turn white the longer he glares at Dmitriy.

Fed up with their staring match, I rise from Dmitriy's lap and walk out. Maybe Dmitriy has a point. Daemon doesn't care about me. And what the fuck is my brain doing? I don't care about Daemon, do I? Is this the point where I admit to myself that I want his attention? Haven't I always wanted it?

As if summoned by the devil, he pulls me to a stop outside the door. "What the fuck, little angel? What were you doing in there with *him?*"

Shouldering past him, I keep walking. The sea of students doesn't part for me like it does for him. I have to shoulder my way through bodies to get away. He's hot on my trail, breathing down my neck. I whirl on him, intent on telling him to fuck off, but he grabs my arm and pulls me to the side.

My back connects with the locker as he corners me with his arms on either side of my head. "Who was she?"

"It's none of your business."

He's so close that his heat warms me through my thin dress. My chest is clogged with emotions that I don't want to feel. If I could purge myself of this need for him, I would.

"I have to go." I try to push past him, but he won't let me. I'm trapped as his fingers dig into my chin.

"I'm not done with you."

"You were done with me when you let that girl sit on your lap."

I shove him off me and set off walking, swiping angrily at the hot tears that seep from my eyes. I wish he didn't affect me like this.

"Aurelia!" he barks, causing me to halt in my steps. I've never heard him use my real name before. I don't turn around. My breaths are coming too quickly. I feel Daemon behind me —his scent, his fingers brushing my hair from my shoulder. I squeeze my eyes shut.

"You can't run from me."

I turn my head halfway, whispering, "I'm not the one running."

It's true, Daemon uses other girls to keep me at bay. He's scared of getting too close. This time when I walk away, he doesn't follow me.

"WHAT ARE YOU DOING UP HERE?" Ronan asks as he sits down next to me on the roof. It's a cold night. My breath is visible in the air, and goosebumps line my arms. I welcome the sharp bite. It keeps the thoughts at bay.

"I wish I could fly up into the clouds."

"Yeah?" His elbow is on his knee, and he's fiddling with a joint. As I watch, he brings it to his lips and lights it up with a click of his fingers.

"How do you do that?"

"Do what?" he asks, blowing out a cloud of smoke.

"Conjure hellfire."

He shrugs, sucking on the joint, then peers at me sideways. "Visualize it."

"It's so easy for you to say."

He doesn't reply, watching me as the embers spark.

I lie back and gaze up at the stars. "Does love exist here in Hell?"

It's a question I've asked myself many times. I see glimpses of it, but then it's extinguished just as fast.

Scratching the side of his nose with his thumb, he takes another deep pull on the joint and looks back out at the trees. "I think so. I wouldn't know."

"Have you never loved?"

"A girl? No."

I reach out, fiddling with the hem of his T-shirt. "It doesn't have to be a girl. Platonic love. Don't you have parents? Siblings? Your friends."

"Do you see them anywhere?"

"No."

"There you go then." He tips his head back and blows a cloud of smoke at the sky. "Love is for the weak."

"That's really sad," I tell him, my fingers brushing over the sliver of skin visible between his T-shirt and jeans. We sit in silence while Ronan smokes, and I trace patterns over his olive skin.

"I think to love is to show strength," I whisper after a while, watching as Ronan flicks his joint over the roof's edge.

"How so?" He lies down next to me.

I peer at his profile, his straight nose, and the sharp line of his jaw. "It takes strength and bravery to be vulnerable. It requires you to see someone for who they truly are and accept them despite their flaws. Love is scary. It sets you up to have your heart broken, so if you have the courage to love someone..." I drift off.

"You think too much, little angel," Ronan says, making me laugh softly.

"Maybe," I admit.

"I'm just happy if I've got a good supply of blood and a willing girl to suck my dick. I don't require much."

"Really? You feel happy?"

He rolls over on his stomach, peering down at me. There's a soft look on his face that I'm unfamiliar with. My heart skips a beat.

"Right now? Sure."

My cheeks heat and I'm grateful the darkness hides my blush.

"Your wings will grow back in and you'll be able to fly again." He stares at the stars overhead while I scan my eyes over his neck and the stubble on his jaw, and his wings that peek out behind his shoulders.

"I will find a way back home."

His eyes come back to me, brown against my blue. "I believe you."

I swallow thickly, trapped in him and the hum of energy between us.

"I can't explain it," I whisper, biting my lip nervously. "But I can feel something inside me. A power of some kind."

He bounces his eyes between mine but stays silent. An owl hoots in the distance, and the breeze makes me shiver from the cold. I don't want to leave. I like this moment here with him—how he looks at me.

"Don't do that," he whispers, with a slight shake of his head.

My brows knit together. "What am I doing?"

"Your eyes, they're all wide and shit. Don't do that girly

thing where you look at me like I hung the moon. I fucking didn't."

Laughter bubbles up inside me. He shifts back onto his knees when I push up on my elbows. "Trust me, my eyes are not 'wide and shit.'"

"Look!" He gestures at my face. "You're doing it now."

I drop my head back and laugh—a carefree sound I haven't heard in a long time. "I'm not doing anything."

When I look back at him, he narrows his eyes. I sit up too, playfully pushing his chest. "Get over yourself. You're not that special."

Dimples pop in his cheeks as he laughs. I've never seen his face light up like this and it steals my breath away.

His eyes settle on mine, soft and searching. "For what it's worth, I'm happy you're here."

Before I have a chance to reply, he rises to his feet and takes off, flying into the night.

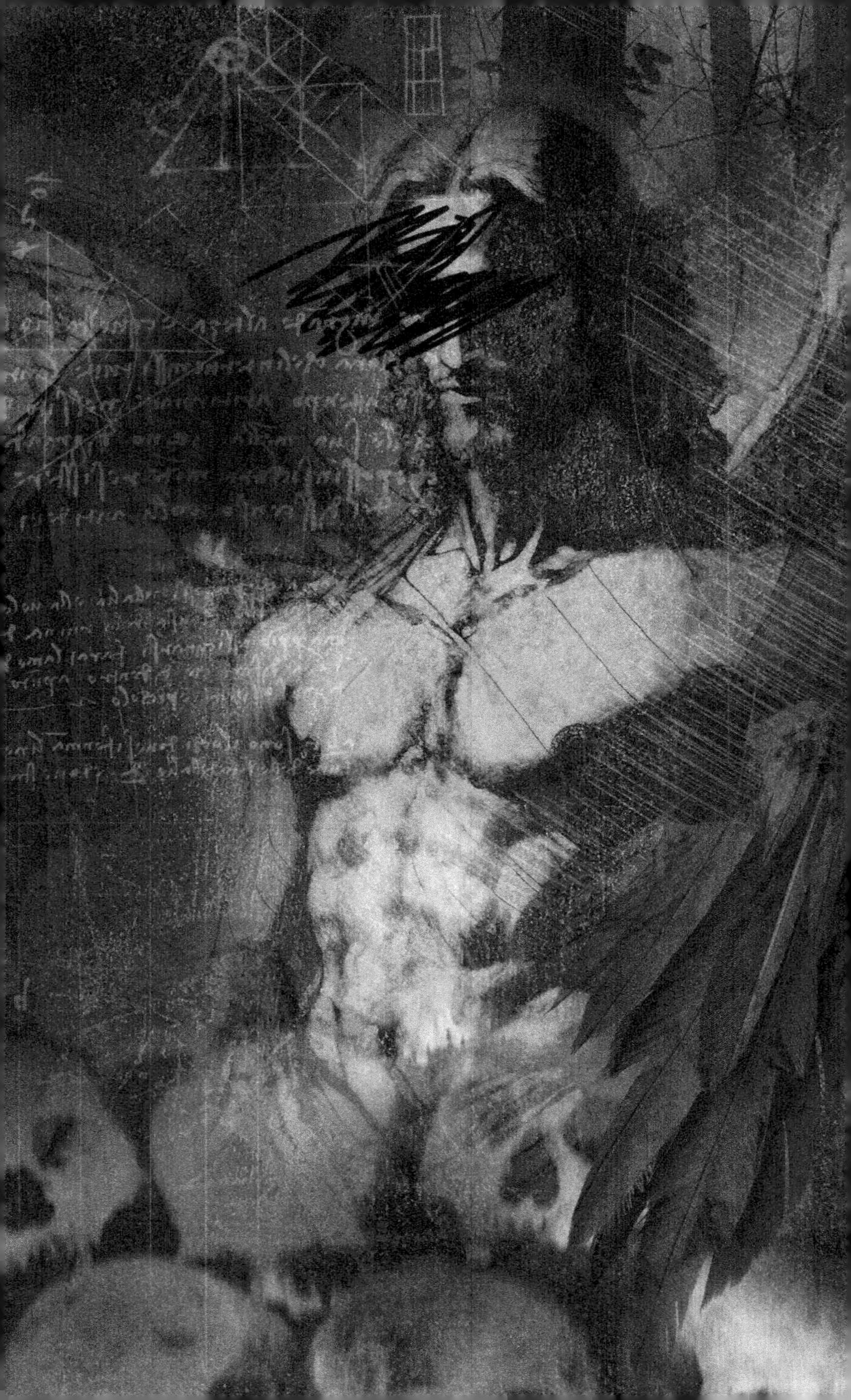

CHAPTER 17

DAEMON

We're back in the human world, on the hunt for food, and our little angel looks anything but impressed as she follows behind us quietly.

I don't like that the fire has gone out of her. But at the same time, it makes me feel in control and I like that. I hate how I feel in her presence—the sheer fucking power she holds over me. No woman should be able to bring me to my fucking knees like she does with one look.

I've tried to lose myself in other girls, but it's not easy when I can't touch them because of whatever voodoo magic she's possessed me with. If I sit on my hands, willing myself not to flee, I can let them have their way with me, but I can't actively participate. It makes me look like a fucking pussy. And what's worse? It's my little angel I see while they get me off. It's always fucking her. I can't get her out of my head. Even though she went behind my back and fucked my cousin.

He's been inside her, tasted her lips, and witnessed her beauty when she comes. I can't move past it. If not for our fathers, I would pluck out his eyes and keep them on my fucking nightstand. I might just do it anyway. Screw my father and whatever punishment he'll dole out. Screw the wider repercussions. Dmitriy is a snake in the grass.

The music in this bar is too loud, and the smell of sweat, alcohol, and pussy is thick in the air. I'm no longer in the mood for this, but we need to feed. I don't want to have to settle for the food in the cafeteria. Scared, anemic girls don't do it for me; their blood doesn't satisfy me.

We reach the dance floor, and I scan my eyes over the throng of sweaty, dancing bodies. My attention lands on a sultry brunette with tits that threaten to spill out of her sequin dress. I would have gladly fucked her if the little angel hadn't cut off my balls. "I'm going in."

Ronan and Alaric stay behind to ensure our angel doesn't do anything stupid like she did last time. Tonight, she'll have to stay and watch the hunt.

The woman notices my approach and offers an inviting smile that says, *take me home, so I can bounce on your dick all night.*

Stepping behind her, I pull her close to my body while keeping my eyes locked on Angel. I want her to watch. I want to see the fire spark to life in her dead eyes. The beat kicks in, and the music sinks into my veins, guiding my movements.

"You know how to dance," the human, who reeks of peach shots and cheap perfume, shouts over the music. I smile against her ear, feeling a sense of triumph when my little angel grits her teeth. I'm hard and it doesn't help that the brunette rubs her pert ass against me.

The moment she falls under my spell, she melts into me, and her arm around my neck slips away like dead weight. I guide her outside into the night air and she willingly follows across the street to a quiet alley, where we disappear into the darkness.

I have her pressed up against the brick wall, my fingers teasing the inside of her thighs, when Angel joins us in the alley. It fucking pisses me off that I can't slide the human's panties aside and feel her wet warmth wrap around my fingers. Angel's gaze flicks from me to the girl and back. She wants to plead for the girl's life.

I quirk my finger at her. "Come here, little angel."

She takes a hesitant step closer, then another, briefly glancing toward the mouth of the alley. There's no one around. We're alone.

"Do you like her?" I ask her as I grab the girl's throat to silence her soft whimpers.

"She's pretty."

"Yes, she is," I agree, mostly to see my little angel's reaction.

She's possessive. It's there in the hardening of her jaw.

"You need to feed," I tell her, pointing out the obvious. It's not something she has figured out yet, but now that she's in Hell, purity alone won't sustain her. Especially not now that she has so little of it in supply.

"I can't drink from her."

The girl whimpers again, and I press my palm over her mouth to muffle the sound. Then, to Angel, I say, "Of course you fucking can. You don't have a choice."

It's the wrong thing to say at the wrong time. Angel puts her hands on her hips, arching her brow. "I don't have a choice?"

I secretly love her sass, but I won't tell her that. She's been depressed for the last week since we found her sitting in a sea of her own feathers. I would lie if I said I wasn't relieved she wasn't let back in. On our way to find her, I kept thinking, 'What if Eden welcomed her home? What then?' That thought scares me more than I want to admit. Hell, she's got me by my balls.

"Feed on her," I order.

Angel shakes her head, looking up at me with her glassy doe eyes. "I've already killed once."

With a groan, I release the girl. She tries to escape, so I grab her arm and pull her back, tossing her into the arms of Ronan. "The sin has already been committed. Your little man in the sky isn't going to place you on a pedestal for *only* killing one human."

She levels me with a glare while Ronan backs the girl up against the back wall. "I will not feed on a human."

Okay, now I'm getting annoyed. I step closer, forcing her back a step. "Tell me, innocent little angel, how will you survive in my world without blood? Your incisors have grown in. You're one of us now."

"Am I?" she argues, half turning, showing me her white wings. "Do I look like one of you?"

It pains me to see the sorry state they're in. The feathers will grow back, but it takes months. Right now, she looks like a distressed chicken.

My hand shoots out, grabbing her jaw. I prod her incisor with my thumb and smile when it sharpens and elongates. She's angry. "Do any of your friends back home have these, huh?" I shove her away. "Your wings may be white, but they fool no one."

Snorting, she strides off. Dammit. Fucking stubborn woman! I chase after her, seizing her arm and dragging her right back. She's not getting away this time. I will get her to feed if it's the last fucking thing I do.

Besides, if she wants her fucking feathers to grow back, she needs to feed. "You're acting like a fucking child!"

Her blue eyes fly up to mine, and there's that fire and defiance I've come to love so much. "A child?! You think I'm acting like a child because I don't want to commit murder?"

Okay, so now I'm laughing. "Murder?"

Angel narrows her eyes to slits and folds her arms over her chest, which only makes me laugh more.

"Are we feeding or debating?" Alaric asks.

I ignore him. The human isn't going anywhere, and Ronan is doing a good job of keeping her under his spell. It's the stubborn little angel I need to work on. No, fuck that. I'm not used to this weird shit. Women fall at my feet. If I click my fingers, they follow orders. They don't glare up at me with their arms crossed and hips cocked. What the actual fuck is this? I'm not fluent in her language. It's confusing as fuck, so I do what I always do when I feel out of my depth. I resort to violence.

Fisting her hair, I force her head back, baring the creamy column of her neck. The pulse point in her neck flutters wildly against her skin, and I can practically hear her hammering heartbeat. The desire is there to discard the food, slam Angel up against the wall, and take what I need.

I haven't fucked anyone for weeks now and I'm not used to dry spells like this. My mouth waters at the memory of her tight cunt wrapped around me and my dick smeared with her scarlet virginity. Maybe I should have made it special for her and treated her like the angel she is. I dismiss that thought. I don't do romance. I take what I want, when I want. And right now, I want the little angel. I want her so fucking much that my skin tingles in anticipation when she's near. All it takes is one defiant look, and I'm hard.

I bare my teeth and growl, "Feed!"

"No!"

Gripping her harder and inching closer, I pull her hair. I want to hurt her and force her hand. The urge to dominate is so fucking strong that I can't stop myself from diving down and dragging my nose over her neck. Her sweet, tempting scent is designed to draw me in like a bee to her nectar.

Her pulse flutters against my lips, and when I threaten to sink my teeth into her creamy skin, she fists my T-shirt.

I give in to the urge and a shudder runs through me at the feel of my teeth slowly penetrating her skin, sinking deeper and deeper. I groan with desire. Her warm blood spills, flowing into my mouth like a river of need. Fucking hell, she's a drug. The urge to drive into her is too much. I slam her up against the wall next to the human girl, yanking her dress up. Her panties have a damp patch and her moans are loud in the quiet alley. This feeling right here is dangerous, and is why I should keep my distance. I've got a meal not five inches away, but I'm drinking my little angel's blood instead. It can't sustain me, but my body sure wants to believe it can.

Pushing off the wall, I stumble back and point a stern finger at the human girl as I growl at Angel, "Fucking feed!"

Amused, Alaric chuckles next to me, clasping my shoulder. "Struggling, brother?"

I swipe Angel's blood off my chin with the back of my hand, my tongue trailing over my teeth. I don't deny it. How can I when she peers at me through lowered lashes, with beads of scarlet trailing down her neck and that glazed look in her eyes? Much to my surprise, she shifts closer to the girl, nudging Ronan out of the way. I can't hear what she's saying, but she talks to the girl in a soothing voice as her hand disappears beneath the girl's skirt. I watch her pleasure her prey; something I can no longer do.

"Beautiful," she whispers, "so smooth and wet."

The human shudders as her lips part. Angel leans in to taste her quivering breath while stealing the whimpers that slip from her tongue.

Ronan and I exchange a look. *How?*

I frown. *I don't fucking know.*

Alaric joins in. *She's making us look like a bunch of incompetent pussies.*

"Tell me about it," I huff out loud.

The woman's eyes roll back as she comes. Angel leans in close and breathes her in before she strikes, causing the human to release a tiny cry.

It gets me hard to watch Angel feed. To see something so pure indulge. I don't know how it happened, but she's the sun in our galaxy now. We're drawn in by her gravity. Three alphas, circling around one angel with wings white as snow. If I'd known this would happen when I stole her from the woods like some fucking prize, I would have stayed well clear. But it's too late to change shit now.

She steps back and smiles innocently at us through bloodied teeth. "Your turn, boys."

Alaric and Ronan surge forward to have their fill, but I narrow my eyes on her. "What game are you playing? First you refuse to feed, fighting me tooth and fucking nail, and now you give me the innocent doe eyes?"

I know I've been played when her long nails walk a slow path up my chest, but I am yet to figure out what playing board I'm on. I thought we were playing chess, but I don't recognize these pieces. The rules are foreign to me. Angel uses it to get the upper hand.

"What was it you said to me, Daemon? Oh, I remember now." As she leans in, her lips curve into a dangerous smile that brings armies to their knees. "Fucking feed."

She leaves me to stare after her like some cartoon character with hearty eyes. It's not my imagination that she puts extra sway in her hips, is it? I don't understand women. She spends a week looking demure—a ghost of her former self—and now she's playing power games with me? She knows I'm a sucker for those.

"The well is drying up. You'll miss out," Ronan warns.

I snap my gaze away from her retreating form and move in, my fangs glinting in the moonlight.

CHAPTER 18

AURELIA

The blood moon hangs low in the sky, close to the Earth, and unusually big. It guides me deeper into the trees. It's quiet. Not even the wind dares rustle the leaves. The single, red door up ahead creaks open an inch, urging me closer as golden light spills out, flooding the ground. With a glance behind me, I squint into the shadows. I'm alone. I turn back around, taking a hesitant step forward, when a twig snaps under my foot. Damp leaves stick to my feet, and the hem of my long white dress is stained from dragging behind me.

Aurelia...

Moving a fir branch out of the way and stepping over a small stream of water, I gaze at the door. It's closer now, my bare feet stepping into the beam of light on the damp ground.

Come closer...

My heart flutters wildly in my throat, and the silence that follows crawls down my neck and over the sheen of sweat on my skin.

Aurelia...

Movement to my left—a darting shadow—startles me, causing me to trip over a root and fall to the ground. My knee explodes with pain that burns and throbs. I wince as I sit up and inspect the wound. It's bleeding, dirt sticking to my skin. I try to wipe it off with my fingers but end up smearing the blood around.

Soon...

The door slams shut behind me, taking the last of the light with it.

SHOOTING upright in bed and breathing harshly, I wipe the damp hair off my sweaty forehead.

Just a bad dream.

I glance over at the clock on my bedside table to see that it has just gone three in the morning. Shifting beneath the warm sheets, I light the bedside candle before throwing my quilt off and placing my feet on the floor. The bite from the chill barely registers while I slowly slide my nightdress up to look at my bleeding knee. Pieces of broken leaves and dirt still stick to the wound.

My dreams are happening more regularly now. I haven't told the boys because I don't know what to say. They saw what happened the day we did the meditation in class, and they dismissed it. Why does all this weird shit keep happening to me? Isn't it enough that I have grown fangs like some fairy-tale vampire?

I slowly make my way downstairs to the kitchen to find something to clean the wound. Alaric once explained to me that houses here have kitchens because some fallen angels keep human blood slaves as pets. Hunger was a fairytale concept until I came here, having never experienced it before. Now I hunger for many things: sustenance, love, power, sex.

"What are you doing up?"

Bent down while rooting through the cupboard beneath the sink, I bang my head. "Ouch." I straighten up and look back at Daemon, who is leaning against the doorway. "I cut my knee. I'm looking for something to clean the wound with."

He pushes off the wall, nudges me out of the way, and reaches into the cupboard. When he straightens back up, he grabs hold of my hips and lifts me up on the counter. In his hands is a glass bottle of pure vodka. His warm fingers slide around my calf and he palms it, bringing it up. My foot rests on his chest as he grabs a towel beside me on the counter. "You good with pain?"

"I'm new to pain, remember?"

He unscrews the lid and flicks it off with his thumb. "I keep forgetting you're not from around here."

"Will it hurt a lot?"

"Yeah, it will."

His warm hand is on the back of my knee, and his brown eyes hold my blue. "You ready?"

For him? No, never. "Yes."

He tips the bottle, and the cool liquid pours over my knee. I release a pained cry. It burns, unlike anything. Setting the bottle aside on the counter, he pats my knee with the soft towel. He's gentle, touching me softly but firmly, and I realize, caught in his gaze, that I'm holding my breath.

My knee is dry, but he doesn't stop touching me. The towel falls to the floor, and his fingers trail a hot path up the inside of my thigh. My lungs burn almost as much as his touch, yet I don't breathe. The throbbing, stinging pain in my knee is forgotten. When his fingers graze my damp panties, oxygen rushes into my lungs.

His other hand lands on the kitchen cupboard behind my head. He's so close, devouring me with his eyes as he hooks his fingers in the fabric of my panties, sliding them aside. My hands fly up to his chest, and he shifts my foot to rest my ankle on his shoulder.

"Daem—" I start, but the words die on my tongue when his fingers press down on my clit. His intense, brown eyes stay locked on mine as he starts rubbing me in slow, torturous circles.

With my breath caught in my throat and my eyes falling shut, I arch into him. The way he touches me... I'm done for. This is not like the other times when he was rough and hell-bent on dominating me. This is slow and sensual. This is for my pleasure only.

"Did he make you feel this way?" he whispers when a shudder runs through me. "Did your skin erupt in goose-bumps at his touch?" His lips are on my jaw, teasing me with his warm breath and nip of teeth. My whimpers grow in volume as his touch travels lower and lower. He sinks a finger inside me, flicking my clit with his thumb.

"No, Daemon," I breathe softly, feeling the slide of his thick digit inside me.

His lips kiss a path down the curve of my neck, over my collarbone and shoulder, then back up to my mouth to steal my breath. He sucks on my tongue before snatching up my lip and giving it a warning bite, the kind that says, *"Don't trust me."*

"Open your eyes, baby," he whispers as he leans back.

I gaze at him through a haze of pleasure while my tongue slides over my lips. As I reach up to bury my fingers in the short hair at the nape of his neck, he moves in, tasting me with hard sweeps of his tongue. His mouth, his touch... I'm in the sweetest Hell. Daemon reminds me with every kiss and sinful word of why I should rejoice that the gates didn't open for me.

"You don't need Eden, little angel. I'm your Heaven and the only one who can make you feel this way. Do you hear me?

No one else can. And if this isn't Heaven," he nips at my earlobe, "then leave me here in Hell to burn for eternity."

"Daemon," I moan as my insides melt and warm.

"I need to taste you." He pulls my ass to the edge of the counter, bending down to lick at my pussy. His warm tongue slides through my wet folds and laps at my throbbing clit.

Fisting his hair, I bite down on my lip to stop myself from coming too soon. I want to savor this moment. Feel every swipe of his tongue, scratch of his beard, and tickle of his hot breath. Daemon stayed away from me this week, and it hurt. I thought I'd lost him.

"Hell, this sweet pussy..." His fingers dig into my hips when he peers up at me from between my thighs. "Tell me he didn't make you feel this good."

There's a vulnerability in his voice that tugs at my heart-strings. "He's nothing compared to you."

He rewards me by sucking my clit into his mouth and groaning deep in his chest. His wings flare out behind him, but not in a display of dominance but one of pleasure. He's enjoying himself.

"Daemon," I moan, my insides tightening. I can't hold it off. The stack of cards comes tumbling down on top of us, and I throw my head back with a moan that's sure to rouse even the sleeping birds in the trees outside. He laps up every drop of cum before dragging his lips up my body, over my dress, and pressing a hard kiss to my lips. My scent lingers on him like an expensive perfume, and it awakens the part of me that wants to possess him.

I grip his stubbly chin, smiling through sharp fangs. "Good boy."

His lips curl back and he bares his own incisors, which are longer than mine and fiercer. "If you try to dominate me again, I'll flip you over and spank your ass raw." His words are a clear threat, but he lets me dig my fingers into his jaw.

The line between us is thin, and I know he wouldn't allow any other girl to hold him in such a possessive grip as I am now. I like that he lets me explore this basic instinct to claim my territory within limits. And I know if I push too far, he'll make good on his threat to slap my ass until I beg for his cock.

He finally tears his chin from my grip, looking down at my swollen pussy and flicking my clit. Then he straightens up and says, "Now, will you tell me how you injured your knee, or do I need to fuck the answers out of you?"

Suddenly nervous, I close my legs, pulling my skirt down as I sneak a furtive peek at the outline of his hard cock inside his jeans. "It's nothing."

"Bullshit!"

I hop down and try to move past him, but he grabs my neck and drags me back. "How did you hurt your knee?"

"I don't even know how to explain," I tell him, fidgeting.

"Did someone hurt you?"

"No, nothing like that."

"Did you fall?"

I suck my lips between my teeth and look to the side. "Kind of."

"Kind of?"

When I don't reply, he pinches my chin between his fingers and brings my eyes back to him. "Kind of?"

Figuring it's best to tell him the truth, I lean against the counter. "Remember the time we meditated in class? My arms were covered in scratches afterward."

His brows pull down low. "Yeah?"

"Well, it's like that. But in my dreams."

He stays quiet, watching me.

"I have these dreams... I'm walking in the woods and stumble upon a door. Just a single door—no house. Like what the teacher told us to visualize during the meditation, remember? It's open, but only enough for light to spill out. And there's a voice coming from inside. It whispers..."

"Whispers?"

I nod, wrapping my arms around myself to ward off the sudden chill in the air. "Yeah. It wants me to step inside."

His deep voice draws my eyes back to his. "And how did you injure your knee?"

"Something ran past me—a shadow—and I tripped on a root."

His dark eyes peer into mine but give nothing away. "You tripped over in your dream and woke up with a bleeding knee?"

"Like that time in class when I scratched my arms on the branches."

"Fuck..." He steps away, dragging a hand down his face.

"What does it mean?"

"I don't know," he admits, looking back at me, "but I bet it ain't good."

I'm glad I told him the truth, relieved even, but I don't like the concerned look in his eyes. Daemon likes to feel in control, and right now, he's not.

"From now on, you're not to sleep alone."

My eyes widen and I push off the counter. "You want me to sleep in your bed?"

Daemon does a double take, his eyes widening, too. "I didn't mean it like that." It's cute how he's rubbing his neck. I try not to smile. "You'll alternate beds."

I cock my head to the side, then let my smile run free over my lips as they spread wide. "Or we could buy a big bed and share."

This time he snorts. "Not fucking happening. Alaric starfishes in his sleep, and the last time I shared a bed with them, I woke up with Ronan's feet in my face and his fucking wing on my cock. Never again."

"You slept naked together?"

The look he gives me is anything but impressed. "Don't get ideas. We'd shared a girl."

I ignore the last part and the twinge of jealousy inside me. "So, there was no sword crossing involved?"

"I was hard, and now I'm not. Thanks, Angel. I can go back to sleep." He walks out, expecting me to follow, which I do gladly now that he has sparked my curiosity. The candles on the wall light up with flames as we pass. It's part of the boys' magic. I still need to inquire about it. How do they make it happen?

"I think it could be hot."

We ascend the steps, and Daemon takes them three at a time as if he wants to escape my line of questioning. The wrought iron banister is cold beneath my palm, and so are the stone steps. I barely notice, keeping my eyes on his broad back.

"You want to watch me with Ronan and Alaric?"

"It could be hot," I admit when we reach the top.

The worn artisan carpet stretches out in front of us. It's soft beneath my feet, staving off the cold.

"I think I would enjoy watching you pleasure Ronan or Alaric."

Opening the door to his bedroom, he watches me walk in. "For your information, they would give *me* a blowjob, not the other fucking way around. I only lick girls."

I was sliding my hand over the black silk sheet on his bed, but at his admission, I whirl around. "Girls?"

Notice the *s* in 'girls.'

Plural.

Daemon pulls his T-shirt over his head, which is a feat with his large wings behind him, and tosses it to the floor. Then he starts on his belt buckle while looking at me from beneath his tousled, dark locks that fall over his eyes. "Yeah, girls."

"Huh?" I say, taking slow steps forward. "That's interesting."

He's clueless, lowering his zipper.

Typical man.

"And I only suck dicks."

No reaction. He kicks off his jeans, and I slide my tongue over my teeth as my eyes flick down to the thick bulge in his boxers.

"Lots and lots of dicks."

He stiffens, his eyes slowly coming to mine. "What did you say?"

With a shrug, I turn around, walking deeper into his room. A deep-green couch is pushed up against the bay window, and the walls are bare except for a framed painting of an angel falling from the sky.

"I said I like cocks."

I feel him before I see him. His heat presses up against my back, and his long fingers curl around my neck. I watch his reflection in the window when he leans down and growls against the curve of my ear, "The only cocks you like are in this house, understood?"

Ignoring the spark in my clit, I fight the urge to lean into him. "And the only pussy you like to lick is mine, understood?"

His grip on my throat is possessive, dominant. His alpha is coming out to play. "No, you heard me right. *Girls,*" he drawls, squeezing me.

My tattered wings erupt, breaking our connection, and my vision becomes a red haze as I slowly turn around. "I think you know I like dicks outside of this house, too."

His own wings unfold, and his teeth sharpen and grow. He stalks me, forcing me backward until the backs of my legs connect with his bed. "If you touch another man again, it'll be the last thing you do."

"And if you ever so much as look at another girl, I'll tear you to pieces."

Daemon throws me down onto the bed, climbing up my body like a fierce, growling lion with its teeth bared. I can't look away from his wings behind him. They're so fucking big, they nearly span the entirety of his room. And when he threw me down, my own wings knocked items off his nightstand.

I don't care about the sorry state they're in—I'm not closing them while he's dominating me like this. I don't care what weird and awkward angle my wings are forced into, squashed up against his fucking furniture. Why can't I have cute little wings like the other girls here? Why are mine big enough to compete with his? It's why we're both peacocking, fighting for dominance over the other. If I had small wings, he'd be my 'alpha.' I refuse to give him the satisfaction.

As if he can't help himself, he grabs my throat and growls, "So fucking defiant with your pathetic wings out. You think I'll submit to you, little angel?"

I snarl, my body vibrating with anger and arousal. We're two animals, giving into our lesser natures. This is what the elders warned us about. Every lesson ever taught to me about sin.

"We both know my wings are anything but pathetic," I hiss, and he pats my cheek patronizingly until I bat him away.

"You want to do this?" he asks, yanking my dress up and slapping my thighs apart. "You really want to taunt my alpha right now?"

My legs fall open in response. I growl low in my chest, making vicious sounds I never knew I was capable of.

Daemon smacks my cheek with enough bite to anger me even more and warns, "Last chance, little angel. Fold your wings."

The growl inside my chest intensifies, and I flip us over on the bed with a strength I never knew I had. My blonde hair falls around us like a curtain as I grit out, "Never." Tearing at his belt, I shove my hand inside his boxers and wrap my fingers around his hard length. "Now, baby," I taunt, sliding my hand over his silky cock. "Be a good boy and pull your wings back in." I lean down and smile a sugary smile against his lips. "And I promise to fuck you until you don't know your own name anymore."

In a blur of motion, we move across the room, colliding with furniture and breaking a floor lamp in the process. Daemon swipes his arm over his desk, sending the content crashing to the floor. "Now, where were we?" he whispers darkly when he has me bent over the desk with my ass bared. "My sweet angel wants me to fuck her tight cunt, isn't that right?"

My fangs cut my bottom lip as I snarl savagely at him. I'm so aroused, my pussy weeps with need.

With his fingers curled around my neck, he kicks my legs apart before rubbing the thick head of his cock between my ass cheeks. "Such a good girl," he taunts, knowing full well how much it pisses me off. "You're going to take my cock like a good little angel, aren't you?"

"And you're going to fuck me like a good boy."

"Shut the fuck up!" he growls, reaching for something inside his drawer. "Remember these?" He quickly and expertly ties my hands behind my back with a length of rope, then stuffs a pair of silk panties in my mouth.

Leaning down, he whispers in my ear. "I gifted them to you the day after we defiled you for the first time in the living room. Remember that time, beautiful? When I licked your cunt for the first time, and we all painted you in cum?" His heat disappears, and I moan around the fabric in my mouth as he kneads my ass cheeks before sliding his touch over my wings. I snarl at him over my shoulder, but he shoves me back down with a hand on my neck.

"Now, now, sweetheart. Don't be so angry." His hard dick rubs over my pussy, and I arch my ass against him. "Such a submissive little angel," he drawls, grabbing hold of one of my wings and filling me up with his delicious cock. I'm so wet the slide of him feels amazing. Every vein and curve rubs up against my inner walls. "Good girl," he breathes. "Keep your wings open for me."

I know he feels powerful fucking and dominating someone with equally big wings. And I would lie if I said I didn't want to keep them open for him, because it arouses me that he gets off on asserting himself over me, even if I want to fight back. Fuck, I want to fight back so damn much. I can't even tell him to fuck off now that I have my panties shoved in my mouth and my wrists tied behind my back. I can't do anything but take it—every delicious inch.

"You feel amazing strangling my dick with your pussy." His hands squeeze me so good—borderline painful—as if it's sweet torture for him to fuck me. I hope it is. I hope he's as lost in me as I am in him. The empty wall in front of me blurs while he pounds me from behind with his hand fisted in my hair. I'll be sore tomorrow. That's for fucking certain.

Flipping me over on my back, he shifts my ankles onto his shoulders, then stares down at his dick as it moves in and out of me. His dark eyes flick up to mine and he smirks, picking up his pace and patting me on the cheek. Once, twice. Three fucking times. Who knew anger could be so arousing? I want to hurt him, but I'm powerless with my arms bound behind me and panties in my mouth.

"There's a good girl," he taunts, slapping me a little too hard to be gentle.

My pussy clamps down on him, eager for whatever humiliating shit he's ready to dole out.

"I love the fucking fire in your eyes," he tells me, squeezing my cheeks before wrapping his fingers around my throat. "I thought it was gone, but now the flames burn higher than ever." As if to make a point, he moves his wings up and down behind him, then winks. *Who's in charge, baby?*

From somewhere deep inside, something truly dark surfaces, and I kick him off.

As he stumbles to the ground, I give a hard yank, and the rope tied around my wrists falls to the floor. I don't stop to question how the fuck I developed such strength. Not when he's lying naked on the floor like a fucking feast.

I straddle his lap, stuff his mouth with my panties, and sink onto his cock, moaning at the delicious stretch. "Fucking hell," I hiss, my nails digging into his chest as I begin to move. "Your dick feels so fucking good..."

He tries to spit the gag out, but I don't let him. When he reaches for it, I grab his jaw, baring the column of his neck. His veiny hands land on my hips. We both know he could throw me off any minute, but he lets me play my games.

"Nu-uh!" I breathe, dragging my tongue up his neck while riding him slow and deep. "You're my good boy, remember? Now you let me take what I need, okay?"

His fingers flex on my hips. He's fighting the urge to teach me a lesson. And he could.

"That's it, baby," I whisper, forcing his dark gaze to mine. "Give me those beautiful eyes." I roll my hips faster, harder. Then I lean back, balancing my hands on his thighs behind me as I let my head fall back.

Daemon shoves my dress down until it bunches around my waist, and then the warm palm of his hand slides up between my breasts and wraps around my neck. He's trying to take back power, but I don't mind. Not when he tweaks a nipple so expertly with his other hand.

"Oh, God," I whimper while bouncing on his dick, chasing the orgasm at the end of the rainbow. "Oh, fuck, Daemon..." My tits bob, my arousal coating his dick and balls.

The sound of slapping skin fills the room. I'm coming apart. I won't survive this climax. It'll be unlike anything I've ever experienced before. "Your dick feels so fucking amazing!" I can't fuck him any harder. My thighs burn from exertion, but I still need more, just a little more. Reaching down, I rub my clit fast and hard until the earth splits open and its core spills out. I orgasm with a scream, collapsing on top of Daemon, out of breath and exhausted.

He flips us over, stuffs my fucking panties in my mouth, and proceeds to fuck me so hard that I'll have friction burns on my back tomorrow. Sweat drips from his nose as he chases his own release. "Fuck, fuck, fuck!" Pulling out, he shifts up my body, his knees on either side of my shoulders. He removes the gag, ordering me to stick my tongue out, which I do very willingly. The corded muscles in his arms strain as he jerks his cock, coating my face with his release. Thick white strings of cum land on my lips and cheeks. "Fuck, little angel..."

I gaze up at him, eagerly catching his cum with my tongue. Every drop. When he's done, and the last spurt of release drips off my chin, he collapses next to me on the bed. Our wings—now tucked beneath us—overlap, his on top of mine, black on white.

"Shit, that was..." he starts, rolling his head on the pillow and sweeping his dark eyes over my face, "...something else."

"Something else?" I burst out laughing, and he soon joins in. We descend into chuckles and giggles that last long into the morning.

CHAPTER 19

AURELIA

"Wake up, sleepyheads!"

Cold water hits me in the face, and I shoot upright, coughing and spluttering. Beside me, Daemon flies off the bed and tackles Alaric to the ground. "You motherfucker!"

Ronan hands me a lit-up joint. "You might want this after last night's sexcapades and this morning's rude awakening by Alaric."

Accepting the joint, I bring it to my lips and take a deep pull. My wet and soppy hair coats my forehead and cheeks. I brush it off, watching the boys roll around like tumbleweeds on the floor. My soaked nightdress molds to my every curve. I'm freezing now but fuck it, this joint is good.

Placing his knee on the bed, Ronan falls forward onto his hands and smiles against my lips. I blow the smoke into his mouth while the sound of a struggle continues. "You're naughty," Ronan whispers, his lips dragging over my cheek to my ear, his breath tickling my skin. "I like it."

I don't answer.

The embers crackle and smoke swirls in patterns. I squint through it at Alaric and Daemon on the floor. They both have bloodied lips and split knuckles, but they're laughing now.

Daemon shakes out his wet hair. "Just you fucking wait until you're asleep next time."

Hopping to his feet, Alaric snatches the joint from me and places it between his lips while I blink up at him.

"Excuse me!"

He smiles at me before pursing his lips around the joint and inhaling deeply. I wait him out, my eyes narrowed. After blowing a smoke ring or two, he puts the joint between his lips again. "Yeah?"

"I was smoking that!"

He shrugs. "Tough."

"Get dressed," Ronan orders, righting Daemon's desk chair before taking a seat. "Dariana will be over shortly."

Daemon is unapologetic about his nakedness. His dick is impressive even when it's not hard. I can't stop looking at it, and he smirks when he notices. Walking up to me, he cups my chin, bringing my eyes up to his. His tempting cock is right in my face, and my mouth waters as I wrap my fingers around his silky length. It soon hardens, brushing up against the happy trail below his belly button. He lets me stroke him while he pulls my bottom lip away from my teeth. But he doesn't take it further, and when I lean in to taste him, he tightens his grip on my chin to hold me back. "Get dressed, little angel."

With that, he walks into the adjoining bathroom.

Not fucking fair.

Just then, the bedroom door flies open, and Dariana joins us in a cloud of spicy yet feminine perfume, her heels clicking on the hard floor. She does a double take when she sees me. "Why are you soaking wet?"

Sprawled on the desk chair, Ronan says, "Alaric woke her up with a bucket of water."

Dariana blinks, and then she blinks again. "Okay, whatever." Hips and boobs swaying inside her minuscule dress, she saunters up to me. "I've got a little something for you." In her hands is a small tub.

"What's that?" I ask as she lowers herself down beside me on the bed.

"Turn around, so your back is to me."

Intrigued, I follow orders.

"My parents know someone who knows someone with special abilities."

I try to turn to look at her, but she won't let me. "Special abilities?"

She hums, unscrewing the lid. "The humans call them witches. In our world, they're fallen angels with unique powers. This particular angel possesses healing powers. She made this balm for you upon my request." She pats my wing. "Open."

I unfold them and feel her rub whatever the ointment is over the areas where I plucked my feathers. She's gentle, touching me as if she cares. My eyes fill with tears as my chest constricts, and I blink rapidly.

"Did it hurt?" she asks in a soft tone.

"Of course it hurt," Ronan snorts, his feet on the desk, his hands clasped on his chest. "Remember when we were kids and would randomly pull a feather from each other because it was fun? That fucking hurt. I can't even imagine tearing off enough feathers to fill pillows for a family of five."

Dariana is quiet behind me, smoothing the salve over my wings.

"I appreciate that you're doing this for me," I whisper.

"Well," she says, "someone has to look after you."

Alaric is gazing out the window with his broad back to us.

His wings are relaxed, grazing the floor. "People are starting to notice you."

Ronan rubs a hand over his face before digging inside his pocket for a packet of cigarettes. He bangs the bottom on his palm and places one between his lips. Every time he travels to the human world, he returns with more packets.

"Now is not the time," he says, lighting one up. With a wave of his hand, the flame flickers out.

Alaric ignores him. "People you don't want to notice you."

Behind me, Dariana screws the lid back on and sighs. "Daemon's father returns tonight, and he wants you to come along to dinner."

"Okay?"

"You're a real angel," she says when I turn to face her.

"I'm aware of what I am."

With her dark, wavy hair that frames her face and falls over her shoulders like a waterfall, she's breathtaking. "Remember what I told you about not trusting anyone here?"

"I remember."

Her eyes briefly flick over my shoulder when Daemon exits the bathroom stark naked, dripping water. "They call it Hell for a reason." Her voice breaks through my X-rated thoughts.

I drag my eyes away from the water droplets on Daemon's back and ass while he roots through a drawer for towels.

"Someone like you is worth a lot of money here."

My brows pull low and I give a shake of my head to clear it. "What?"

Dariana taps her nail on the tub of salve in her hands. "I don't know how much the boys have told you... Daemon's father is a powerful man."

When I don't reply, she continues, "He received a bid for you yesterday."

The atmosphere in the room turns icy. Daemon slams the

drawer shut so hard, it doesn't surprise me when it breaks and hangs sideways. "How do you know this?"

"A little bird sang."

"What. Little. Bird?"

Dariana juts her jaw out. "I'm not telling you. If I do, you'll go after them. We can't afford to lose informants."

"Fucking fine!" he growls. "Who made a bid?"

Uncertainty flickers in her depths, and I don't blame her. Daemon is fucking scary. The vein in his temple pops when he fists her hair.

"Tell me right the fuck now so I can kill them!"

"Your uncle."

Daemon drops her and stumbles back against the dresser. "Why the fuck would he do that? And why the fuck would my father go along with it?"

Alaric turns around, his hands in his pockets. "Your uncle offered to step away from active royal duty in exchange for the girl."

Active royal duty? What does that mean?

I open my mouth to speak, but before I can get a word in, Daemon spits, "No fucking way. They've fought wars over my father's throne my whole fucking life. Why would he suddenly offer to step down in exchange for the angel? It doesn't make sense."

It's Ronan who breaks the ensuing silence. "A few reasons. He's playing the long game. When your father defeated your uncle after he attempted to overthrow him, he forced him to sign the treaty. Your uncle was backed into a corner. The next heir to the throne is you, Daemon, not Dmitriy."

"I know all this. What's your fucking point?" Daemon says, pulling on a pair of jeans and leaving them unbuckled.

Ronan points the fingers with the cigarette at me. "You don't want to admit it, but she's become your weak link."

Daemon throws his arms out, laughing disbelievingly.

"Steal the girl, and the future heir to the throne topples over like the queen on a chessboard. Your uncle wins. His son gets the girl and then the throne when your father dies. Voila, family fortune secured."

Daemon starts to pace.

"Remember what it says in the contract signed by both Amenadiel *and* your father. If you hurt your cousin or uncle, the throne diverts to them. This is what they want. They expect you to come for Dmitriy."

"FUCK!" Daemon roars, picking up his nightstand and throwing it across the room.

I stare in disbelief at the splintered wood while Daemon continues pacing like a caged animal.

"I need to speak to Father. I need to stop this."

"What good is it going to do? He can't see reason right now, not when your uncle is dangling a worm on the hook. Do you seriously think he'll listen to you? Angel is nothing but a girl to him. He's wanted your uncle to step away from the royal family as long as I've been alive."

The royal family? Contracts? I'm so fucking confused.

"So we let him give up active royal duty, and then we kill Dmitriy," Alaric says, running a hand over his face.

Blowing out a sigh, Daemon shakes his head. "It doesn't work like that. Even if he gives up his title and steps away completely, the throne still reverts back to him if either I, my father, or anyone connected to us hurts my uncle or cousin. The contract is watertight. My father was adamant about keeping the peace. And the throne."

"Must have been some family rivalry for your dad to take such drastic measures," I comment drily. It makes sense now why Dmitriy prepositioned me at school. Even if I don't understand fuck about the 'throne.' "What happens if they hurt *you?*"

"They lose their titles and access to the family fortune."

"So this dinner tonight—" Dariana starts, but Daemon cuts her off.

"She's not going."

"You know your fath—"

"I don't fucking care! My uncle doesn't lay a finger on her. He isn't allowed to fucking look at her!" To Ronan, he says, "What was the other reason?"

"What?"

"Your words were 'a few reasons.'"

Ronan blows smoke circles before shrugging and placing his feet down on the floor. "Daemon, she's an angel. Do I need to say more?"

"Yes, you fucking do!"

Groaning, Ronan gets to his feet and walks up to Daemon. "Man, why the fuck are you torturing yourself like this?"

"Spit it out!"

Ronan gets up in Daemon's face and shoves him back a step. "She's an angel. Your uncle will most likely sell her unless you do something stupid like offering them the throne on a silver platter. Can you imagine how much fucking money she's worth? I'm surprised no one has tried to steal her from us yet. If we were smart, we should have kept her hidden in the fucking basement."

My mouth falls open. "Fuck you!"

Turning toward me, Ronan laughs. "It's for your own good, sweetheart."

Alaric begrudgingly nods his head. "Ronan has a point. If he sold her, I bet he could get enough money to rival your father's fortune."

"If I'm worth so much fucking money, how come you haven't tried to sell me yet? How come you've left me out of your sight at the academy?" I fold my arms over my chest, treating them all to my best glare.

"Because," Daemon says, "no one would fucking dare try to steal you. Why haven't I tried to sell you yet? I'm already rich. I don't need to sell you. I was having way too much fucking fun opening your eyes to all the shit your elders kept you ignorant about. The fucking look on your face—your doe eyes—when you saw an erect cock for the first time sealed your fate. I wasn't going to give that up. Money is fucking boring. Money doesn't scream the fucking house down the first time it experiences an orgasm. It doesn't crawl on its knees with innocent, wide eyes to pleasure three horny fallen angels. And it certainly doesn't tell me no while challenging me with unfolded wings."

I shoot to my feet so fast, it's a miracle I don't hit the roof. "You piece of shit!" I'm in front of him in a flash, jabbing my finger into his chest. "You didn't think to sell me because 'you were having fun?' I was *fun* to you, was I?"

"Yes, you were fun. Look around you. This world of darkness isn't exactly exciting. I can have anything I fucking want at the click of my fingers. But then you came along with your refreshing innocence and blazing attitude. So yes, you were fun!"

"You stole me from my home because you were bored?!"

"You were in the fucking woods!" he roars, forcing me back a step. "Monsters lurk in the shadows, Angel." Grabbing my jabbing finger, he continues, "*I* am that monster! You walked into *my* territory. I saw you. I wanted you. So I took you. End of story. I'm not going to fucking apologize!"

My hand flies out and smacks him hard across the cheek. Seeing his head whip to the side makes me feel marginally better.

When his eyes come back to me, they're cold and soulless. "Maybe I should let him buy you, after all."

He walks out and slams the door behind him. The others shuffle awkwardly when rage, unlike anything I've known, bubbles up inside me. My feet move, following him out into the hallway. "There you go, running away again. It's what you do, Daemon. You're weak and pathetic!"

He whirls on me and slams me up against the wall just as the others come tumbling through the door. "Call me weak and pathetic one more time, little angel!"

I shove him back, and he falls against the wall opposite, causing a mounted painting of a portrait to fall to the floor. "You're weak, Daemon. Weak and pathetic!"

His smile is cruel when he comes for me, and his eyes are dark pits of fury. "You think you're so fucking special, Angel? You think I would fucking care if my uncle bought you?"

"Daemon," Alaric says, his voice carrying a warning, "think about what you're saying."

I stand my ground, refusing to cower, no matter how much taller than me he is.

His hand shoots out and he grips my throat, pulling me into him. "You're just a willing pussy."

My throat clogs up with emotion, but I force it down. He's right. I'm no one in their world. "I should have taken Dmitriy up on his offer. He was right when he said he would never treat me as badly as you do. It looks like I'll be in good hands."

He drops me like he's been burned, and then he steps back and shoves Alaric out of his way as he makes his escape.

"Run, Daemon. It's what you're good at!" I call after him, ignoring the strong urge to chase after him. "Fucking asshole!" I do a double take when I notice the others staring at me. "What?"

They exchange glances. "You're toxic when you're together," Alaric says, looking uncomfortable.

"Because he's a prick, and I'm fucking over it!"

"And you like to attack his pride every damn time," Alaric retorts, shaking his head. "Daemon is a powerful angel and used to getting his own way. He's not used to this-this..."

"This what? Spit it out!"

"You defy him all the fucking time." Alaric kills the distance between us before ducking down and forcing me to look him in the eye. "I know he has a shit way of showing it, but he's in love with you."

My mouth falls open. I scoff, then laugh. "Are you on drugs?" I make quotation marks with my fingers. "You're just a willing pussy."

Alaric averts his gaze, staring at the wall for a long moment. Then he rubs his hand over his face and looks back at me. "Whatever. Believe what you want, Angel. Just know that you did more than just slap him here today. Daemon is nothing if not destructive. If you attack his pride, you need to understand there are plenty of female angels willing to help build it back up to unreachable heights. Are you okay with that? Someone else on his lap, whispering sweet nothings in his ear, because you lashed out in anger?"

My shoulders square as I curse the tears in my eyes. "Why are you making me out to be the villain in this story? He stole me!" I point to my chest. "I didn't ask to come here. I didn't ask for this." I gesture at the floor, the walls, them. "I didn't ask for any of it!"

Alaric looks away, better at keeping his anger at bay than Daemon and me. "I don't know what you want me to say." When he looks back at me, there's a hardness in his eyes. "Hell is a cruel place, full of cruel people. It's not Heaven. The sooner you realize that, the easier life will be for you."

He walks off and Ronan follows him.

Sinking back against the wall and sliding down to the floor, I let the tears fall. Everything is such a mess, and I don't know who I am anymore. I don't know who I'm supposed to be in this world. Dariana crouches down in front of me, takes my hand in hers, and squeezes it. "Everyone fights sometimes. He'll come around."

The framed portrait painting on the floor is cracked. I did that. I ruined it. Like I ruin everything I touch.

Dariana's soft fingers wipe the tears from my cheeks. "Arguments suck. Anger sucks. I know what it's like. I've lived here my entire life, remember?"

I appreciate that she's trying to make me feel better, but I feel like shit.

"Do you know what helps after an argument?"

I sniffle pathetically, wiping beneath my nose and shaking my head. "No..."

"Dancing and alcohol. Lots of it. Come with me. Let's get you dressed and dolled up and forget about all this for a while." Rising from the floor, she holds her hand out. I stare at her manicured nails and olive skin before clasping her hand and letting her pull me to my feet.

CHAPTER 20

AURELIA

The music is so loud, I can feel the base in the floorboards beneath my heels. Dariana dressed me in a short, glittery black dress, far more revealing than anything I've ever worn before, and I feel pretty.

We're in the human world, back in the club where they come to hunt. Mortal men flirt with us, and we let them buy us drinks. I'm having fun—a novel concept.

"Why is there fruit in my drink?" I ask, squinting at the pieces floating in my drink.

"It's a gin and tonic. It's supposed to have strawberries," she shouts over the music. "Try one. Best combination ever."

"You know, I'm only just getting used to blood, and now you're introducing me to alcohol mixed with fruit? Wait, I thought you didn't eat food?"

Her mischievous, scarlet smile draws my eyes while she scoops one up and places it on my tongue.

My eyes widen. "It's sweet."

"Good, right?"

"Oh, yeah!" I groan, wiping droplets of strawberry juice from my bottom lip with my thumb. Dariana's black dress has a dangerously low neckline, and her silver necklace disappears into her cleavage. I want to follow it with my tongue. Alcohol makes me horny—well, more horny than usual.

"He's cute!" She points to a human man over by the bar. I take in his white shirt, the two top buttons undone, and his black slacks that hug his thighs just right. The rings on his tattooed fingers glint in the lights behind the bar as he lifts his beer to his lips.

"We should share him," she whispers in my ear, and my eyes snap to hers.

"Daemon will kill him."

Scooping a strawberry from my drink, she pops it in her mouth. "Daemon isn't here."

My gaze is fixed on her lips.

"He's probably with some girl right now."

I look down at my drink, swirling the straw through the pieces of fruit. "Don't remind me, please."

She watches me throw my drink back. I'm already feeling the effects of the alcohol. "Are you not hungry? When was the last time you fed?"

I went all my life without feeding on humans, and now I crave blood like some mythological vampire. Just one more negative thing to add to the list of reasons why it's a bad idea to sneak out of Eden.

"Let's share him," she coaxes. "It'll be fun. Just you and me and a hot human man."

"But Daemon—"

"So what if he kills him? We'll kill him anyway."

I wince and she pinches my chin, forcing my eyes back to hers. "It's nature. Why would your God create predators if we weren't meant to hunt prey? Why do spiders eat flies? And lions, antelopes? We're just higher up the food chain than him."

I consider her words while I study the human man. He has a nice smile, straight white teeth with a dimple on his cheek, and a tattoo on the side of his neck. His brown hair is kept short on the sides and longer on the top.

"Do humans fuck as good as angels?"

Dariana chokes on her drink and it takes her a moment to stop coughing, but her eyes glitter with amusement when she does. "Why don't we find out?"

"I don't know," I say, dropping my gaze to the floor. "Daemon—"

"Stop worrying about Daemon. Let him fucking stew."

"Do you think that's fair?"

"Yes!" she exclaims, exasperated. "I think it's fair. He stole you from Eden. When you arrived at his house, you'd never felt anything but complete contentment. Now you feel all these emotions that you don't know how to handle. Daemon, on the other hand, has no excuse for his behavior. He's had a lifetime to learn how to wrangle his explosive temper, but you, little angel, you've only had a matter of months. He said it himself: he saw you and he wanted you, so he took you. Now, you want to feed on that human, so go over there and take what you want. Do something for yourself for once. Put yourself first."

"You're very eager for me to betray Daemon."

"Oh, for fuck's sake," she growls, "you're about to seduce your meal. That's not cheating. What do you think the boys do before they eat? They seduce those girls every damn fucking time." She takes my hand and steers me over to the man, who lowers his drink when she trails her manicured fingers up his chest.

"You look like you know how to show two women a good time."

He swallows the beer in his mouth as his hazel eyes trail over to me and dip to my chest. "Want another drink?"

Dariana darts her tongue out, sweeping it across her bottom lip. "Why don't we skip the formalities and jump straight to it? Hmm? Why don't you take us somewhere more private?"

Placing his beer down on the bar, he pushes off and slides his arms around our waists. "Let's go."

HIS APARTMENT IS flashy in a way I didn't expect. It's open-plan and spacious, with shiny, dark marble floors and windows that span from the ceiling to the floor. There's even a balcony that overlooks the city. The couch in the living room is black leather, the kind of modern design that screams bachelor. No woman would have a couch like that without at least a dozen throw pillows.

"Angel," Dariana giggles between kisses, stumbling toward the bedroom with the human. "Join us."

Dragging my eyes away from the silvery moon outside, I follow them into the bedroom, where they fall onto the bed in a tangle of limbs. I'm unsure what to do, and when Dariana reaches for my hand, I let her pull me onto the bed. The human, who we found out is named Cole, pushes up on his knees and removes his tie while Dariana slides the straps down my shoulders before capturing my nipple between her plump lips. She sucks eagerly, and pleasure trickles down to my core. Cole tosses his tie to the floor and starts on his shirt buttons.

"Isn't she so pretty?" Dariana says, gripping my jaw and smiling up at Cole. "Don't you just want to fuck that pretty mouth?"

Cole palms my naked tit before shrugging out of his shirt.

His ripped abs ripple as he unbuckles his belt. There's a script tattoo on his ribs, and more tattoos than I can count cover his stomach and chest. He's even got his birth year tattooed in large numbers on his chest.

"She's the prettiest thing I've ever seen," he agrees, shoving his jeans down and stroking his hard length. My gaze slides down and then back up. I didn't think humans had big dicks, but he's impressive in the anatomy department. Not as big as my men, but definitely not small. *My men?* Shut up, brain. They're not my men. They're three captors that keep me like a pet because they're bored.

Dariana lies down beside me, cupping my cheek and bringing my eyes to hers. "Open your legs, baby." Sliding her fingers down my stomach and between my thighs, she begins to circle my clit. "Yes," she breathes, "take what you want, little angel."

Do I want this?

Cole's big hand presses down next to me on the pillow as he settles between my legs. He tears a condom with his teeth, sheathing his length. "Look at me with those pretty eyes," he orders, and Dariana giggles, flopping onto her back. She's drunk. I am as well, but I'm not too drunk to realize this feels wrong, and when Cole crowns my entrance, I shove him off.

Dariana laughs next to me. "I knew you couldn't go through with it."

My cheeks heat as I sit up and hold my dress over my tits.

"What the fuck is wrong with you?!" Cole growls, glaring at me.

Beside me, Dariana shifts onto her hands and knees and crawls up to him. "Relax, lover boy. You'll get to come." After removing the condom, she takes him in her mouth, and I peer up through my lashes as her head bobs on him. Meanwhile, his dark, heavy eyes stay locked on mine the entire time.

"You like that," she teases, licking him from root to tip.

His gaze snaps to hers, and he traps his bottom lip between his teeth before shoving her away and climbing off the bed. He leaves the room and returns shortly after with a bottle of champagne. The lid pops and he takes a large sip as he walks up to me. Then he fists my hair, yanks my head back, and presses the rim to my lips. "Drink, Blondie."

The cool bubbles sparkle on my tongue and pour down my chin and throat.

"There's a good girl." After handing the bottle to Dariana, he grabs my chin, bringing my lips to his. "Why'd you deny me?"

I try to move away, but he tightens his grip, freezing me.

"You frigid?"

Dariana chokes on her drink and falls back, laughing on the bed, the bottle extended in the air. "My girl is not frigid."

"Could've fooled me." He shoves me away, then climbs back onto the mattress and takes the bottle from Dariana. His throat bobs as he swigs it. Then, when it's empty, he tosses it to the side and circles his fingers around my ankle. His grip is rough, and I let out a surprised sound when he drags me down the sheets. My skirt rides up around my waist to expose my pussy.

Cole grabs my wrists, forcing them up over my head. "You didn't come here to watch me fuck your friend, did you?"

My mind is hazy with alcohol. I don't like his touch at all. It doesn't feel like when Ronan, Alaric, or Daemon touch me.

His makes me feel cheap.

"Such a pretty pussy," he says as he drags his fingers through my slit. I'm dry, so he spits on his digits and tries again, rubbing my clit. Behind him, Dariana sits up with a raised brow, smeared lipstick, and tangled hair. The challenge in her eyes is not lost on me.

I shove him off, straddling his lap. His cock is right there, nestled between my legs and sliding against my pussy. If it were

Daemon, my body would tremble with need and I would be begging him to fuck me, but he's not Daemon. He's not Ronan or Alaric, either. He's prey, and I'm the cat toying with my mouse.

"Do you know what I like?" I whisper, slowly unfolding my wings behind me. Dariana's eyes widen. "My friends don't like to feed on frightened prey. They use their power to place their victim in a trance, if you will. Personally, I think it's dull." My teeth slowly grow, glinting in the light from the bedside lamp.

His eyes widen.

Suddenly, he can see my wings, too.

With my eyes locked on Dariana, I lean in close to him and whisper, "I like my prey awake and screaming with fear." I strike, tearing into his neck until it's in shreds. His terrified cries that echo through his apartment soon die down. Dariana is in fits of giggles. I spit out a thick lump of flesh, curling my finger at her. "You've got to stop playing me like that."

She crawls forward, hips swaying, with a seductive, erotic smile. "I knew you wouldn't really fuck him."

My hand flies out and I grab her by the throat. "I don't like that you had his cock in your mouth."

Her dark eyes glitter beneath those long lashes. "I like this possessive side of you."

Covered head to toe in blood, I crawl over the dead body, covering Dariana with mine. I fist her skirt in my hand and shove it up. Then I press my thigh against her pussy, slowly beginning to move on top of her. "You like that?"

"I like you covered in blood and gore." As if to prove her point, she removes a shred of flesh from my hair. "You're vicious."

I grind against her, my hand wrapped around her slender throat. "I liked it."

She whimpers, her lashes fluttering. Looking down at my

naked breasts, she palms them and tweaks my nipples. "He's bleeding out on the bed. We're waisting blood."

"I've had my fill," I tell her. "Why don't you feed."

"I would, but you feel so good on top of me." She lifts her head off the pillow and sucks my hard nipple between her teeth.

I lose myself in her for all of two seconds before climbing off. "Feed. I didn't kill your prey for you so the mattress could soak it all up."

As she settles over his body and begins to lap at the blood that trickles in a steady stream from his neck, I crawl up behind her and grab her ass. The scent of her pussy is everywhere, enticing me to hook my thumb in her panties and slide them aside so I can feast on her cunt.

She moans, spreading her legs wider and rocking back against me while I circle her tight entrance with my tongue. I suck on her soft, soaking folds, dragging my tongue from her clit to her anus. My hand slides over her ass, leaving a trail of blood in its wake as I tease her pussy with my crimson fingers.

"Dammit, I'm trying to focus on feeding here," she laughs.

I slide two bloodied fingers inside her, watching them disappear into her slick heat. "Fuck, you're so warm, tight, and greedy." Leaning in, I sink my fangs into her ass, ignoring her fierce snarl. She can fucking take it! Pumping my fingers, I lap at the trickle of blood from the incisor wounds. My wings bump into the walls on either side of me, but I don't care. I'm too busy feasting on her pussy.

That is, until the bedroom door flies open and three very angry angels tumble through. Dariana and I pop our heads up. What a sight we must be: Dariana feasting on a dead corpse while I'm eating her out from behind.

"Hi, boys." She giggles. "Turns out our girl is a psychopath."

"What the fuck?" Daemon bats my wing out of the way as

he takes in the scene of me half naked, the dead guy with the floppy dick, and Dariana's ass in the air. The chunks of flesh strewn here and there on the sheets.

"Damn," chuckles Alaric. "We missed quite some party."

Ignoring them, I lean back in and circle my tongue over Dariana's throbbing clit. She's an addiction, and I want more.

"Fuck," she whimpers, pulling on the man's short hair and dragging her tongue over the last trickle of blood on his neck. "Unfortunately, you're too late, boys. We already drained him dry."

"By all means, continue," Alaric comments, flopping down onto the couch across the room that's conveniently placed to offer a prime view of the bed.

Ronan chuckles on his way over and lowers himself down next to Alaric. "Daemon, man," he calls out, "let the girls finish."

Daemon's footsteps retreat. I don't care to check his anger levels, not now when I have Dariana's pussy pressed up against my lips.

Priorities and all that.

CHAPTER 21

AURELIA

Aurelia...

I step out from the spindly trees, their branches reaching far and wide. My breath is visible in the air with every breath as the scent of fir and damp moss tantalizes my senses. My feet stop moving. There, in front of me, is the door, and it's closed—an old wrought-iron key glows beneath the silvery moonlight.

As I take a hesitant step forward, the branches snap back into place. The silence that presses in around me is absolute.

Almost suffocating.

A deafening void.

I climb over a broken log, slimy between my bare thighs, and pieces of rotten bark come away beneath my nails.

Aurelia...

My breath catches in my throat when a light flicks on behind the door and floods through the gap at the bottom. Then it shifts as if there's someone on the other end.

I backpedal a step, and the log behind me connects with

the backs of my ankles. I fall backward—my dress snagging on a thin branch—and when I sit up, a piece of fabric has been torn from my dress. It's stuck to the branch like a quivering leaf, but that's not what's got my attention. I'm bleeding profusely from a deep, throbbing cut on my thigh.

"Fuck," I whimper, touching my fingers to the slippery blood. It's too dark to see how deep the wound is. Climbing to my feet, I leave a trail of dripping blood behind as I hobble closer to the door. The wound stings with every step. An icy yet burning pain.

I come to a stop in front of the door, staring at the chipped red wood and the wrought-iron key. It's old, as if time itself is carved into the metal. Reaching out, I trace the unique bow design with the tips of my fingers.

Aurelia...

I pause, retracting my trembling hand. Nothing else happens, so I reach back out. My fingers grip the end and turn it slowly.

It clicks.

Holding my breath, I shift on my feet, steeling myself as I slowly push down on the handle. The sliver of light floods over my bare feet and ankles, growing larger and climbing up the muddied fabric of my skirt.

MY EYES FLY open and I shoot up, my gaze darting around the bedroom. I'm in Alaric's bed. The breeze from the open window whips through the curtains, and the single sconce on the wall beside the door is lit up, the flame flickering angrily.

Alaric's side of the bed is empty. I shift my legs beneath the quilt but wince in pain when the damp sheet slides over my thighs.

The dream...

My heart starts racing. I strike a match and light the

bedside candle before kicking my legs out from underneath the quilt. Now that I know something is wrong, the pain is an insistent throbbing.

As I slide the torn black dress higher up my thigh, my eyes widen. Blood trickles from the wound, soaking the sheets. The gash is deep enough that I can see the stark white of my bone.

My palm flies up to my mouth, and my other hand presses down on my thigh to stop the bleeding. It doesn't work. Warm, slippery blood seeps between my fingers as panic swells within me.

In a flash, I'm out of bed, hobbling downstairs and wincing with every step on the staircase. Behind me is a trail of scarlet and bloody footprints. Feeling dizzy, I flatten my hand on the stone wall to steady myself. I don't know if it's because I'm losing blood or breathing too hard.

"Alaric? Daemon?" My mouth is dry and I swallow before croaking, "Ronan?" I grip the handrail as I descend the stairs, leaving a bloodied handprint behind on the wall. By the time I reach the landing, my stomach churns with nausea.

"Oh, God," I whimper, falling back against the cold wall to steady myself. I'm losing blood too fast. The ends of my wings dragging behind me on the floor are smeared scarlet. My baby feathers don't look so cute now. Bending over, I tear the hem of my skirt, and the ripping sound is loud in the quiet hallway. I quickly tie it tightly around the upper half of my thigh with slippery fingers. Then I straighten up, dragging in steadying breaths.

What the fuck am I doing? Where are the others? "Daemon?" I call out again, stumbling forward. "Ronan?"

When I round the corner, I finally hear voices. The relief I feel has me toppling to the ground. I sit up, lifting my skirt to inspect the wound. Why won't it stop bleeding? I release a pathetic sob, and the voices in the kitchen fall silent.

Heavy footsteps sound on the floor. Alaric stumbles

through the door first, followed by the others. They stare at me wide-eyed before taking in the blood on the floor and walls. Daemon shoulders past the others. "Fuck, Alaric. You shouldn't have left her alone."

My head feels heavy. I can barely hold it up. Boots appear in my vision and Daemon crouches down, parting the curtain of hair in front of my eyes. His fingers stroke over my cheek. "My little angel?"

I smile weakly, but even that's an effort.

After standing back up, he bends down to scoop me up in his arms. "What happened this time?" The sconces on the walls burn brighter as we pass.

"I tripped over a log."

"You're very accident-prone in your dreams."

"I'm sorry."

He frowns. His brown eyes are tight and worried. "Don't apologize for falling over a log." To someone else, he says, "In there. Alaric, contact Dari. We need blood."

"No." I reach up, touching the stubble on his sharp jaw. My arm feels like lead.

His eyes come back to me, scanning my face.

"I'm sorry for what I said. You're not weak and pathetic. You're strong. You're—"

"It's okay." He lowers me down on something soft—a couch—and I sink into the throw pillows. Ronan pulls a few out from underneath me, tossing them to the floor.

"Light up the fireplace. She's cold," Daemon barks.

"It hurts," I whimper.

"I know," he soothes, his fingers brushing my thigh as he lifts my skirt to inspect the wound. "I'm impressed you know how to tie a tourniquet, but it's not tight enough to stop the bleeding." He swiftly unties it, then pulls it even tighter. I wince while he softly inspects the wound.

"The fire is lit," Ronan's voice drifts back over. "How bad is it?"

"It's bad enough that shit won't end well unless Dariana arrives soon with the human."

"It's deep," Ronan observes.

"She's lost too much blood too fast to heal on her own. Fuck! Where's Dari?"

Alaric walks into the room. "I'll clean the wound."

"The fuck you will!" Daemon snatches the bottle of vodka out of Alaric's hand. Then his fingers are on my cheek, cupping it gently. "Remember when you hurt your knee? Remember the vodka?"

"Hmm?"

"It'll be like that, only a thousand times worse, okay, beautiful?" He unscrews the cap and says to the others, "Hold her down."

Warm hands grip my shoulders and knees.

"I need you to be very fucking brave for me, little angel. Can you do that?"

My eyelids are heavy. I look at him, but he seems so far away. "I ruin everything, Daemon."

The boys exchange a glance.

"I say things I don't mean."

"Quiet!" There's a warning in his tone, one I'm all too familiar with. "I don't care about any of that shit, get it? We need to rinse out your wound."

"Okay."

His jaw tics and he gives my good leg a squeeze. "You ready?"

"Just do it."

"See Ronan?"

I do. His hands are firm on my knees.

"You focus on him. Whatever you do, don't look away

from his eyes, okay? Let him be your anchor. I'll count to three."

A tear slides its way down my temple to my hairline.

"Three."

Blinding pain sears through me. I try to look Ronan in the eye. I try so fucking hard to be brave. But I'm not brave, and in the end, I squeeze my eyes shut and scream.

CHAPTER 22

AURELIA

A drop of blood falls on my lips, followed by a second that rouses me when it trails through the seam of my mouth and onto my tongue.

"Drink, baby."

I blink my heavy eyes open to find Dariana smiling down at me softly while a human girl sits beside me on the edge of the couch with her wrist pressed firmly against my lips. I frown, trying to piece together what's happened. I had a dream. I injured my leg.

Now the girl?

"Don't think so hard. Just drink."

Judging by the dazed look on the girl, she's not fully here, realizing what's happening. Maybe her mind is still in the human world. She's definitely not an enslaved person in these lands. Her blood is too rich. Too potent.

"Good girl," Dariana encourages, brushing my hair out of my eyes when I grip the wrist tighter and take deeper pulls. My body takes over, shutting away my innocent angel in a back room where she can bang her fists against the wall all she wants. *We need to feed to regain our strength,* my body says, retreating back to the here and now and the healing blood that's slipping down my throat.

Daemon is pacing over by the mantelpiece like a caged, feral animal. The flames in the fire are high and flicker wildly. "Why isn't she healing?"

"Relax," Dariana says, watching me. "It takes time."

My eyes roll toward the back of my head. I dig my teeth in even further, relishing the girl's pained whimpers. No one says a thing; they wait while the human's heartbeat slows before stopping altogether. The last weak thump is loud in the room. The ensuing silence is even louder. Daemon chews on his thumbnail as he continues pacing. Ronan sits on one of the armchairs with his elbows on his knees, his face in his hands, and Alaric toys with a yo-yo of all things. Up and down it slides, again and again. It seems to be the one thing keeping me grounded. That yellow spinning circle—a splash of color in a dark world.

"Anything?" Daemon snaps.

Dariana slowly removes the girl's wrist from my mouth, ignoring my snarling. "The human is dead. There's no more blood to be had."

The girl slumps over on the floor, empty eyes gazing upwards.

I shoot upright, snarling when Dariana touches my thigh.

"It's okay," she soothes my animal. "I'm not going to hurt you."

Soft fingers trail over the damaged skin, too gentle to hurt. I breathe harshly through my flaring nostrils. Pain is all I've known here in Hell. Pain in all its forms. Life outside of Eden hurts in more ways than one. I'm starting to see now that there's a sharp thorn for every fragile petal of pleasure.

"It's healing. Let her rest."

"One of us needs to stay with her at all fucking times. If she got this injured today, fuck knows how bad it'll be next time."

"What did she say happened?" Ronan asks, looking up.

Daemon rubs his hands over his face. "She said she fell over a tree trunk."

Dariana knits her brows together, glancing between the boys. "And this started with the meditation?"

"Yeah, she said she scratched her arms on the tree branches. After class, she had scratches all over."

"And now it's happening in her dreams?"

"What's your point?" Daemon asks, exasperated. "How the fuck can she hurt herself in her dreams like that?"

"I don't know," Dariana says quietly, "but I think we need to accept the fact that she's an angel, and we know nothing about 'true' angels."

"She's changing," Alaric comments without looking up, and they all glance over at him. "Her wings stay white, but she's growing fangs and thirsting for blood. I bet she'll be able to master fire soon."

"So she's becoming a fallen angel?" Ronan asks, leaning back in his chair and placing his ankle on his knee.

Alaric lets the yo-yo spin out, leaving it dangling in the air. "Scrap what I just said. She's not changing. She became a fallen angel the moment she snuck out of Eden because of her own curiosity. Curiosity, which, might I add, has no place in Eden."

Daemon throws his arms out. "So?"

Pocketing his yo-yo and walking over to one of the spare armchairs, Alaric plops down, kicking his shoe up on the footrest. "What does it mean to be a fallen angel? You say she's *growing* fangs? But besides the color of her wings, she's not physically different from us, which must mean the fangs have always been there, unused. To be a fallen angel simply means a fall from grace. Take Adam and Eve, for example. They were blissfully unaware of each other's nakedness until Eve took a bite out of the apple from the Tree of *Knowledge*. It wasn't until we took her in that she opened her eyes. *We* are the apple she bit into."

Ronan snorts with laughter but stifles it when Daemon shoots him a glare.

"Go on," Daemon says to Alaric.

"I'm just saying, she's not turning into a fallen angel; she already *is* one. She fell from grace. She took a bite out of the apple of knowledge—"

"I don't give a shit about the fucking apple," Daemon growls.

"Knowledge, Daemon! Think about it. She knows about sex now. There are no cravings in heaven. She now has desires and needs because of her newfound awareness. The promise of fulfillment is the driving factor behind a lot of her decisions. She's had a taste of blood and death, so she now hungers. How can you ever feel hunger of any kind if you've never tasted sustenance?"

"That makes no sense. Surely they must have some fucking desires in Eden? What do they do all day?"

The others shrug.

"What has any of this got to do with her dreams?"

"It hasn't," Alaric shrugs. "My point is simply that we don't know anything about true angels. I mean, look at us. We've evolved black wings to blend in with the dark environment. An angel with black wings in Eden would stand out like a sore thumb. But a safe assumption is that angels are born with the highest potential. Why would she suddenly grow fangs because she walks through a gate? She wouldn't. The potential for hunger—to become a predator—was always there. She was born with a clit, right, so the potential to feel horny was always there. She just needed to *see.* Get it? Don't ask me why they don't fuck like rabbits in Eden, because I don't fucking know. Maybe they're all Eunuchs. But that's beside the point. What's happening to her now is not new. It's not that she's changing. Her knowledge is expanding, and her form is blossoming into its highest potential. Does that make sense?"

Daemon blinks. "No, it doesn't. It makes no sense whatsoever. How is that supposed to help us? We are nowhere near figuring out how the fuck she can hurt herself when she's meditating or sleeping? And blossoming? Really? Who the fuck talks like that?"

"Wait, wait, slow down," Dariana says, cogs ticking over. "The part you mentioned about our feathers evolving to help us blend in with the environment. Centuries have passed since the fall, right?"

"So?"

"We've adjusted to our environment. Sure, we came to our full potential, as Alaric put it, but we have also evolved. Take hellfire, for example. Do you truly think a true angel can conjure fire? Think about it! Fire is unique to Hell. What, then, is unique to Eden?"

Ronan's eyes widen and he straightens. "Light!"

"Exactly!" Dariana snaps her fingers. "Light! Somewhere inside her, she must have access to the light."

Alaric stands up and starts pacing, dragging his thumb across his lips. "The Bible speaks of redemption. If Eden can let her out, there must be a way back in."

"I'm so fucking lost," Daemon says, throwing his arms up. "Who the fuck cares about the Bible?"

"I'm just saying, the God of the Bible is a God of love."

Daemon snorts with disgust.

"She can turn away from the light, but she can't be apart from the light," Dariana murmurs.

"We don't have time for philosophical bullshit! How do we keep her from getting impaled by a fucking tree branch in her sleep?"

"A tree branch?" laughs Ronan, and Daemon's head snaps his way.

"What I want to know is what's behind that door?" Dariana murmurs, looking back at me. I'm too exhausted to follow their back and forth. The pain in my thigh is slowly ebbing away.

"You said she can turn away from the light, but she can't be apart from the light," Alaric muses, leaning with his hands on the mantelpiece, watching the flames burn brighter. "What happens if she turns toward the Light?"

"And how would she do that, huh?" Daemon comments drily. "Eden refused her entrance when she was begging outside to be let back in."

"She's not of the dark. Do away with the dark, and only light remains. The light is who she is," Dariana says.

"This philosophical shit is getting on my last nerve!" Daemon flops down in one of the armchairs, rests his head on the back, and stares up at the ceiling. "She's not returning to Eden. She tried that, and it didn't work. The meditation exercise was meant to teach us to tap into our power. That's what her dreams are about: her accessing her power. And somehow, for some reason, she gets hurt. Maybe because she hasn't learned how to harness it yet."

"Who's the deep one now?" Alaric teases, pushing off the mantelpiece.

"We're screwed either way," Ronan says, his eyes on the fire. "If her power is directly connected to the Light, we can't help her. We have no experience with anything holy. Throwing fireballs is not in the same league as the Light."

"And then there's your fucking uncle," Alaric comments. "We can't catch a fucking break."

Their voices drift into the background as exhaustion drags me into a dreamless sleep.

CHAPTER 23

AURELIA

I wake up to voices drifting in through the gap in the door where it has been left ajar. The last of the embers crackle in the fireplace. Ronan, who was left on guard duty, is asleep in the armchair. He looks younger in his sleep, his sharp features smoother.

I push myself up to sitting. The dead girl is gone, and my dress has been changed. The one I have on now smells faintly of soap and midnight. It must belong to Dariana. I'm shorter than her, so it falls around my knees when I push to standing.

Lifting the skirt, I inspect my thigh. It's healed, and my skin is smooth and void of blood, as if last night never happened. They must have cleaned me, too. Not wishing to wake Ronan, I pad barefoot to the door, careful not to make it creak as I slip outside. I can make out the deep timbre of Daemon's voice up ahead. "What can you tell me of the Light?"

"Why this newfound interest all of a sudden?" The other voice with him is new.

"You've seen it."

Curious, my feet slow as I reach the doorway to the kitchen. Maybe they want privacy? I should turn around and walk back upstairs to my room. It's what I should do, but I don't. Instead, I take a hesitant step forward and peer into the room. The man with Daemon is an older copy of him, with short black hair, a sharp jaw, and the same straight nose. Fine lines frame a deep set of the brownest eyes I've ever seen, except for Daemon's.

You would have to be blind not to notice their similarities. The man wears a black button-up that stretches tight across his broad chest. His slacks are fastened with a black leather belt, and the buckle draws my eyes when it catches the light above the sink. His wings are large and inky black. Even folded, I can tell they're impressive.

When he turns, he spots me, and I don't know how to feel about the smile on his lips. It's the kind of smile that draws you in, hoping you'll get another flash of straight teeth, but there's also a darkness to it. Before the man has even uttered a word, I know he's dangerous.

"You must be Aurelia."

Daemon's head snaps toward me in the doorway and he grinds his teeth so hard, it looks painful. "What are you doing here?"

"Don't be rude, son." To me, he says, "Come here."

The air crackles with tension. I should have stayed with Ronan or walked upstairs to my room. What I shouldn't have done was to come here. I know that for certain when the man sweeps his eyes down my body like I'm a curiosity—one he's no stranger to.

"Well. Well. I never thought I would see the day." He holds his hand out. "Perhaps I should introduce myself. I'm Daemon's father, Lucifer."

I freeze, my eyes widening. "Lucifer?"

He shakes my hand with a firm grip. "I'm sure you will have heard of me."

"Yes," I reply, but the quiver in my voice betrays me. Lucifer was the first fallen angel to choose evil and turn away from God. The first angel to fall from grace. *The original.* Seven more angels rebelled and joined him soon after.

He tsks, sliding his hand out from mine. "You shouldn't believe in everything your elders teach you. What do they call me now? Satan? The Devil? Do I still torture human souls for eternity in a pool of hellfire?"

My mouth has gone dry. I'm as terrified, standing here in front of him, as I am fascinated. Lucifer is a man of myths and legends, the monster in every fairytale. I'm also strangely intrigued by him. He was the first angel to look up at the shimmering gates with curiosity and a desire to discover what lurked outside of Paradise. No other angel before him had the same curiosity. Not until me. What about the other seven angels? Lucifer convinced them to join him by telling them there was more to life outside God's paradise. If not for Lucifer, they wouldn't have left Eden. The man in front of me is a man I can relate to more than any angel back home.

Lucifer smiles tightly, and the way his dark eyes burn into me awakens my flight instinct. My heart starts racing in my chest. I will it to stop.

"I have somewhere else I need to be. I look forward to seeing you at our family dinner tonight."

Family dinner?

Daemon's eyes stay glued on mine as his father clasps his shoulder. "Don't be late, son."

As soon as his father is gone, Daemon surges forward and traps me against the counter. "Why did you leave the living room?"

He's so close that my breath gets caught in my throat when his masculine scent tantalizes my senses. My gaze travels up his chest, past his collarbones and long throat, to his devastatingly handsome face. Dark stubble on olive skin gives way to sharp cheekbones and stormy eyes.

I shouldn't have set sail in these treacherous waters by escaping Eden. I was done for the moment I crushed my compass beneath my shoe and set course for the dark clouds on the horizon. But I couldn't stay moored any longer.

"You should have stayed in the fucking living room."

His voice drifts into my consciousness. I don't care that I'm drowning in his eyes; death can't come soon enough.

Wait? I frown, giving my head a shake to clear it. "Did you just say I shouldn't have left the living room? Am I your prisoner now?"

Placing his hands on the countertop behind me, he leans in. "I stole you from your precious Eden and treat you like shit, remember? Those were your words."

My gaze falls to his lips, only to flick back up. He's so close, his breath dances across my face.

"My father is not a good man. You'd do well to stay clear of him."

"You're not a good man either."

He takes his hand off the counter and toys with a strand of my hair, the backs of his fingers brushing my collarbone. "I'm the Devil's son, sweetheart. The minute you snuck out of Eden, you entered my land."

"It's not your land yet," I hiss, lifting my chin defiantly. I can't believe he never told me who he is. All this time, I never realized.

"Touché," he chuckles before stealing my breath with a single look that makes my toes curl in my shoes. "I'm the next heir. My father may be immortal, but even the immortal pass away."

I'm drawn like a moth to the flames that flicker in his eyes. If I don't wrangle this desire, I'll burn myself. Still, I can't resist singeing my fingers on his hard chest. The black fabric creases in my hands as I press up on my tiptoes to place a kiss on his jaw.

The second my lips connect with his stubble, his hand flies up. He grabs my jaw, forcing my mouth to his. His kiss is hard, ruthless, and fucking delicious. I moan as his sharp teeth sink into my bottom lip, and the taste of copper teases the back of my throat. I'm just about to beg him to take me when Ronan stumbles into the kitchen, bleary-eyed and yawning.

Daemon steps back, adjusting his dick in his pants. "Our little angel ran into my father thanks to you falling asleep on guard duty and allowing her to sneak around the house."

Ronan lowers his fisted hand from his mouth. "Shit, man."

"Yes, shit."

"What did he say?"

"He was here to remind me of the family dinner tonight."

"How do these family dinners work?" I ask, looking between them. "Does your dad have women tied to poles in the dining room?"

Daemon doesn't even bother with a reply. It's like I'm not here anymore. "He's curious. I could see it in his eyes."

"Yeah, but that doesn't have to mean anything."

Their voices drift away when they walk out. Left alone, I blink as my lips tingle from Daemon's kiss.

CHAPTER 24

AURELIA

Daemon is stiff next to me as we ascend the weather-beaten stone steps to his father's house. If you can even call it that? It looks more like a Gothic castle or a church than a cozy family home. It's hard to imagine Daemon growing up here, playing on the grass beneath the statues of scary angels with sharp teeth and dead eyes.

We reach the top step, slowing to a stop. Daemon reaches for the door handle but changes his mind.

"What?" I ask.

Staring at the floor he leans with his hand on the door, his ankles crossed. The world weighs his shoulders down. His eyes slowly come to mine, sweeping over my features, before dropping to the black silk dress that hugs my curves, trailing behind me on the ground. "Let me do the talking tonight."

I frown, gripping the clutch bag in my hands. I'm cold, but his eyes warm me enough to ward off the chill. Daemon lowers his lips to mine, close enough to make me tingle in anticipation but not close enough to ignite sparks. "Can you keep those pretty lips shut for once?"

I wet them, ignoring the fluttering of butterfly wings in my belly. "You don't get to tell me what to do, Daemon."

His breath gusts over my chin and his teeth grind as he hovers with his lips over mine. "Why are you so stubborn?"

"Why are you so grumpy?" I counter.

"I'm trying to keep you safe." He shifts infinitesimally closer as I hold my breath against the onslaught of his intoxicating, masculine scent and his heat. He's built like a tank, towering over me. If he touched me now, my queen would topple. I need the shield of board pieces to guard me against him. Especially when I feel the heat of his fingertips slide down the thin strap on my shoulder. His lips follow, a soft press on my creamy skin. As he straightens back up, my lungs burn from the need to inhale fully.

"Stay close to me tonight." He opens the door and guides me inside with his hand pressed to my lower back. I hastily pull the strap back up while he steers me deeper into the belly of the mansion. My heels sink into the red plush carpet on the stone floor. Cast iron sconces flicker, creating shadows that chase us along the walls, and the air smells of long, dark winters and damp stone. I always imagined Hell as a warm place, with burning flames designed to entrap your soul, but it's cold, and the flames on the walls don't ward off the icy bite in the air.

Voices drift closer, causing Daemon to stiffen beside me as he pulls on his tie. It's the only outward sign of his unease. His face remains a hard, impenetrable mask.

As we enter a large sitting room, my gaze dances over the plush couches in front of the most impressive mantelpiece I've ever seen, and the intricate carvings in the stone draw my eye as we walk closer.

Flames flicker wildly, the occasional spark quickening my

heartbeat. Three men sit on the couches, and when they spot us, their conversation falls silent. Lucifer is the first man to stand up. His dark eyes fall up and down my body, noting every curve and crease in the expensive silk. It's difficult not to fidget beneath his scrutinizing gaze. Lucifer strikes me as a man whom nothing gets past. He sweeps his hand out and says, "Meet my brother, Amenadiel."

The man in question walks up to us and holds his hand out for mine. "It's a pleasure to meet you again, *Angel.* We met on your first day at the academy, remember?"

I don't like the way he emphasizes my nickname. It feels wrong. My skin crawls when I slide my hand into his.

Pressing a kiss to the backs of my knuckles, he smiles. I know him from the stories told to me as a young girl. Amenadiel is Lucifer's oldest brother and one of the fallen angels that walked out of Eden. "I believe you've met my son *Dmitriy?*" he asks.

I snatch my hand away out of instinct. "I have."

Memories of Dmitriy's hands on my body flash through my mind as he steps up to us with a smirk. "Hi, Angel."

Next to me, Daemon vibrates with anger. If he could, he would wrap his fingers around Dmitriy's throat and squeeze.

"Have you settled in well in Hell?" Amenadiel asks.

I snap my eyes away from Dmitriy and try to focus on his father's question. "As well as can be expected."

He hums, his gaze dragging over my white wings and pale skin. "And the academy? Are you enjoying it?"

What is this?

Why the millions of questions?

I look to Daemon, but his face is a stony mask while he glares at Dmitriy. "Um, yes, I enjoy it."

"Excellent," Amenadiel says.

Lucifer lifts his hand, wiggling his finger impatiently while clearing his throat. Out of the shadows appears a waiter with a tray of tumblers filled with an amber liquid. They all help themselves to a glass. Lucifer hands me one, watching me closely as I bring it to my lips for a hesitant sip. The bitter burn warms my stomach. Amenadiel holds my gaze with his dark eyes, smirking behind his glass. There's something not right about him. The true devil isn't the man in the room who bears the name, but the man watching me with cold, dark eyes that are void of any warmth.

"How long did it take for your wings to turn black?" I ask him, causing Dmitriy to choke on his whisky.

Amenadiel slowly lowers his tumbler, his lips quirking in an even slower smile—a smile with a hardness to it. Next to me, Daemon stands frozen. I know he asked me to stay quiet tonight, but my curiosity can't be leashed. Lucifer and his brother have both walked on the same green grass and climbed the same tall trees as me. They both had white wings that were brighter than snow and felt the sun heat their cheeks. I'm a stranger to their world, but they're not a stranger to mine.

"A long, long time, sweetheart. It might not happen for you."

The worm dangles on the hook just below the surface, squirming and wiggling. I'm circling the bait; we both know I'll bite. "Why wouldn't it happen for me?"

Bringing the tumbler to his lips, he winks, pulling the worm out of the water. "Curiosity leads to trouble."

I narrow my eyes on him as I take a sip of whisky, relishing the burn and how it gives me something to focus my nerves on. Amenadiel likes to play games. I'm starting to think it's a family trait. "And yet, life is meaningless without trouble."

Dmitriy looks bored, and Daemon stares into the distance like a silent statue behind me. Only Lucifer is paying close attention to our exchange.

Amenadiel's cold eyes sparkle in the glow from the fireplace. He likes to challenge me. "The trouble with trouble is that it starts out as fun."

I raise a brow, but just as I open my mouth to speak, Lucifer cuts in, "Let's retreat to the dining room."

Next to me, Daemon is a statue. I can't read him and it's making me jittery. His hand returns to my back, leading me out of the room. I like his touch too much. It's dangerous to seek safety in a pack of wolves when you're a lamb.

Lucifer walks ahead and I'm unable to look away from his impressive wings. The black feathers shine, reflecting light from the candle-lit chandeliers overhead as we enter the dining room. I instantly want to tuck tail and run, but I keep my mask firmly in place when I feel Dmitriy's father watching me closely, hunting for cracks and weaknesses in my armor. Terrified, whimpering human women, shackled naked to the long bench at the table, fall silent. One of them is struggling to keep her panic at bay, and when she rattles the handcuffs behind her back, a guard steps out from the shadows and slaps her hard. "Behave!"

Something inside me breaks at the sight. I've seen and tasted cruelty on my tongue since I got here. I even liked it. But the darkness, alive and breathing in this room, chips away at the goodness inside me. Amenadiel smirks knowingly on his way past. I'm not surprised at all when he walks straight up to the terrified girl and fists her hair, pulling sharply to bare her neck for his elongating teeth. The man is a sadist. He hasn't just fallen from grace; he's so far down the pit he can't be reached.

Lucifer gestures for a waiter, who collects our tumblers. "Unlike my brother, I pride myself on being a gentleman. Go on, Aurelia. Pick a girl."

I'm paralyzed by the fear that trickles down my spine.

"Go on," he urges, nudging his head. "I left Paradise once too, remember? I know you hunger."

"You know nothing," I hiss before I can stop myself.

Beside me, Daemon turns to stone. Not a single breath slips from his lips. Amused, Lucifer chuckles. Then, to Daemon and Dmitriy, he says, "Choose your meal, boys."

The warmth of Daemon's hand on my back slips away, leaving me cold and unable to take a full breath. Lucifer circles me, a predator sizing up its prey. He steps up close behind me, the heat of his breath teasing my cheek as he leans in and whispers, "My son is not for you."

I watch in horror as Daemon slides his chosen girl onto his lap and sinks his teeth into her neck while his eyes stay locked on me. Breathy chuckles dance across my skin. "This game you're playing with my son won't end well. For anyone."

"I'm not playing games."

"Tut, tut," he whispers, his fingers sliding over the silk fabric that covers my stomach. "Lying doesn't befit you."

My throat is clogged with something other than aching sadness for the horror in front of me. Burning flames lick their way up my throat. I whirl in his arms, baring my throbbing teeth in a show of defiance. "Your son kidnapped *me* for his own amusement. If anyone is playing games, it's Daemon. I'm simply trying to survive this world I have found myself in. I'm a fighter, unlike you."

His eyebrows shoot up, and he regards me. "You don't think I'm a fighter?"

"You're a coward!"

That makes him laugh, and it strikes me how much Daemon resembles his father. "Tell me, sweet girl, how am I a coward?"

My soles itch to run away as I press up on my tiptoes and whisper, "I left the garden on my own. You didn't have the fucking balls. No, you had to convince seven other angels to join your boys' club."

His smile falls and he grabs me by the throat. "You have

guts, I'll give you that much, but your foolish bravery will get you killed in my world." As if he didn't just threaten my life, he lets go of me, then makes his way over to the others, where he bends over the back of his girl of choice and drains her blood while squeezing her small breasts.

Unsure what to do, I shift. The lone girl who's meant for me sits with her head bowed. Her stringy brown hair falls in a curtain around her face. I killed that man the other day without blinking, but this feels different—cold and callous.

The girl in Amenadiel's arms slumps forward. I don't need to look up to know she's dead. Slapping his hand down on the table, he says, "Bring the whisky and cigars." His cold eyes come to me and he cocks his head to the side. "Why don't you join us, Angel. Let's get to know each other a little better."

With his teeth buried deep in the girl's neck, Daemon's eyes track me as I take hesitant steps closer to the table. The worst part is that my fangs throb with hunger, their sharp tips grazing up against my bottom lip.

Amusement sparkles in Amenadiel's eyes while he drags the pad of his thumb over his chin to catch the droplets of blood. He shoves the girl off his lap and rests his elbows on the table. "Sit down."

It's not like I can say no and walk out the way I came. I'm here now and they won't let me leave. I slide in on the bench across from him and look around the room nervously while his eyes stay fixed on me. A waiter turns up out of nowhere with a tray of alcohol. After pouring whisky into one and handing it to Amenadiel, he puts a glass in front of me and pours blood-red wine into it. It glugs, sploshing against the sides.

"To new adventures," Amenadiel says, holding his tumbler up.

I raise my wine glass and clink it with his, watching him closely the entire time. He looks down the length of the table to his brother, who discards the dead corpse like she didn't have a beating heartbeat five seconds ago. Straightening back up, Lucifer runs a hand through his hair and accepts a tumbler of amber liquid. When he smiles at me, a shiver runs down my back. His teeth are coated in blood, revealing his true monster behind the veil.

"Shall we discuss business matters?" Lucifer rounds the table until he's right next to me, and I sit frozen with my breath caught in my throat as his fingers brush my hair behind my ear.

"Father!" Daemon's voice is filled with smoke and tension. The girl on his lap lies slumped on the table, her cheek pressed against the worn wood, her dead eyes staring at nothing. There's only one poor human girl alive, and she's not making a sound.

Lucifer ignores his son while brushing the tips of his fingers over my jaw and cupping my chin. "Such a pretty girl." He looks at his brother. "Though I have to say, it sounds like a foolish wish to give up your royal title for a girl."

My heart beats like a frightened rabbit's inside my chest when Amenadiel chuckles and rises to his feet. His footsteps are slow and measured, just like his approach on this chess-board. How can Lucifer be so blind? Amenadiel has changed tactics. Lucifer is quick to act, going after what he wants with putrid hatred in his heart and guns blazing. On the other hand, Amenadiel waits and observes. He acts behind a closed curtain, choosing instead to strike his opponent when they're weak.

"She's an angel. You can buy gold and diamonds, but you won't find another *true* angel."

"Don't tell me you're feeling sentimental, brother. You were never a collector of rare things before." Lucifer steps away from me, and while they discuss, my eyes clash with Daemon's. I've never seen him this angry before. It's electric, hovering over him like a dark storm cloud. It's the pressing heat before the whip of lightning across the sky.

Dmitriy looks bored as he slides across the seat to the poor, sobbing human. I look away when he brushes her hair from her shoulder in a gentle caress. He likes to hurt pretty things, but first, he likes to be the hero.

"So, if I let you have the angel, you'll stand down completely? Forgive me, brother, if it sounds too easy."

That's because it is.

My attention gets drawn back to the two men circling each other like vultures. At first glance, Lucifer looks calm and composed, but I don't miss the tic in his cheek. He doesn't trust his brother.

"Come on," chuckles Amenadiel, his hands clasped behind his back. "Are you not bored with this feud between us? How many years have we been at each other's throats?"

"Too long."

"Don't you think it's time we bury the hatchet?"

They walk away to converse over by the fire. I try to listen in, but they're too far away. My poor heart beats in a staccato rhythm, and my breaths are shallow. While I'm fully aware Daemon kidnapped me, it hasn't truly dawned on me that I'm a prisoner until now. They're discussing my future like I'm nothing more than a piece of furniture or one of the dead girls in the room. I'm struck with a sudden pang of homesickness that coils itself around my heart. Tears sting my eyes, but I don't let them see. Instead, I hide away behind a curtain of blonde hair and proceed to pick at my cuticles until they bleed.

Soft fingers slide beneath my chin and tilt it up. "Are you okay, Angel?"

Am I okay? I don't think I'll ever be okay again. My head shakes and the tears spill over, trailing a hot path down my cheeks. Daemon swipes them off with his thumb before dipping it into my mouth. His touch is gentle in a way I didn't know him capable.

"This is cute," Dmitriy drawls across the table. The girl is dead. He shoves her off and slowly rises to his feet while wiping off a trail of blood from his chin with the back of his hand. "You better enjoy each other now while you can."

Snarling deep in his throat like an animal, Daemon bares his teeth. "Stay the fuck away from her, or I'll peel your fucking skin off your body!"

"Now, we both know you won't do that." Dmitriy chuckles, continuing his slow approach. "I'm untouchable, cousin. Your girl here *is not.*"

Ice runs through my veins at the dark look in his eyes when he releases a deep, taunting chuckle.

"I've got to say, she has the tightest pussy I've ever fucked."

All hell breaks loose. Daemon flies at him with his wings on full display as a terrifying snarl rips from his lips. They crash into the table and fall to the floor. It all happens so fast. With my hands pressed to my mouth, I watch Lucifer calmly walk over and haul Daemon off Dmitriy like he weighs nothing.

"Enough!" His voice is sharp, cutting through the ensuing silence like a whip. The glare he gives his son could kill a man on the spot, but Daemon is unfazed, breathing harder than a provoked bull.

"You're not this fucking naive!" Daemon growls, low and threatening. "You know exactly why they want her."

Lucifer stays calm, giving nothing away, and his dark eyes remain cold and detached. "Calm yourself down, son."

Rising to his feet and smirking at me, Dmitriy walks past, whispering, "I'll see you at school, Angel."

CHAPTER 25

AURELIA

The night air is cool, and the chill in the breeze turned my nipples into hard pebbles the second we stepped outside. It's a short walk back to the house, and while Daemon could fly us, he chose not to. I get the sense that he needs the icy breeze to clear his head before he explodes with anger.

His father and uncle continued talking business like I wasn't sitting right there. I don't know what this means for me or what has been decided, but I would rather try my luck out in the woods than move in with Dmitriy and his uncle.

"I told you not to speak!"

I hug my arms around myself, rubbing my bare skin. "I had no choice."

"The fuck you did. You could have kept your lips shut!"

My breaths are visible in the air as I whirl on him. "Fuck you, Daemon! You didn't say shit back there. Someone had to talk. But, you... You were too busy touching that human girl and drinking her blood."

With his hands in his pockets, he throws his head back and laughs bitterly. "Is that what bothers you about everything that happened tonight? Not that my father and uncle discussed you as part of a sale?"

When he fists my hair to keep me frozen, I squeeze my eyes shut.

"Fucking look at me!" Daemon jostles me, then pulls me in closer. His breath is hot on my lips, his anger stoking my own. "Look. At. Me."

I reluctantly open my eyes, gasping when he dives down and kisses me hard. Our teeth clash, and our breaths become one as he drinks my moans from my lips like nectar.

My son is not meant for you.

I break away from Deamon's kiss but barely manage a breath before his lips are back on mine, dragging me beneath his waves. I resurface, whispering, "Who are you meant for?"

The statement has bothered me ever since his father whispered the words in my ear like a taunting lullaby. The icy air frosts over, and Daemon turns to stone in my arms before slowly leaning back and flicking his eyes between mine. I hold my breath, scared of what he's about to say. My hands fall away from his shirt when he turns around and walks away without another backward glance, the silvery moon reflecting off his inky, black hair and feathers.

I take chase, lifting my skirt off the damp ground. "Wait."

He doesn't. He keeps walking, his shoulders tense, the air crackling around him. I pull him to a stop, and when he wrenches his arm free and turns to walk, I round him, blocking his path. "Can you stop running away?"

The muscle in his jaw clenches, his eyes burning with flames while he tries his damnedest not to throttle me.

"Who are you meant for?"

"No one!"

"That's not what your father told me."

"He will tell you anything to secure his kingdom. If he can auction you off to his brother to secure the entirety of the kingdom, he will do it in a heartbeat."

"That's not true."

"No?" He steps closer, tall and imposing. "What do you know about my father?"

"I'm still here with you, aren't I?"

"For how long?"

My back connects with a tree trunk, and he wastes no time cornering me.

"I don't understand why you're so bothered, Daemon. They can only use me as a weapon against your father if you let them."

"You don't understand why I'm bothered?" There's an indent in the skin between his eyebrows. "How can you say that shit?" Reaching up, he trails his calloused fingers down the column of my neck, over my racing pulse, and back up into my long hair. As he leans down, I push up on my tiptoes and we hover, lips brushing with every breath. "When you escaped Eden, you tilted my fucking world on its axis."

"Don't," I whisper as he tightens his grip on my hair.

"Why not?"

I wet my bottom lip, and he snatches it up with his teeth.

"Tell me," he breathes out.

Pulling him down to me by his neck and diving my tongue into his mouth, I tug on his soft, raven hair. *Fuck,* every time he kisses me, he chips away at my heart, collecting piece after piece.

He grabs my waist, hoisting me up against the tree and guiding my legs around his waist. Behind him, his wings erupt, blocking out the moon's silver glow. I come alive, breathing him in with every swipe of my tongue. His calloused fingers drag up my thighs and pool my skirt around my waist before squeezing my ass and spreading me apart. He rocks against me until I break away from his lips, breathing heavily.

"I'm scared, Daemon," I whisper.

"Good." His scorching lips descend on my neck, kissing and nibbling. Then his mouth returns to mine to steal his name from my lips. With my hands buried in his raven hair, I freeze as he lowers his wing, and I catch a glimpse of the door behind him. He notices the shift in the air and blocks it out with his worried eyes. "What's wrong?"

I tap him on the shoulder in a silent command to let me down, and he sets me on my feet, then follows my line of sight. "What are you looking at?"

"Can you not see that?" I whisper, slowly stepping toward the floating door.

It's ajar.

As I move closer, a light flicks on and floods the ground through the small gap in the door. I swallow thickly, then look at Daemon behind me. He's frowning, his shoulders tense. "The door, Daemon. Can you not see it?"

"What the fuck are you talking about?"

Aurelia...

My breath catches, and I look back at the door as my heart thunders inside my chest. "It calls my name."

"The fuck?!"

Another step closer. Daemon yanks me back by my arm. "Where the fuck are you going?"

His grip hurts, but it grounds me enough to peer up at him. Daemon looks adorably confused, and it would be cute if not for the whispers coming from inside the door, urging me closer.

As I take a step back, his hand shoots out and he grabs the back of my neck, then pulls me into him. I stare in horror as his sharp jaw starts to melt away like candle wax. His cheeks slowly slide down to reveal flesh and bones, the corners of his mouth turning downward. "Where are you going, beautiful?"

"Daemon?"

Cruel, masculine laughter bounces off the trees, echoing all around me. I look back, but Daemon is gone. Before me is Amenadiel, who takes a menacing step closer. I dart my gaze around for an escape, but there's nowhere to run. He's bigger, faster, and more powerful.

Smiling cruelly, he grabs me by the throat and leans down. "You look scared, Angel."

"Let go of me!" I shove him off, then stumble back and fall onto my butt.

The wet grass soaks through my skirt that's pooled around my waist, but modesty is the last thing on my mind as I scramble away, my heels sliding on the grass.

"Did you think Daemon was the worst wolf in these woods? He's a cub, Angel. Trust me, you'll soon learn the true meaning of hell when I get my hands on you."

I roll onto my stomach, push myself up to my feet, and run toward the door. His taunting laughter dances across the sheen of cold sweat on my skin while my heart gallops wildly. Before I reach the door, he grabs my hair and pulls me back against his hard chest. "Where are you off to in such a hurry? I'm not finished playing yet."

"Please," I whimper, trying to push down on my panic. Amenadiel hums and buries his nose in my neck. He breathes me in, causing my skin to swell with goosebumps as I struggle in his arms. It's useless. He's much stronger than me.

"Sssh," he soothes, his lips curving into a smile against my neck as he strokes his hand down my hair. "I won't hurt you... much. What do you think it'll take for Daemon to snap? Will it be enough to fuck this sweet cunt?" Ignoring my soft pleas for him to stop, he palms me through my dress. If anything, my fear turns him on more. "Or if I cut off your wings and nail them above my fireplace?"

I push free and run, but he yanks me back by my blonde hair and shoves me to the ground.

Slap.

Blood fills my mouth and my ears ring. Amenadiel crouches down, grabbing a handful of my hair and flipping me onto my back. "How long will it take before your *hero* comes to the rescue?"

"Fuck you!" I roll over on my side, spitting out a mouthful of metallic blood. Thick, putrid hatred courses through my veins when I feel his touch on my cheek.

"You're not ready for me yet," he taunts as he tucks my hair behind my ear. "I like pain and a lot of it. Little innocent angels like you don't come out alive, and we can't kill you too soon. Not until the kingdom is mine and I have your wings and my brother's head mounted to the wall above my fireplace."

I make sure he sees the hatred in my eyes—the sheer force of it. It's yet another feeling to add to the scroll of emotions forced on me since I set foot in this world.

"Ah!" he says, cupping my chin. "Can you feel it darkening your soul yet, Angel? Snuffing out the last of the light until only darkness remains." Still crouching, he grabs my hair and forces me onto my knees in front of him. "It's a shame to ruin such perfection." His lips descend on my neck, and he whispers, "Scream for me, beautiful." Then he strikes, sinking his teeth into my neck.

I WAKE UP SCREAMING, startling Ronan next to me, who lights up the lantern on his bedside table. Shadows dance across his face as his eyes widen when he spots the blood pouring from between my fingers on my throat. "Shit!" He tears his T-shirt off, ordering me to use it to apply pressure to the wound. Then he jumps out of bed and disappears through the door, leaving me alone with the hazy remnants of my nightmare. Hot tears stream down my cheeks as I try to calm my breathing, but I can still feel Amenadiel's touch on my skin and his sharp teeth tearing into my neck.

The door flies open, and Daemon and Alaric tumble through with Ronan hot on their heels. When they spot me on the bed, they pause. Trails of crimson run down my arm, and my matted, sweaty hair sticks to my cheek.

"What happened?" Daemon demands, striding forward. The bed dips beneath his weight as he lowers my hand to inspect the damage.

"She woke up screaming," Ronan replies as he starts to pace. "Someone attacked her in her dream. Fed on her."

"How the fuck is that even possible?" Alaric growls, rubbing his face. "This clusterfuck makes no fucking sense."

Pressing the T-shirt back on my neck, Daemon's eyes fly up to mine. "Who did this to you?"

My mouth slams closed. If I tell him, Amenadiel wins. He wants to rattle Daemon and push his buttons until he's forced to act.

"Answer me! Who the fuck fed on you?!"

"An animal."

His gaze hardens, and he removes the T-shirt before shoving the blood-soaked fabric into my mouth and fisting my hair. "You're lying! An angel fed on you in your dream."

My eyes burn with defiance while we stay locked in a stare-down. He grabs my jaw, digging his fingers into my cheeks as he tilts my chin up. His threat crawls beneath my skin and burrows deep. "If you don't fucking tell me who hurt you, I'll fuck the answers out of you, and I won't be gentle."

My nostrils flare. It's not like I can tell him with Ronan's T-shirt in my mouth who hurt me, and Daemon knows it.

He's waiting for a sign to signal my willingness to talk so he can pull the gag out. If I don't, he'll keep me gagged for no reason other than because he can. His grip tightens, and the flames in my eyes burn brighter. "Who. Hurt. You?"

Shifting closer, Alaric and Ronan frame Daemon's big body—three avenging angels hungry for flesh. Daemon's warm hand slides lower, wrapping around my throat. Blood seeps between his fingers as he starts to squeeze. "Not going to talk, huh?"

Behind him, Alaric pulls his T-shirt over the back of his head before unbuckling his belt. Daemon's eyes remain on me, watching my reaction closely while Ronan starts undressing, too. My throat jumps beneath his tight grip on my bloodied, slippery neck.

"You're our slut, little angel. Our fuck toy. It's time you show us how much you fucking like it when we touch you." Releasing me, he climbs off the bed and removes his T-shirt while Alaric drags me down the bed by my ankle before flipping me over. His hand comes to the hem of my T-shirt, and he shoves it up, his fingers brushing over my skin.

I crane my neck to look at him over my shoulder, and his lips curve in a menacing smirk. Alaric holds my gaze as he slowly leans down and presses his lips to my creamy skin. A shiver runs down my back, chasing his lips on their way to the curve of my ass. Biting the globe, he drags his palm up my back, between my shoulder blades, and then back down. His fingers reach for the hem of my T-shirt and tear it off my body. I'm naked, at their mercy, with Ronan's T-shirt stuffed in my mouth. At least the blood on my neck has slowed to a trickle.

Alaric smacks me, and I yelp. The bed shifts again as Ronan kneels in front of me, sliding his long fingers into my blonde hair. His cock rests heavily in his palm, and my mouth waters at the sight when he drags his hand over the veiny length.

"I suggest you tell us who hurt you." Ronan pulls the gag from my mouth, then massages the swell of my bottom lip with his thumb. "What we're about to do to you will sentence you to Hell forever."

I snatch his thumb between my teeth and suck it deeper into my mouth while holding his gaze. Behind me, Alaric rubs my clit in slow, torturous circles. Daemon is leaning against the wall, watching the show unfold with a cigarette pinched between his fingers. He brings it to his mouth and squints as he takes a deep pull on the cancer stick. As angels, we can't suffer human diseases. But we sure as fuck can enjoy human pleasures. A primal moan slips from my lips when Alaric fills me up with his fingers, hooking them just right to make my lips fall open.

Ronan slides his thumb out and cups my chin, rocking his cock against my mouth. It slides up my cheek before he leans back, prodding my mouth with the bulbous head. "Open wide, baby."

Just then, Alaric smacks my ass hard, and I gasp as I jerk forward.

With my hair fisted in his hand, Ronan thrusts his cock into my mouth until I feel him down my throat. "Take it," he growls before pulling out and sliding back in, slower this time. His eyes are intent on my face, the tears in my eyes, and the drool on my chin.

"I want to fuck her." Alaric pulls me off Ronan, then climbs onto the bed. He lies back and guides me over his cock as he grips my hips. "Ride me until I come, Angel."

Sinking down onto his length, I reach for Ronan, who shifts closer, watching me purse my lips around the crown of his cock.

"Yeah, you like that," he breathes out, brushing my hair out of my eyes. "You like it when we take you."

I moan, sucking him deeper. Beneath me, Alaric slaps my

ass, impatient for me to bring him a taste of Heaven. His warm mouth envelops my aching nipple while he reaches up to squeeze my breast.

Daemon flicks his cigarette through the open window before walking up behind me. The bed shifts, and then he's there, his big palm gliding down my spine and over my ass cheek. "Fuck, such a pretty whore."

I jut my ass out, inviting him. I want to feel them all inside me, moving together and ruining me. My soul burns in their flames.

Daemon leans forward to grab something from the bedside table, and humiliation heats my bloodied cheeks when he spits on my ass and rubs the saliva over my exit. Then he squirts lube over my ass and inserts his thumb. It burns, but I soon find myself pushing back against him. My eyes threaten to fall closed until Ronan slaps my cheek.

"Keep them open."

I gaze up at him as he pulls out and smacks his dick over my mouth while Daemon replaces his thumb with two fingers. A soft whimper escapes me, and Ronan shuts me up with his cock.

"That's it, good girl."

More lube, more fingers. "This will hurt, Angel," Daemon warns me as I hear the telltale sound of a buckle being undone. "I won't take it easy on you, beautiful. I'll fuck you until you tell me who the hell fed on you. I don't care how much you beg me to stop."

Alaric bites my nipple, then soothes the sting with his hot tongue as he drags it over the hardened peak. Pleasure bursts behind my eyelids, trickling down my stomach in a race toward my throbbing core. Daemon grabs my hair while working the tip of his cock inside my ass, and the burning pressure has tears rolling down my cheeks. Ronan swipes one up and winks at me as he wraps his lips around his thumb.

"Fuck," Daemon growls, digging his fingers into my hipbone with his other hand. "Fuck, she's tight." The tip finally pops inside, and he slowly thrusts forward until he's balls deep. Then he starts to move, and the slide of their cocks becomes too much—too overwhelming. It hurts, but it also feels good. I want them off me, and I want them closer. I want them to consume me, fuck me until I'm ruined, and then take me again.

Daemon rides me from behind and his grip on my hair is so tight that strands get torn from their roots. The burn has nothing on where he's entering me again and again. I welcome the pain. I own it like a fucking trophy.

Snaking his hand beneath my body, he begins to rub my clit while Alaric sucks on my sensitive nipples. It's sensation overload.

"Give me those beautiful eyes," Ronan orders as he stares down at me. The slide of his cock in my mouth, Daemon's rough grip on my hair to keep me in place while he takes what he needs, and Alaric's hot mouth on my tits—it's all too much. I don't ever want it to end. The elders were wrong. This isn't Hell; this is Heaven. I'm completely at their mercy and there's nowhere else I would rather be than here, every hole filled by them.

My fallen angels...

"Fuck, little angel. You feel so good," Ronan grunts, picking up the pace.

"That's because she's a piece of Paradise," Daemon tells him, sliding his hand up my back and over a wing. I try to snarl, but Ronan shoves me down on his dick, keeping me frozen while they grab a wing each and pry them open.

It's the ultimate humiliation.

Degradation at its finest.

It only makes me angrier and wetter.

"Ready to talk yet?" Daemon asks, already knowing the answer.

I would shake my head, but I can barely fucking breathe through the snot and saliva. They can fuck me all night—I won't complain—but I refuse to tell them about my dream. The last thing I want is Lucifer's downfall because his son is a possessive asshole. This moment is mine. I'm not theirs, and they're not mine. When this is all said and done, I want them and their kingdom safe. The forces of Heaven and Hell are bigger than me. I'm just an angel who let her curiosity lead her into a shitload of trouble. And that trouble is currently fucking me so hard, I won't be able to sit for a week.

Pleasure builds low in my belly as Daemon rubs my clit in firm circles, determined to push me over the edge. "You're just a greedy little slut, aren't you, Angel?"

I try to peer at him over my shoulder, but Ronan guides me back and takes my mouth, groaning low in his throat. "I'm close."

"Fuck, so am I! We're going to stuff your holes with cum, Angel."

We're a heap of rocking bodies chasing release. I choke on Ronan's dick, and it's such a turn-on that I clamp down on Alaric's thick cock. Daemon bites down on my shoulder while rubbing my clit harder and faster. His lips brush up against the shell of my ear, and he whispers, "Let go, Angel. Let us have you."

I come. My entire body tenses up, every muscle contracting when a wave of intense pleasure washes over me.

"That's it, little angel." Ronan slides his cock down my throat as my cunt continues pulsing and strangling Alaric's dick. "Come for us. Let us hear how much you enjoy it."

Fuck. I don't recognize my own sounds. I'm trembling and moaning, taking everything they give me.

Ronan curses, spilling his salty seed down my throat. *"Fuck!"*

I greedily swallow every delicious drop, and just when I begin to think it's never going to end—that they'll make true to their promise to fuck me until I divulge who fed on me—Daemon and Alaric stiffen behind and underneath me as they fill me up with their release.

Ronan pulls out of my mouth and tucks himself away, leaving his jeans unbuckled. He walks over to Daemon's desk, snatches up a packet of cigarettes, and bangs it on his palm.

Daemon collapses next to me on the bed, an arm slung across his face. With a soft sigh, I rest my cheek on Alaric's chest, listening to his pounding heartbeat beneath my ear. My eyes soon fall closed. I'm content for the first time in my life and happy to lie here in Alaric's arms while he catches his breath.

"Damn, Angel. You're killing us," chuckles Alaric, and I love the deep rumble in his chest.

The chair scrapes on the floor when Ronan pulls it out and plops down, his elbows on his knees. Smoke swirls around his face as he scratches below his lip with his thumbnail.

Soft fingers brush my hair away from my cheek. It's deceptively gentle until Daemon pinches my chin and moves in close. "You think you won this round? Think again. You will tell us who fed on you."

"I told you it was an animal."

He shoves me away before climbing out of bed and tucking his dick away, leaving his pants unbuckled.

I lift my head off Alaric's sweaty chest to watch Daemon disappear into the adjoining bathroom.

The shower turns on.

"Don't even think about it," Alaric says, fisting my hair and forcing my lips to his. "You're mine until he returns."

Behind us, Ronan chuckles. He takes another pull and the

embers crackle, glowing orange in the dim room. "How many orgasms will it take before you sing like a lark, Angel?"

When I peer at him over my shoulder, Alaric grips my chin and yanks me back. "The first two or three feel like heaven. But that pleasure soon becomes too much."

"I'm trying to protect the kingdom. Trust me, you don't want Daemon to find out."

"Daemon will find out anyway. Nothing and no one can stop him when he sets his mind on something."

"Good thing I'm no longer a stranger to pain."

Alaric's raspy chuckle dances across my lips. "Careful, beautiful, or we'll tear you to pieces." He nips my bottom lip and slaps my ass before flipping me onto my back. My smart reply dies on my tongue when he kicks my legs apart with his knees and sinks into me.

CHAPTER 26

AURELIA

I'm on my way to the library when Dariana catches up to me in the hallway. "You have that glow," she teases.

"What glow?"

Her hair is up in a messy bun, and her black dress flows around her thighs. She smiles at me through her red-painted lips. "Like you've had them all at the same time."

My eyes widen as I pause in the middle of the hallway. "They told you?"

Waving me off, she continues walking. "Relax, no one said a thing. It was a lucky guess." She looks at me over her shoulder and winks. "And I was right, judging by the blush on your cheeks."

Okay, so maybe I'm smiling a little too big. Sue me. "I don't know what you're talking about."

"Right, right." She nods as we enter the library.

I love the silence and the smell of old books, the wisdom that whispers in the air. The lady behind the counter looks up from the novel splayed in front of her before lowering her gaze back down and turning the page. We walk deeper into the library until we reach the back, where there's a small seating area. Lanterns sit in the middle of the circular table, and the soft glow from the flames throws shadows across Dariana's face as she takes a seat in one of the chairs.

I pick up a lantern, using it to peruse the books on the nearest shelf while she watches me. Feeling self-conscious, I peer at her over my shoulder. "You're staring at me."

"What are you looking for?"

The flame of the candle flickers wildly as I hold it up in front of the books. "Something to shed light on my dreams."

Surely, there must be information in a library this old. The chair scrapes on the stone floor, and then she's behind me, reaching over my shoulder to drag her fingers over the spines. Her nails are painted red to match her lipstick, and she's wearing a golden bracelet with a small heart charm.

"What are we looking for exactly?"

I try to focus, but it isn't easy when she's so close and her warm breaths dance across my bare shoulder. "Something about doors, maybe?"

"Doors, maybe? Or dreams about being attacked by Lucifer's brother."

My eyes widen, the flame flickering wildly inside the lantern as I whirl around.

"What's the matter?" she says, before I've had a chance to utter a word. "Didn't think we would figure it out?"

"Oh, my God," I whisper shakily. "I don't want them to do something stupid."

She lifts her hand, twirling it through the air. Then she clicks her fingers, and the fire in the lantern goes out, bathing us in darkness. My heart starts pounding. "Dariana?"

With another click, a small flame flickers to life in the palm of her hand. She brings her eyes to me, watching me over the flickering fire. "Daemon will stop at nothing to keep you safe."

It's why I need to find a way to escape. "You're friends with him; he'll listen to you."

"No," she replies, blowing out the flame. "He won't." Shifting closer and sliding her hand into my hair, her lips curve into a smile against my neck. "He'll burn the whole world down for you."

"I need to escape."

"Don't you get it?" Dariana whispers, lowering herself down onto her knees and tossing my leg over her shoulder. "There's no escape." She drags her warm tongue up the inside of my thigh all the way to my aching pussy. She's just about to taste me when Dmitriy's voice drifts through the shelves. Dariana stiffens, her hot breaths tingling my sensitive skin for a brief moment before she lowers my leg back down and rises to her feet. Her hand clamps over my mouth as she whispers, "Quiet, baby."

"She's not going to go with me willingly."

"Then you need to work your charm, don't you?"

My eyes widen in the darkness. What is Amenadiel doing here at the academy?

Dmitriy snorts. "They've got her wrapped around their little fingers. She's untouchable in these hallways."

"You've fucked her before—"

"She came to me."

"It doesn't matter. I've found a way into her mind. If she doesn't come to you, we'll get her somewhere they can't reach her."

My pulse is beating against the pulse point in my neck. So, he was real and not just an apparition in my dream?

"I don't have your powers, Dad. I can't do what you do."

"Don't worry about that. You do your part and I'll work on the rest."

"What about Uncle? Will he go along with it?"

"Lucifer is blindsided by the promise of me stepping

down. He can't see reason. To him, she's just another girl. He can't see how she's become a weakness to his son and a weakness to the kingdom."

"What's so fucking special about her anyway? So, she has white wings? Big deal."

"Besides the fact that she has God's light within her, something no one in this kingdom has." Amenadiel chuckles. "Daemon likes a challenge."

"I still don't fucking get it. You used to live in Eden, too."

"I did, but my light burned out a long time ago. Hers is still there. She's about to be yours soon, son, so you'll have plenty of time to explore the ins and outs of it then."

Their voices drift away.

Dariana conjures a new flame. Her wide eyes take me in before she whispers, "We need to tell Daemon and the others."

My throat jumps and I quickly shake my head. "No, we don't. Listen to me. That's what they want. Amenadiel is trying to force my hand. Don't you see? If I tell Daemon, he'll attack Amenadiel or his son." I wave my hands around the room. "Amenadiel wins. He doesn't really want to give up the power he holds now. If he can find a way to make Daemon break the treaty before then, he will."

Dariana looks unconvinced. "What if he kills you in your dream next time?"

Pushing off the shelf, I walk back to the circular table and plop down onto one of the chairs. Dariana puts out the flame in her hand and sits down, too. I'm getting a headache. Massaging my temples, I try to think. "There must be more to this?"

"You're asking the wrong person. I stay out of their millennia-long argument. No one even knows how much time has passed since the fall. Only they do and the other angels involved... but it's been a very fucking long time."

"I can't get between Lucifer and Amenadiel." I lower my hand, meeting her gaze.

"No, you can't," she agrees. "Lucifer will kill you if he thinks you're a threat."

"I don't get this. Daemon doesn't even like me that much. We fight most of the time."

Her hand slides across the table and she trails her fingers over mine. "You don't have to understand it. Daemon is a powerful man, the next heir. Everything comes easy for him. Well, it did until you. You're different, and not just because of your wings. You have a spark and a fight in you that very few possess here. Daemon never stood a chance. None of us did."

Compliments make me uncomfortable. I shift, hiding my blushing cheeks.

"It doesn't change the fact that Amenadiel could kill you in your sleep. We have to tell Daemon."

I pull my hand away from hers and grip the edge of the table as I lean in. "We don't tell Daemon anything. Amenadiel won't kill me."

"How do you know?"

"I just do! If he kills me, he has no leverage over Lucifer and no way around the contract. He needs Daemon to break, and that way is through me. Let's not tell Daemon anything until I figure a way out of this."

Dariana's eyes flash with uncertainty, but she backs down. "I have a bad feeling about this."

"We have two options right now."

She stiffens, piercing me with her gaze. "I don't like the look in your eyes."

I ignore her comment. "I go willingly with Dmitriy, or I disappear."

Leaning forward, her hand shoots out and circles my wrist. "No. Fuck, no!"

I'm so tired. Ever since I got here, I feel like I haven't slept.

"It's not up to you, Dariana. I'm Daemon's weakness, and you know it."

"If you disappear, he'll burn down the entire kingdom to find you!"

"And if I go willingly with Dmitriy?"

She lets go of my wrist before leaning back in her seat and folding her arms over her chest. Her unyielding eyes hold mine. "He might just lock you in a cell in his basement and never let you out."

Her words make me shiver because I know she's right. Daemon wouldn't hesitate to take away my freedom. "Promise you won't tell him?"

Her gaze burns into me, and for a long moment, I worry she won't answer me. "I can't promise you anything."

My throat swells with emotion and I avert my gaze. Of course her loyalty lies with Daemon—I expect nothing less—but I'm trying to protect him. Why can't she see that? "Dariana... I care about Daemon. I wouldn't do this otherwise. I'm just a girl; there's nothing unique or interesting about me." I shrug, my eyes brimming with tears. "He'll find someone else. I'm not special enough to be the catalyst for war in Hell. I don't want to be the reason for Lucifer's fall."

Rising to her feet, she leans over with her hands on the desk. Shadows dance across her face from the flame inside the lanterns. "You're not home anymore, Angel. We don't do what's good or *right* here. We take what we want. Stop trying to be the fucking hero. You're dangling the light inside you—that spark of goodness—like a worm on a hook. Sooner or later, the fish will bite."

I rise to my feet too, when she turns to leave, throwing my arms out. "What the fuck do you want me to do then? Nothing?"

She comes to a halt and looks over her shoulder. "I don't know, Angel. Maybe you should fight for us, too? You accused Daemon of running away. Who's doing the running now? Who's letting the enemy win?" She turns fully. "Daemon isn't the only one who cares about you." The stoic quiver in her voice squeezes my heart like a vice. "You must clearly care so little about us if you can just walk away."

She leaves, and the tears in my eyes finally spill over, trailing a hot path down my cheeks. I wipe them off, but more fall. How fucking difficult is it to make her see that I'm not running away? I want to stay. I want it more than anything. At first, I wished so desperately to return home and be let back into paradise. But now...

I leave the way I came, keeping my head low so the other students don't see me cry. The hallways are empty except for a handful of boys standing by the lockers. Everyone else is either in the cafeteria or outside. By the time I reach Mr. Kozlov's classroom, my tears have dried. I raise my hand and knock on his door three times.

"Come in."

No one pays attention to me as I enter the classroom. The teacher sits behind his desk, grading papers. At the sound of my heels clicking on the floor, he looks up and straightens in his chair. "Aurelia, I didn't expect to see you here."

I'm unsure how to broach the subject with him, and my nails dig into my palms to give me something to focus on. "Remember when we did the guided meditation class?"

He regards me before gesturing to the chair across from him. "Have a seat."

Lowering myself down, I place my hands in my lap. He's halfway through the stack of papers on his desk and one of the sheets has fallen to the ground. Leaning down, I pick it up and hand it to him.

"Thank you. What about the meditation class?"

"I have dreams."

He pauses in his mission to straighten the stack of papers on his desk. "Dreams?"

Chewing on my bottom lip, I nod. I'm unsure how much to share, but if I want answers, I have to open up sooner or later. "There's a door in my dream."

"A door?"

"Yes. Just a door, like you asked us to visualize during class. No house or anything."

His brows pull down low and he slowly leans back in his seat, motioning for me to carry on. "What else can you tell me?"

Rain patters on the windows to my left, and I study the droplets of water on the glass before whispering, "They're not regular dreams, Mr. Kozlov. They spill out into this reality, too."

Silence, except for the rain outside. "What exactly do you mean by *spill out?*"

I figure the best way is to show him, so I brush my hair aside and bare my neck. "Something attacked me. And the time we meditated in class, well, I had scratches on my arms after."

His eyes are wide. "It shouldn't be possible for your mind to bleed into this reality. Somehow, the veil between the two worlds is torn."

"I don't understand."

Leaning forward, he pins me with his gaze. "It means whoever attacked you could have done so in this reality, or they could have stepped through the veil."

"Can anyone do that?"

He shakes his head, loosening his tie. "No, only someone powerful can step between realities."

My brain is trying to process what this all means.

"The meditation," he starts, "was to explore the power residing at your core." He hesitates, rubbing his fingers through his beard. "You mention a door. Have you ever tried to step through?"

"No. I turned the handle once."

"I think you'll find your power behind that door."

There's a hard knock, and Daemon and his entourage walk in before Mr. Kozlov has given them permission to enter.

"It's time to go, Angel," Alaric barks while Daemon glares at the poor teacher.

I shoot Mr. Kozlov an apologetic glance and scoot my chair back. "Thanks for your time."

"I wish I could have been of more help."

Daemon pins me with his glare as I walk past him on my way out. The guy is always grumpy. "What was that about?" he asks as soon as the door clicks shut. The hallway is slowly filling up with students on their way to class.

Ignoring Daemon behind me, I walk away. It goes down as well as could be expected. He allows it for all of two seconds before seizing my arm and hauling me back. I collide with his hard chest.

"Answer me!"

"Let me go!" I growl, my heart fluttering at his proximity.

"Not until you answer my fucking question."

Why does he have to smell so nice? It makes it hard to think. "I needed help with my homework."

"What homework?" chuckles Ronan beside us.

I shoot him a glare, and he winks at me.

Daemon jostles me like he wants to shake the truth out of me. "What were you doing in there?"

My mouth slams shut, making him growl. I frustrate him, but that's okay. He frustrates me, too. My arms are bruised from his tight grip when he lets go. That's Daemon for you—always too rough, always too much. Still, I need more. Maybe that's why I keep poking the sleeping bear.

As one, they turn and walk back the way they came.

I blink.

What the fuck?

Chasing after them, I pull on Daemon's arm, but it's like trying to move a tank. "Where are you going?"

Alaric answers for Daemon, "Since you won't tell us, we'll beat the answers out of the teacher."

I fall behind and my eyes widen with panic. I run after them again, launching myself at Daemon's back like a spider monkey. It's not fucking easy to cling on when his wings are so damn huge.

"Don't touch him!" I growl through a mouthful of feathers.

Reaching behind him, he lifts me off and sets me to my feet like I'm nothing more than an annoying little child. Then they set off walking again, parting the sea of students like Moses.

"I asked about my dreams," I shout, and they draw to a halt.

Daemon turns back, shoving me up against the lockers and trapping me in. I can't see past him, he's so big. "What did he tell you?"

"Nothing of great importance."

He slams the locker so hard that I startle. "Tell me the fucking truth."

My eyes burn with hot tears. I'm vibrating with anger. "He said my mind is bleeding into this reality."

"What else?"

"The veil is torn."

Growing still, he pushes off the locker and turns to Ronan. "If the veil is torn, someone powerful enough can enter through, right?"

Why does he have to be both big and smart? Could he not have muscles and a peanut brain? It would make my life easier right now.

Ronan nods slowly. "The only angels powerful enough are—"

"My father and uncle."

"An animal attacked me!"

Ignoring me, Daemon slams his hand over my mouth to shut me up. "So if my uncle can step through the veil…"

"He's the one who attacked her," Ronan finishes for him.

Fucking, annoying dickheads. I tap Daemon's hand on my mouth, but the boys keep talking like I'm not here. Beside me, Alaric smirks, nudging my shoulder with his. To the others, he says, "Maybe we should listen to what the lady has to say."

Tensing up, Daemon grinds his molars and lowers his hand. "Let's hear it then."

"Mr. Kozlov pointed out that he thinks my power lies behind the door. That's what we should focus on. Not your uncle."

Students hurry past when the boys laugh. My comment wasn't that funny, but it sure sounds like it.

"So, what do you suggest, Angel?" Daemon asks, leaning next to me on the locker, his ankles crossed. "Should we do nothing and let Amenadiel attack you in your dreams? What's to stop him from killing you?"

Rolling my eyes, I walk away, calling out over my shoulder. "It was an animal, Daemon. You're being paranoid."

"It's cute when you lie," he says, following closely behind. I try to pretend I'm not affected by his six-three height and two hundred and fifty pounds of muscle build.

"It doesn't change the fact that I'm going to kill him."

I halt in my step and turn around. It's a big mistake, because now I'm staring at his chest and the black T-shirt that stretches tight over his pecs. I crane my neck to peer up at him. "Why won't you listen to me? It was an animal. I won't let you break a contract and put Hell at risk because of your enormous ego. Amenadiel is an ancient Fallen Angel. You can't defeat him." I poke him in the chest to emphasize my point, and as soon as I fall silent, he looks up from my finger and grabs my wrist.

"What I do is none of your business."

"It kind of is when you want to start a war because of my nightmares."

"Your nightmares," he growls, leaning in close, "nearly got you killed!"

I wait for a group of students to walk by before I lower my voice. "Don't you get it? This is what he wants. You're playing into his hands."

Releasing me, he walks by and carries on down the hallway. Confused, I blink as Alaric puts his arm over my shoulder.

"Baby, you've got to stop angering him like that."

"Me angering *him?*" I laugh. "He's the one being unreasonable."

"You insulted the heir to the kingdom by accusing him of not being powerful enough to protect you."

My mouth opens and closes, and then I blurt, "Because he's not!"

Ronan shakes his head and then walks off too, leaving me to stare after him. When I look up at Alaric, he's got an amused glint in his brown eyes.

"It's the truth!"

Removing his arm from around me, he pats me on the top of my head and says, "Keep telling yourself that."

As he walks away, I huff an annoyed breath before flipping him off, making a group of students laugh nearby. "You know I'm right!"

CHAPTER 27

DAEMON

I sit in my father's office with my ankle crossed over my knee, watching him stare at the moon through the tall window. Its silvery glow floods the room and travels across the stone floor. His face is in shadow when he slowly turns, his dark eyes burning into me as he nears. With his hands clasped behind his back, he takes measured steps. "I understand you're fond of the girl?"

I stay quiet, my jaw clenched. He called me in here for a meeting. Whatever he has to say, I won't like it.

"You know the deal, son—"

"I haven't forgotten!"

He regards me as he lowers himself down onto the edge of the desk. "Good. She's a pretty girl, but there's a bigger picture. We can't afford to get sidetracked."

"I won't get sidetracked."

Flashing his perfectly straight teeth, he smashes his hands together. "That's the right attitude. I've spoken to your uncle, and the deal will go ahead as planned. They'll collect her this coming weeke—"

I shoot up so fast, the chair falls over, crashing loudly on the stone floor. "Over my dead fucking body! He's not having her."

My father narrows his eyes at me but keeps calm. Unlike me, he's not as quick to anger. "She's not for you."

I snort. "She sure as fuck is not for Dmitriy!" The thought of him touching her again makes me want to destroy something. Preferably my cousin and his smug smile. I feel sick thinking about him parading her down the hallway like a prize, because that's exactly what he'll do.

My father waits for me to finish raging before folding his arms over his chest and spreading his legs. "You knew from the beginning that you wouldn't be able to keep her."

I'm pacing again. Okay, sure, I stole her for a bit of fun. She was a novelty. But it's not fucking fun anymore. She has burrowed her way under my skin, unlike any other girl. I'm not giving that up. I'm not giving *her* up. I don't care what it takes.

My father, perceptive as always, rises to his feet and kills the distance between us. We're matched in height. There used to be a time when I was shorter, and he would use it against me, but those days are over. I'm in my prime, and he's not.

"She's become your weakness, son, and we can't afford weaknesses. Enemies will take notice, and they will use her against you. Besides, she's an *angel.* It won't be long before word spreads about what we're keeping hidden here at the academy."

I hate that he's right. I would kill for her. Fuck, I *have* killed for her. At this rate, I would probably *be* killed for her, too. She'll get me into a shitload of trouble, if nothing else.

"Dmitriy can't have her," I repeat.

The thought makes me fucking nauseous. How can I

watch him parade her at school, knowing he slides between her thighs at night? I shake my head to clear it of those sickening thoughts. If I'm not careful, I'll go after him. That can't happen. Angel is right—I'm playing into my uncle's hands. They're doing this to provoke me, and I'm letting it happen. My father knows it too, but he's too razor-focused on convincing my uncle to relinquish his title. Meanwhile, my uncle is poking me with a stick time and time again, just waiting for me to snap and do something stupid. Which I will.

"Unfortunately," my father says, placing his hand on my shoulder, his grip tight, "you have no choice. He's collecting her on Saturday, so make sure her bags are packed and she's ready to leave by seven p.m sharp."

"And if I refuse?" My voice is a low growl.

My father flashes an easy smile, but it has an edge. Darkness which birthed Hell. "We wouldn't want to see anything happen to Angel, would we? She's a smart girl who could have a bright future here at the academy." He lowers his hand, takes a cigar out of his breast pocket, and puts it between his lips. After lighting it up, he puffs on it, squinting at me through the smoke. "I will not allow for weaknesses, son. Not now that we're so close to our goal. I understand it's easy to be blinded by pussy, especially someone as fine and rare as her, but don't lose sight of what's important."

Clapping me on the shoulder, he walks to the door, but before he can leave, I blurt, "Do you really think it's wise to give up the only pure angel in the land? There's no one else like her."

My father's gaze meets mine over his shoulder as he half turns. "You forget one thing. I used to be just like her. She's nothing special." He walks out, leaving me to brood alone in his dark office.

I've never before felt like my hands were tied. I fucking hate it. I'm going after my uncle, but how? If I step out of line, my father will lose the throne. But I need to do something. I can't just sit back and let them take Angel. Why do I even care so much? When did I let her get under my skin?

As I walk through the front door, I hear them in the living room. Angel is laughing, and the light, airy sound travels through the walls, chasing away the shadows. Sprawled on the couches in the living room, their heads turn in my direction when I enter.

My eyes seek out Angel like a moth to a flame. She's breathtaking with her blonde hair, big blue eyes, and that glow she has about her. It strikes me like an arrow to the chest every time, but behind the beauty lies fire and attitude. It's what I love the most. She doesn't take my shit. Before she came here, I pictured true angels as meek. Boy, was I wrong.

"Daddy looks grumpy," she teases, lighting a match to my fire. Just like that, I'm hard and ready to choke the attitude out of her. I flop down onto the armchair beside the fire and pat my lap.

Shifting from her spot between Alaric and Ronan, she slides down onto the floor and crawls toward me while I crack my neck and adjust my aching dick inside my jeans. Fuck, the sight of her on all fours with her ass in the air and her eyes on me—how can I not want to kill for her?

When she nears, I keep quiet, curious to see what she'll do. Her blonde hair is a mass of wavy strands, thanks to the rain outside. *Thank fuck for Mother Nature.* I'm dying to pull on it until her eyes tear up.

"You look like you've had a bad day," she says with a smirk as she kneels between my legs and runs her hands up my thighs. Fingernails with black, chipped nail polish—courtesy to Dariana—inch closer to my crotch. Just as she's about to hit holy ground, she stops, peering up at me through long, dark lashes. "Promise me you won't do anything stupid?"

My throat goes dry when she walks her fingers over the hard bulge inside my jeans. What a fucking tease. I snatch up her wrist, gripping her tight enough to make her lips part. "You can bat your pretty lashes all you want. It won't get you what you want. Not with me. Now, by all means, go ahead and convince me with your mouth why I shouldn't do something stupid."

A feminine voice from the doorway breaks our stare off. "I'm just in time for the party, I see."

Dariana's thick and shiny hair is down, and her little black dress has a slit up the thigh that goes all the way to her hip. Her perfect tits almost spill over the low neckline, but none of her physical beauty compares to the girl between my legs. Angel's creamy skin makes my palm itch with the urge to mark it. The flames in her eyes burn brighter when I try to assert myself over her, which makes me want to do it more. I want to corrupt her. Own every part of her. I don't know if it's because she's from Heaven and I'm from Hell. But it's such a fucking turn-on to see her beautiful lips wrap around my cock.

Angel tries to wrench her hand free, but I pull her in closer, fisting her hair with my other hand and forcing her eyes on me. To Dari, I confirm, "You're just in time for the party. Let's play with our toy."

My little angel has expressive eyes that speak a thousand words while her mouth remains shut. Right now, she hates me a little bit.

"Flare your wings," I order, because I want to see them spread out in all their fucking glory while she chokes on my dick.

Dari ignores me, walking deeper into the room. "What did your father say?"

My grip on Angel's hair tightens until she slowly unfolds her wings. *That's my good girl.* "I don't want to talk about my father. I want my fucking dick sucked."

Used to my shitty attitude, Dari rolls her eyes as she takes a seat on the coffee table.

"Unbuckle my belt."

Of course Angel doesn't listen, and I love her a little more for it. It makes me fucking ache with desire when she fights back.

I groan, letting my head fall back against the couch. The chandelier overhead has enough spider webs to make my house look like Dracula's abode.

"Amenadiel turned up at the school today," Dari says, causing my head to snap up.

Angel sets to work on my belt, no doubt trying to distract me. I shove her off, ignoring her protests when she falls to the floor. "You saw him?"

Dari smirks. "And heard him."

Jumping up to her feet, Angel steals my attention for a brief few seconds when she begins swaying her hips in front of me, dancing to an imaginary tune my dick sure can hear. Her slender fingers slowly inch her skirt up her thighs until I catch a glimpse of her silk panties.

Dari clicks her fingers, stealing my attention. It's difficult to drag my gaze away from Angel's smooth skin and that tiny triangle of fabric that hides Nirvana. "What did he say?"

"Why don't you ask the seductress over there."

Angel glares at Dari. "I'm trying to prevent a war here. You're not helping."

"I never thought I'd witness the day an angel from Heaven would use sex to stop a war."

Alaric and Ronan chuckle. I join in as Angel's cheeks heat with embarrassment.

"Go on, tell them, baby," Dari urges, looking amused while our little angel fidgets. When she doesn't reply, Dari says, "Fine, I'll tell them. Amenadiel attacked her in her dreams. He even admitted it."

Waving a hand dismissively, I grab Angel by the hip, then pull her into me and flip her skirt up. "That's not news."

Dariana falls silent. She expected me to rage and fly out of my chair, but I'm too distracted by these damp silk panties to point out that we got Angel to admit the truth—well, sort of.

I hook a finger in the fabric, sliding them aside and baring her soft little pussy. Angel looks down at me with her big doe eyes, and I'm struck with the urge to nail Dmitriy to a fucking cross and leave him to die while I show him exactly all the things I want to do to *my* angel. I'll gladly come out to play if he wishes to raise the fucking Devil from the flames.

"Daemon, fuck! Can you focus for one second?"

"I'm good at multitasking," I tell her, teasing Angel's slit with my finger.

"The fuck you are," Dariana growls, moving Angel out of the way. Her skirt falls back down—a tragedy of epic proportions.

Bringing my finger to my nose, I breathe in her heavenly scent while keeping my eyes locked on hers. *This is what you do to me, Angel. The power you hold.*

Smoke fills the air, and Ronan tosses me the cigarette packet across the room. I catch it effortlessly. Let's face it. If I were human, I would be the best star receiver their world has ever seen. Banging it on my palm, I bite one out and light it up before shaking my palm to extinguish the flame. Jealously swirls in the depths of Angel's blue eyes. She wishes she knew what her own powers are. I would lie if I said I wasn't curious, too.

"So, what's the plan?" Dariana asks while I sweep my gaze down Angel's long, smooth legs. Her toenails are painted black too, and there's something so inherently rebellious about it that I want to spank her ass for thinking she'll ever fit into our world. "We kill him."

"Just like that?" Dariana sounds incredulous.

I admit that my plan isn't very well thought out, but we can get to the ins and outs of tearing his head from his body *after* I make Angel scream my name.

"This is exactly why I was trying to distract him," Angel argues, waving her hands, "but you had to remind him again of his revenge plans."

Ignoring her little temper tantrum, Dariana walks up to me and steals the cigarette from my lips with a wink. She takes a drag, squinting at me while holding the smoke in her lungs before blowing it back out. "Your lack of a plan is ridiculous. You can't just kill a centuries-old Fallen Angel. Besides, do I have to remind you of what's at stake here? Your father has ruled Hell since the fall."

Shrugging, I lean back in my seat, picking imaginary lint from my jeans. "Amenadiel isn't immortal. He can die, and he will. I'll make sure of it."

Ronan speaks up, "Until he's dead, how do we protect our angel in her dreams?"

"We need to enter her dreams, somehow."

Alaric laughs. "Are you serious right now? We're not powerful enough to enter someone's mind."

"Well, what else do you have in mind?" I counter, annoyed. I fucking hate common sense sometimes, and my friends have a lot of it.

Leaning forward with his elbows on his thighs, Ronan says, "We need to find her a way out of the dream. A way for her to wake up."

Exhausted, I scrub my palm over my face. Why can't it just

be fucking straightforward? Kill the guy and have it over and done with. Why the stupid treaty? "How do we do that? She needs to realize she's in a dream first."

A thick and heavy silence falls on the room. The truth is, we don't know the answers. We're backed into a corner. Amenadiel plays dirty by attacking from the shadows, and my father is too blinded by the promise of ultimate power to care about anything else. We're running out of time.

CHAPTER 28

AURELIA

I'm exhausted and terrified of sleeping in case Amenadiel decides to visit me again soon. I dread what he'll do next time.

How far will he go to push Daemon past his breaking point?

Dariana stops outside the doors to the cafeteria and sweeps her eyes over my face. Her worried eyes take in the shadows under mine. "You need to feed soon—well, that and sleep."

She's right. I haven't fed in too long, and it's making me weak. But the thought of feeding on the scared humans in there turns my stomach.

"We'll take a trip to the human world later."

I nod, hugging my books to my chest.

Reaching up, Dariana strokes the backs of her fingers over my cheek. "Are you sure you want to wait out here?"

"Yes." I don't enter the cafeteria willingly.

"Okay, I'll be back soon."

She doesn't want to leave me out here alone, but she needs

to feed. With everything that's happened lately, she hasn't returned to the human world, and neither have the boys. They're all in there now.

"Just go."

"Fine, stay here."

"I'm not a dog," I say with an eye roll and a smile, but I'm only half joking.

Dariana hesitates for a short moment longer before opening the door and slipping inside.

Moving over to the side, away from the doors, I slump against the wall.

I'm weaker than I let on. Exhaustion weighs heavily on me, and my eyelids threaten to close the longer I wait. I need a good night's sleep, and I also need to feed. It's at times like these that I miss Paradise. I never hungered for anything back home.

"Falling asleep in the hallways?" Dmitriy asks, making my eyes fly open. He's right in front of me with his hands in his pockets, his eyes sparkling with amusement. His black shirt is unbuttoned at the top to offer a glimpse of his tanned, olive chest, and his dark hair is shorter than the last time I saw him. He's had the sides cut short, but his hair is still long enough on top to give him that 'I just fell out of bed' look. I'm once again struck by how similar he looks to Daemon.

"Are you out here by yourself?" He tsks, inching closer. "Your guard dogs shouldn't leave you alone and unprotected. You never know what dangers lurk in these hallways or who might try to steal you away."

My teeth grind as I refuse to look at him. "You don't have to *steal* me, remember? You're collecting me like a cash prize on Saturday."

"Oh, yes." His smile is too wide and his expression is too smug. "I'll be back then to take you home with me."

When he cups my chin, I wrench free, but he pinches it

between his fingers, forcing my eyes onto his. "Word of advice, beautiful. Don't fight me, okay? Daemon won't react well if you do, and you don't want to cause a scene."

I give him my best glare, telling him without words just how much I hate him. "You don't need to worry. I won't put up a fight."

It's true. I'll do whatever it takes to stop Daemon from hurting his uncle or Dmitriy. Ronan and Alaric aren't as volatile as their leader, so I don't worry about them. But Daemon... He won't sit back and watch Dmitriy haul me away into the night without a fight. Whatever happens, I can't let him break the contract.

"Good girl," Dmitriy whispers, caging me in against the wall. "My father wants the kingdom; to take his brother's throne, but my wants are much simpler." His lips brush the curve of my ear. "I want Daemon to squirm like a worm on a hook while I slip between his girl's thighs every night, knowing he's tearing his room apart in anger. Trust me, Angel, I'll fuck you every opportunity I get just to spite him, and there's nothing he can do."

My teeth grind, but I stay quiet, keeping my anger firmly locked down. I'm an angel in Hell. This isn't my world. I'm now a weapon to be used among men for power.

"Angel," he trails his fingers down the side of my jaw, "don't look so angry. I'll take good care of you, I promise."

"You're as sick as your father!"

"That may be so," he admits, staring at my mouth while pressing down with his thumb on the swell of my bottom lip. "It doesn't change the fact that you're going to be mine, so I suggest you work on your attitude. I am a patient man, but even my patience has limits."

Just then, the door to the cafeteria opens, and Daemon, Alaric, and Ronan walk through, laughing. They soon stop when they look up.

Any other angel would have jumped back and fled for their life, but Dmitriy knows he's got the upper hand over Daemon. He uses it to his full advantage as he slowly lowers his hand from my mouth. "Just getting reacquainted with my new girl before we pick her up this weekend."

"You motherfucker!" Daemon surges forward, shoving him off me, but before he can throw his fist out, Alaric and Ronan pull him back.

Dmitriy laughs as he straightens his shirt, throwing me a wink. "See you on Saturday, Angel. Wear something nice."

As he walks away, Daemon struggles against Ronan and Alaric's restraints.

"Calm the fuck down," Ronan orders, stepping in front of him, but Daemon shoulders past him and traps me against the wall.

"Did he hurt you?"

"No."

He looks unconvinced. "What did he say to you?"

"Daemon," I whisper tiredly before ducking beneath his arm and making my escape.

Of course he doesn't let me.

"Get the fuck back here!" He pulls me by my arm. It's impossible not to get lost in his brown eyes, even when they flash with annoyance. He's got a permanent crease indented between his eyebrows from his constant frowning. I suppress the urge to smooth it with my finger.

"You've got to let me go, Daemon. The stakes are too high—"

"Shut up," he growls, but I'm not finished talking.

I dig my finger into his chest. "No, I won't be quiet. You listen to me! I don't *want* you to disobey your father because of me. I will leave with Dmitriy on Saturday, and you will let it happen. You won't fight hi—"

His hand shoots out, and he wraps it around the back of

my neck, shoving me into him. Our lips brush against each other with every harsh breath. "You won't be going anywhere."

Just then, Dariana leaves the cafeteria and walks past us. "Possessive as always, I see." The humor in her voice brings a smile to my lips, despite the rough grip Daemon has on my neck.

He's still trying to calm down.

Students hurry past, sparing us brief glances. I'm sure they can sense the anger radiating from the man in front of me, and no one wants to get on the wrong side of Daemon besides me, apparently.

My lips tingle with anticipation, and when he finally slams me up against the wall and crushes his mouth against mine, I kiss him back with everything I've got.

Who cares who sees? If anything, I want the girls here to watch me claim him. Daemon isn't the only one who can be possessive. I am too, and he's *mine.* I don't care that we're not meant for each other. It doesn't matter that I have to leave with Dmitriy soon. All that matters is this one moment with his lips on mine, despite the wall that scrapes my back while I dig my claws into his heart.

We finally come up for air and he cups my chin, trailing soft, searing kisses along my jaw to my ear. "If you don't want me to lose my father's kingdom to my uncle, you shouldn't kiss me like that."

I stare after him as he walks away, flaring his wings to scare off a group of students in his way. They scatter like cockroaches.

I'm pulled into a warm chest, and when I look up, Ronan smiles down at me. "You're always causing mischief," he teases, rocking us back and forth. "Come on, let's get to class."

CHAPTER 29

AURELIA

It's another sleepless night. The window in Daemon's room is cracked open an inch, and the cool breeze feels nice on my skin next to his warm body. Even asleep, he radiates heat. The worry lines between his eyebrows have been smoothed out by sleep. He looks younger, almost boyish.

The embers in the fireplace crackle as sparks shoot into the air, and it draws my attention away from the sharp contours of Daemon's face. One of the photographs on top of the mantelpiece catches my eye, and I slowly slide out from beneath the sheets. The cool stone bites into the soles of my feet as I pad over and pick up the frame. It's gold and carved in a language I can't understand. Daemon stands with Dariana tucked underneath his arm. Alaric is in the background, his eyes glowing red from the camera flash. They most likely stole it from one of their victims.

Brushing my finger over their carefree smiles, I sigh. Their lives were easier before I entered. Nothing good came from my curiosity.

"Stop thinking and get back into bed." Daemon is lying on his front, his arms tucked beneath his pillow. I place the photograph back on the mantelpiece, climb back into bed, and lie down on my front too.

Daemon's brown eyes make me feel things I shouldn't as they gaze into mine. "Can't sleep?"

My head shakes. "It won't come."

He's silent for a moment before shifting onto his side and reaching out to stroke my hair behind my ear. "You don't always have to be strong."

"Who would be strong for me?" I ask. "You?"

His fingers trail down my cheek and he cups my chin, his thumb tracing over my lips. "You're not alone anymore."

The intensity in his eyes makes my throat go dry. "Dame-on..." I whisper, but he won't let me continue.

Leaning in, he brushes his lips over mine in a soft, sweet caress.

My heart feels too full.

"You're not alone, little angel." Deepening the kiss, he shifts on top of me, then clasps my hands on the pillow. His weight pushes me down on the mattress until I can't breathe, but fuck if I want to feel him everywhere.

"Baby," he whispers, trailing his nose over the bridge of mine before placing a soft kiss on my forehead. He lingers, his eyes squeezing shut as if he's in pain, and I hold my breath. "I never fell from Paradise. That's the heritage my father gave me, but I sure as hell fell for you."

"Daemon," I breathe out, but he presses his forehead against mine.

"No, you fucking listen to me, Angel. Just keep your pretty lips shut for once and let me tell you how I feel. Fuck..." His breath gusts over my lips, and his grip on my wrists tight-ens. "It doesn't fucking matter where you are. I'll follow you into Paradise and bow to the fucking Light. I'll beg on my knees for forgiveness. Power means nothing to me, Angel. Not anymore. Don't you fucking get it? I'm in love with you, and Heaven or Hell can't keep me away."

"Daemon," I try again, but his lips on mine silence my words of reason. The embers in the fire spark again and the flames rise, casting flickering shadows across the walls.

When he enters me, I cry out, fighting against his tight grip on my wrists. I need to touch him, leave my mark on his broad back, but he holds me spread for him while he steals more pieces of my heart like a man completing a puzzle.

Determined to own all of me, he takes me with slow, deep, and delicious thrusts that hurt worse than the sharpest knife. My heart splinters in my chest, knowing I can never be his, and the pleasure he wrings from my body is bittersweet. As I yield to him, he swipes his tongue over my kiss-swollen bottom lip, sucking it between his teeth.

"Your moans belong to me," he whispers, nudging my jaw with his nose, baring my neck to his sharp teeth that gleam in the flickering flames from the fireplace. "*You* belong to me."

With his next thrust, he pierces my skin with his incisors and my eyes fly open. I fall apart, spasming around his cock as he continues drinking from me. There's something so erotic about this moment. To be completely at his mercy.

He rolls us over and fists my hair at the same time his right hand slides down and palms my ass. "Drink from me, sweet angel."

His pulse flutters steadily beneath my tongue as I drag it up his throat to his ear.

Fuck, he's perfect.

"Do it, Angel."

I know without asking that Daemon has never willingly let anyone feed from him before, and it should make me feel good knowing I'm entirely his in this moment, but it hurts instead.

Love breaks you apart, piece by piece, and when the storm settles, you're never the same again.

As I sink my teeth into his neck, he digs his fingers into my ass. His grip on my hair tightens to the point of pain, but he doesn't stop me.

"That's it, baby. Take what you need."

His coppery taste slides like the finest scotch down my throat, warming my insides and swirling up a storm of complicated emotions. Tears wet my lashes, but I keep drinking, stealing his essence and his heart. More warm and coppery blood pools in my mouth with every heavy thump, awakening the slumbering darkness inside me. I don't retract my fangs, and as I straighten back up, the blood on my chin trails a path down my throat, chest, and in between the swell of my breasts. Rising up on my knees, I guide his cock where I need him before sinking back down.

He grunts, his fingers digging into my thighs, his eyes entrapping mine.

My head drops back on a moan.

The slide of his cock, his rough touch, his burning eyes... I won't survive this, *him*. "Daemon..."

"Good girl, ride me."

Our eyes clash, and I dig my nails into his hard chest as I roll my hips. The bed creaks, my breasts bounce, and my breath catches.

I don't stop.

I ride him faster and harder.

I ride him until my thighs quiver and my hair sticks to the sheen of sweat on my body.

Reaching up, he palms my left tit and tweaks my nipple.

"Daemon," I moan as he shifts onto his elbow and takes the rosy bud in his mouth.

He swirls his tongue while his gaze burns into me, and the intensity in his brown depths slays me. How can I not hand my heart over to him when he fucks me like he wants to imprint himself on my soul? He doesn't need to worry; he's written all over it like felt-tip scribbles on a bathroom stall.

His elongating fangs graze his bottom lip and then he strikes the swell of my breast, but the sharp pain gets swept out to sea with the next roll of my hips. Moaning his name like it's the holiest of prayers, I fall apart for a second time while clinging to his shoulders.

Daemon shifts me onto my front, pulls my hair, and then sinks into me from behind, chasing his own release. He fucks me hard and fast, letting go of my blonde, tangled strands to grab my neck. The headboard bangs against the wall with every brutal thrust, drowning out my loud moans and his deep grunts.

"Fuck, Angel," he groans, stilling on top of me as every muscle in his body tenses. Rocking slowly but so fucking deeply, he fills me up with his cum while pushing me down into the pillow with a firm grip on the back of my neck. I take it all. I let him use me until he's spent and wrung out. Then he collapses beside me, dragging me onto his sweaty chest and wrapping his arms around me. He kisses my head, and it's so sweet that I squeeze my eyes shut. "I won't ever let you go."

That's what I'm afraid of.

"Sleep, baby," he whispers, covering us with the blanket as my eyes grow heavy. "We'll figure it all out tomorrow."

CHAPTER 30

AURELIA

"What the fuck was in that drink?" Dariana laughs while I press my hand on the brick wall outside the club. I'm laughing, too. "We're angels. How can we get this drunk?"

The night is warm here in the human world. Warm and clammy. Music pulses through the thin walls as the bouncer looks over at us from the doorway.

"Sshh!" Dariana giggles, pressing her soft finger to my lips. "Don't give our secret away."

My eyes grow wide. "Oh, shit!" Descending into giggles, I pull her into me and lean my head back against the brick. I hiccup, smiling. "We should do this more often."

"How long until your bodyguards find us?"

Another hiccup. I shake my head. "I'm surprised they haven't yet."

Dariana's smile widens before softening. "You need to feed. Let's find you a juicy meal."

"A juicy meal," I laugh, the world spinning around me.

Instead of moving away, Dariana shifts closer. "Do you want a man or a woman?"

"I want you."

She smiles, biting down on her lip as police sirens wail in the distance. "You have me."

More laughter. I can't seem to stop.

The stars twinkle overhead.

"That was cheesy."

"You think?" Her smile rivals mine.

"Yes."

She leans in, but I place my hands on her chest. "He's watching us."

"Who?" she asks, looking to the side. "You mean the bouncer?" When her eyes return to mine, they sparkle with mischief. "Let him look."

"You're trouble." I giggle.

Her hand slides up my chest to my throat. "You have no idea."

My breath gets caught in my throat when she nips my bottom lip with her teeth. Then she dives in and plunges her tongue into my mouth, her grip tightening on my throat. She tastes of gin, strawberry lip balm, and the enchanted night.

With her eyes still closed, she swallows deeply before leaning back. She's breathtakingly beautiful. So beautiful that I want to kiss every inch of her and explore every soft curve. My heart hammers inside my chest as I reach up to cup her face, and my trembling breaths, visible in the night air, mix with hers. "It's just us. I don't think they're coming."

She leans back in and whispers against my lips, "They'll come."

Something sharp digs into my chest, causing me to frown as I break away from her parted lips. My hands fly up to my mouth when blood begins to pour down her chin. Dariana's eyes widen before she's yanked off me.

Amenadiel pulls her into his chest, pressing the sharp edge of his bloody knife against her throat. "Angel, did you think you could hide from me in the human world?" He tsks, tightening his grip on Dariana while she struggles in his arms. "You can't hide anywhere."

Dariana's wet coughs and the blood that pours from her lips has tears trailing down my cheeks.

"Don't hurt her. I'm here. You have me."

His dark chuckles echo against the brick wall. The bouncer is gone, and the music is silent. It's just us, my loud, beating heart and his crazed smile.

"Please."

Tilting his head to the side, he says, "The angel begs."

With my hand outstretched in front of me, I push off the wall and take a careful step forward. "I'll do anything. Just let her go."

"Do you know how to kill an angel?"

More tears. Why am I so fucking weak when I need to be strong? I should have fed. "Amenadiel, you don't need to do this."

"Answer the question."

Dariana's breaths are coming fast, her dark eyes pleading with me not to do anything stupid. "Run," she chokes out.

I tear my gaze away from her, shaking my head. "I don't know the answer."

"They don't teach you anything in Eden."

A scream leaves me when he slides the gleaming knife across Dariana's throat. Blood pours from the cut, and her eyes grow wide with fear as she gurgles.

Throwing her against the wall, his hand shoots out and tears her heart from her chest. It beats in the palm of his hand, grotesquely beautiful. Crimson blood drips from his fingers as he holds the torn organ out to me. Dariana's lifeless body collapses in a heap on the cobblestones.

"You stole her heart with your blue eyes and heavenly light. It's only fitting that you should have it." He fakes concern. "What's wrong, Angel?"

I turn, fleeing down the alleyway. Fear chokes me, but I don't look back. If I stop running, even for a second, he'll be on me. Every nerve ending in my body knows it. My blonde hair flies behind me and I lose my shoes. They lie abandoned on the cobblestones, like in a scene out of Cinderella. Loose rocks dig into the souls of my feet, but the pain doesn't register through this haze of panic. I have to keep running. I need to get away.

"Angel!" he calls out behind me, above me, all around.

A sob rips from my lips as I turn the next corner. The main street is empty. Even the bars, which were buzzing with nightlife earlier, are now dark, their windows bordered shut with wooden planks. The world is void of life, as if I've stepped onto an apocalyptic movie set.

"You can't run from me."

I don't know how many shopfronts I run past before I collapse to the ground, unable to breathe through the clogged fear in my throat. Stumbling back to my feet, I keep running. Blood pours from a stinging cut on my knee, and my black dress has turned white, trailing behind me on the ground and disturbing the low-lying mist. I look like a runaway bride.

"How long until he comes to save you, Angel? Can you hear him?"

Amenadiel's words give me pause and I halt, turning in a circle as Daemon's deep voice echoes against the buildings. I'm in a town square. The fountain in front of me is empty of water.

"Angel, wake the fuck up!! Fuck, what do I do?!"

I whirl around at the sound of heavy footsteps behind me, my white skirt dragging on the ground, my blonde hair plastered to the sheen of sweat on my cheek.

"Angel," Amenadiel says, advancing on me slowly. "Why are you running?"

"Angel! Wake up!"

"They can't save you now." Amenadiel cocks his head, listening. "Your friends sound pretty desperate, don't you think?"

"Fuck you!"

"I would much rather hurt you."

"WHAT DO YOU WANT?!" I scream so loudly, my throat hurts. Fear trickles down my spine the closer he gets. His dark shirt doesn't hide Dariana's smeared blood on his neck and chest, where the buttons have come undone.

"What do I want? It's easy. I want to peel your skin off your body while lover boy watches on from the other side of the veil. How much damage can I do before he flips? How long until he seeks out my son or me? By then, you'll be dead."

Behind me, my wings erupt, flaring beneath the dim streetlights as I bare my fangs with a hiss.

Coming to a halt, Amenadiel raises his brows. He looks amused. "Would you look at that? Your light is already beginning to flicker out."

My ankles connect with the fountain as I step back. I'm trapped with nowhere to go.

Daemon's voice filters back through. *"Angel, hold on! Ronan, we have to enter through the veil somehow."*

"How? Fuck!"

"I don't fucking know! We're running out of time!"

I squeeze my eyes shut, trying desperately to center myself. This is my fucking dream, and Amenadiel is an impostor. I'm in control here. Not him.

"Are you ready to die yet, Angel?"

As I open my eyes, I'm met with empty air behind me.

The fountain is gone.

My breath gets caught in my throat as I turn to see the

door with its cracked wood and peeled paint. A light flicks on beneath the gap as if someone pressed a switch.

Turning around, I look at Amenadiel, who cocks his head. His eyes travel past me to the door, and he visibly gulps before his eyes harden.

"I think your power resides behind that door."

I take a step back, closer to the door, and he narrows his eyes. "Angel..."

"Know something I don't?"

His lips curve into a dark smile. Following me step for step, he clasps his hands behind his back. "All I know is that you won't find what you're seeking behind that door."

You said she can turn away from the Light, but she can't be apart from the Light. What happens if she turns toward the Light?

"That's interesting," I muse, my skirt dragging on the cobblestones while I smile at him. "I think I'll find exactly what I need behind that door."

Chuckling, he runs his hand over his beard. "The thing about you, Angel, is that your curiosity will always lead you back here. You can't escape until you leash your darkness. Or *unleash* it." His smile widens and he lowers his hand. "We're not so different, you and I."

"Get out of my fucking head!" I hiss.

His cold and cruel laughter lifts the hairs on the back of my neck.

"Fuck, Angel! I can't lose you! Wake the fuck up!"

Amenadiel's laughter stops just as suddenly as it started. "Sounds like lover boy is desperate. You have truly wrapped Lucifer's son around your finger."

Fast as lighting—faster than I can react—he strikes out with his knife, slashing my arm. Pain sears through me and I stumble back, falling on my ass. The blood pouring from the flesh wound stains my white dress, filling the gaps in the cobblestone. Daemon's roar cracks like thunder in the sky.

Whimpering, I scramble back as Amenadiel advances, his tongue dragging through my blood on the sharp blade. "Now, let's rip Daemon's heart from his body."

I jump to my feet, tripping on my skirt as he advances. It all happens so fast. One minute I'm standing up, ready to run, and then the next, I'm flat on the ground. The cobblestone scrapes my knees, and searing pain radiates through my wrists from the impact. I cry out in agony and look down. My broken wrist bone sticks out through my split skin, stark white against the red blood pouring from the wound.

I lift my gaze.

The door is ajar.

Planting his feet on either side of me, Amenadiel fists my hair and yanks my head back, pressing the sharp blade against my throat. The triumph in his eyes devours the defeat in mine. "Any last words, Angel?"

She can turn away from the Light, but she can't be apart from it. So what happens if she turns toward the Light?

I swallow against the sharp blade, feeling it nick my skin. "I unknowingly broke the veil. I can mend it again." Reaching my hand out, my fingers graze up against the elongated light beam on the ground. I close my eyes.

"The God of the Bible is a God of love."

"I think you'll find your power behind that door."

Drawing in a sudden breath behind me, Amenadiel stumbles back, whispering, "It's not possible."

Rolling over on my back, I gasp. Light streams from my hand, too bright to look at directly. I shield my eyes as it shoots up and spreads across the starry sky like pulsating veins. I can see it: the crack. It's right there, slowly filling with the warm light that pours from my hands and body.

Amenadiel is staring up, wide-eyed, and too shocked to

move. My breath catches in my throat, and tears stream unchecked from my eyes as love, pure and unconditional, pours from my every pore into the universe.

Every inch of me is alight.

This is who I am. I am love... *peace.*

Every beginning and every end.

The light slowly retreats from the sky, and like a boomerang returning home, it seeps back inside my center, where it has always resided.

I laugh through my tears, ignoring the throbbing pain in my broken wrist. "What are you going to do now? You're trapped here."

His eyes snap to me and he hisses through deadly fangs. "You fucking whore!"

More crazed laughter. I hurt so fucking bad.

Launching himself at me, he lets out a roar and I throw my hands out, clutching at loose rocks while he drags me farther away from the door. "I'm going to kill you so fucking slowly."

My nails snap off and grit sticks to the exposed flesh on my wrist. The pain is so intense, I can't stop more tears from falling. "If you kill me, you die. There's no way out. You'll forever live inside my mind."

"And haunt your fucking nightmares," he growls, flipping me over onto my back.

I can't hear the boys anymore. Not now that the veil is closed.

"You think death scares me, Angel?" Amenadiel's smile is deranged. He's got nothing left to lose. Raising the knife, he strikes.

I roll away just in time and the knife connects with the cobblestone. Pain radiates through my wrist as I push myself up to my feet and run as fast as I can. It's not fast enough. His shadow is gaining on me.

"I'll drag you down into the darkest fucking pits of Hell with me!"

My heart pounds in my chest while I sprint for the door. Every instinct I have tells me this is my last chance. The light pours out across the bloodied cobblestone like an outstretched hand.

"*What happens if she turns toward the Light?*"

His fingers snag in my hair, tearing out a clump from its roots.

With a scream, I throw myself at the door. It gives way and I fall through into the blinding light. Amenadiel's deep voice is the last thing I hear before it slams shut behind me.

"Don't go to sleep, Angel!"

"AURELIA, WHAT ARE YOU DOING?" Freya, my best friend, asks, causing me to startle and snap my wings shut behind me. She laughs. "Sorry, I didn't mean to scare you."

My heart is still in my throat as I drag my gaze away from the tall gates.

When I don't reply, she follows my line of sight. Her throat jumps before she circles her fingers around my arm, steering me back to the path that leads to the village. "You know we shouldn't be out here."

"Is this real?"

"You can't tell anyone I let you talk me into coming along. The elders won't be happy."

I pull her to me and wrap my arms around her small frame, squeezing the life out of her. After I release her, I palm her cheeks. "Are you real?" I turn in a circle, squinting against the bright sun. The walls are as tall as I remember, enclosing us from the outside world. From fallen angels, inky black wings, brown eyes, and scorching kisses. From death. Life.

"Aurelia?"

My eyes snap back to Freya's. "You're naked." I look down at my body and let out a gasp. The sun warms my bare skin, the mild breeze licking at my nipples. Raising my hand in front of me, I stare at my wrist, unable to believe my eyes. There's not a scratch on it, as if it was never broken.

"Why are you acting so weird?"

I slowly lower my hand and look at Freya for a short moment before taking off in a sprint down the path.

"Where are you going?"

Fear constricts my throat, a feeling I had never tasted before I left Eden.

"Come back!" Freya runs after me.

I don't stop. I run as if I can outrun this rising panic inside. I can't. It chases me down the hill like an avalanche. Any moment now, it'll crush me.

"Aurelia!"

I launch myself at the gate, but no matter how much I pull on it or bang my hand against it, it doesn't budge. I'm trapped. Swinging around, my gaze lands on a tree. The hare nearby flicks its ears as I throw myself at the lowest branch, hauling myself up. I've climbed this tree since I was a young girl. It's different now. I'm not scaling it with a curious mind. Fear pushes me higher through the branches, and my heart aches with every beat while I push myself to the limit.

How am I back here? Was any of what happened real? Was it all a dream? But no, it can't be. I didn't know about kisses, emotional pain, or this drowning fear before. I didn't know Deamon's smell or Dariana's laughter, like that of chiming bells. Or the coppery taste of blood.

I emerge through the tallest branches and stare out over the wall. Beyond it, the dark forest stretches out as far as the eye can see. The screaming silence drowns out everything except my thundering heartbeat. I slip but right myself, clutching onto the branch.

"Aurelia!" Freya calls out from below. "What are you doing?!"

Tears burn my eyes as reality comes crashing down on me. I'm back here. Only it's no longer home. It's out there, amongst sin, death, and inky black wings. It's calling me. It's calling me home.

"The Bible speaks of redemption. If the Garden can let her out, there must be a way back in."

To be continued.

Also by Harleigh Beck

The Rivals

The Rivals' Touch

Fadeaway

Counter Bet:

Counter Bet

Devil's Bargain

Standalones

The King of Sherwood Forest

Kitty Hamilton

Novellas:

Entangled

Sweet Taste of Betrayal

Acknowledgments

I love writing outside of my comfort zone, and this was so far outside that I'm still lost in the woods somewhere, running from the starving wolf. I had so much fun writing it, though. I hope you enjoyed it, too. Next up is *Touched by Darkness,* and I hope you'll stick around for that one.

Firstly, I would like to thank you, the reader, for giving this book a chance. It means the world to me. If you read this far and enjoyed it, please leave a review. It helps us indie authors tremendously.

I have a few individuals I would like to extend a special thank you to.

My hubby — Authoring is fun, but it's not easy. You see me at my highest and my lowest. Thank you for supporting me every step of the way and for reading all my dark and depraved smut without running for the hills.

Paula — How can I write my acknowledgments and not include you? You're the angel in my life. You're the first one who read this book before it became an opinion piece. Thank you for loving it. Thank you for loving *me.*

Courtney — You have no idea how brightly you shine. I love our chats. I love that you're always there for me. I love how genuine you are. I love that you bolster me when I have a bad day and that we celebrate each other's word count each day. No matter how big or small. You once said authoring is a lonely business. I agree. So thank you for making it less lonely.

Kimberley — Thank you for editing my baby. You said

something that stuck with me ahead of this release, and I'll keep it close to my heart.

Ndune — I love chatting with you, hun. You're amazing! Thank you for your support and for being such a lovely person.

Heidi — You've got this, hun. Uni. New flat. Everything. Keep shining bright.

Nisha — Thanks for your hard work on promoting my books. I love that you put up with my unorganized ass. While I can write a full-length book, I sure as hell can't decide on teasers or write a list of trigger warnings or a blurb in a timely manner.

I feel like I'm missing lots of people. You all know who you are. You're all special to me.

Much love,

Harleigh.

ABOUT THE AUTHOR

Harleigh Beck lives in a small town in the northeast of England with her hubby and their three children. When she's not writing, you'll find her head down in a book. She mainly reads dark romance, but she also likes the occasional horror. She has more books planned, so be sure to connect with on her social media for updates.

Printed in Great Britain
by Amazon

29237150R00199